SOME SOUL
TO KEEP

SOME SOUL
TO KEEP

J. CALIFORNIA
COOPER

ST. MARTIN'S
GRIFFIN
NEW YORK

Published in the United States by St. Martin's Griffin, an imprint of St. Martin's Publishing Group

SOME SOUL TO KEEP. Copyright © 1987 by J. California Cooper. All rights reserved. Printed in the United States of America. For information, address St. Martin's Publishing Group, 120 Broadway, New York, NY 10271.

www.stmartins.com

Designed by Meryl Sussman Levavi

The Library of Congress has cataloged the first St. Martin's Griffin edition as follows:

Cooper, J. California.
Some soul to keep.
I. Title.
PS3553.05874S6 1987 813'.54 87–4414
ISBN 978-0-312-19337-9 (trade paperback)

ISBN 978-1-250-85760-6 (trade paperback)

Our books may be purchased in bulk for promotional, educational, or business use. Please contact your local bookseller or the Macmillan Corporate and Premium Sales Department at 1-800-221-7945, extension 5442, or by email at MacmillanSpecialMarkets@macmillan.com.

Third St. Martin's Griffin Edition: 2024

10 9 8 7 6 5 4 3 2 1

DEDICATED WITH LOVE TO

Joseph C. and Maxine Rosemary Lincoln Cooper, my parents
Paris Williams, my chile

Roland H. Crane   *Christine Coleman*

Alexis Ron'ee   *Mary Janice*   *Williams Lurlene*

REMEMBERED

Hattie   *Mahala*   *Ellen*   *Jack*   *Arthur*
Homer   *Edessa*   *Opal*   *Renee*

VERY SPECIAL OTHERS

Nelson and Winnie Mandela and all South Africans fighting
for Freedom

Fannie Lou Hamer   *Harriet Tubman*

El Haj Malik Shabazz

Diop   *Ivan Van Sertima*   *Martin Luther King, Jr.*

OTHER SPECIALS

Fats Waller   *Billie Holiday*   *Erroll Garner*
Eugene O'Neill   *Dinah Washington*   *Paul Robeson*
Orson Welles

TO ALL CHILDREN . . . ESPECIALLY THE ABUSED.

CONTENTS

AUTHOR'S NOTE

Some people say, with a smile, "You write all love stories." Well . . . I say . . . I try to write about needs . . . and Love is our greatest need . . . after health.

Now . . . I am reaching out to write a novel.

On my journey to that novel, my mind stretched itself, digging in deep places and dusty corners of my imagination. Pulling my soul hither and yon, looking under mental carpets of my imagination I did not know were there, in my soul.

On this journey through my imagination these long-short stories came to me. They, now, come to you with pieces of my soul.

So . . . I named this book what I offer you. . . .

Some soul to keep.

SOME SOUL
TO KEEP

SISTERS OF THE RAIN

You know, life goes a long way, don't it? Just is all around you . . . filling up all the tiniest places, so you got to watch round you and keep it all together. Watch it, so to take care of it best you can, with whatever you have to work with.

Sometime something happen to you today, done reached way back, way back, to your grandmothers and great-grandfathers, then done found it's way on down to you. Or, you reach back for it . . . and bring it on up to you. Either way, if you ain't watching life, you won't know what to do with the life you got in your hands.

Reason I say that is cause what I want to tell you starts way back, way back, even further than I can go. But I'm starting where I can.

I have been a schoolteacher for many years. I go way, way back. Have watched many births, lives and deaths. Some of my schoolchildren's lives I watched closer than others because they seemed to have something, be something, but just couldn't get above their life where they could use what they had in them. And I couldn't get the time with them where I could try to shape it. I'll tell you what I mean.

One day, many, many years ago in a sparsely peopled farming settlement, a twelve-year-old, barefoot girl was walking home from school down a long, winding dirt road.

Her face was an old face, not from lack of innocence but a lack of carefree childhood and that special joy of living, given, almost alone, to children. Her lips pressed tight over her teeth, eyes almost closed in the way she had when she was thinking hard, dreaming, with her bare feet sinking into muddy places in the road. She was thinking about the book pressed tight under her arm.

This book she looked at every few minutes, and squeezing it tighter, she would cry for joy. Ahhhh, imagine . . . a child crying for joy over a book! For this child, the well that held her joy had held mostly tears, so it was natural for her to cry in joy. She wanted to stop, open and look through the book again, but she kept a steady push homeward. She knew her mother was sick and that she was needed at home and in the fields. She was the second child of four and, as one of the oldest, was needed everywhere. In the house all the time. In the fields at planting or harvesttime. Since she was four years old.

Each year tho, for the past three years, her mother had insisted she go to school for at least a month, or two if possible (to her keenest joy). Each year also her mother had grown sicker and weaker, miscarrying stillborns, walkin round with a piece of pneumonia and other miseries. Having no money for white doctors and having no Black doctors to owe.

The mother could no longer do her own work, much less any part of her daughter's. The mother was dying. This morning she had insisted, again, that her daughter go "one more day" to walk the five miles to school. To take a note to the teacher with the one word she knew how to write . . . "PLEASE," taught to her by a white lady she had worked for once. To ask for one book, any old book, to bring home, for her daughter to keep, so her daughter could continue to learn to read.

The mother knew if she should die, her daughter would never get to school again; only into the fields to work and someday to the bed to give birth to a screaming future, and then to the silent grave, as she herself was doing. Had done. Not because the father was cruel and drank, dodged work and had other women, but because he was poor, and misused by the whites that owned the land, gin mills, seed and tool stores. He must feed, clothe and provide a home for his family . . . and he must use them to help him do it on this land even as they dropped from the womb. Indeed, sometimes they were born in the field. Off a piece from where the mother had been working.

The father, also (of course) was caught in this briar patch of human egos and lies, hatred and ignorance. Not ignorance that if other people had known better they would have done better, but ignorance of the type they didn't have sense enough to know better. These people's lives was all about women (sex) and money. Take one away, they be alright maybe. Take both away and they knew nothin else to think about or do, cept try to steal at least one back. The world is run today by these two things, but the places are changed. It's now money and sex.

Anyway, the only home he could provide from his stand so near his own grave was two rooms. One, he and the mother and the youngest child slept in. The other for the three older children, and the kitchen, a outside privy and a well. A box house of rough wood, with many drafts that would not, could not, be stopped. Causing constant colds in the family. Crude wooden slats that covered window openings so that they are closed off from the whole world when they huddled within . . . only each other to look at. One kerosene lamp, an old unsafe fireplace.

In the father's heart, the aches as well as the hopes are cracked and broken. He is too worn and tired for either hope or hate, but both were there in the cracks and among the broken pieces of a ignorant youth's dreams. Dreams that started with a new, smiling wife, hot biscuits and bacon before going to the fields to work. Dreams gone down to a sick wife, hungry children and a cold biscuit on the way out the door to the fields, sometimes to pull the plow hisself! It was a prison . . . the walls of which have no end to them, no height or length.

Except . . . for the mother, dying, who wanted a book for her daughter, for her family, to learn to read. To seek a gate in the prison wall.

As the young girl neared her home, she heard the wagon coming that carried the white children home from school, rain or shine. She looked for a place to hide, because it was the white children's pleasure to store up rocks and throw them at the Black children they saw on the road walking. Even in the coldest weather, they never thought to give them a lift and the adult who drove them did not think of it either . . . wouldn't dream of thinkin it!

The girl stepped off the side of the road, less afraid of the snakes. Seeking the tall grass and thickets, she stooped, hiding, holding her book; letting it fall open, she looked at it. She wasn't afraid if she knew they would not see her. The fear had left the Black children after it had become a habit to hide. Just a thing you have to do when white folks are around. Sometimes not as feared as resented. As being poor is resented, as others who do so much less have so much more, just because they are white.

The wagon passed and the girl carefully moved from the thicket back to the road. Looking down at her muddy feet, wet dress torn by an obstinate branch through the weak and worn material, the scratches on her arms, the blood on her hand, which she wiped off the book before she cares for her hand. She cries. She is not crying for herself, she is crying for her mother and has no words to say why. When she reaches home . . . her mother is dead.

Neighbors bring little things, but no one can bring Mother back. The door to the world of childhood closes behind her forever and she is in the whole new world of headwoman of the house. She does not cry this time. She does not feel the difference in her position. She just does what she has to do.

No more school to look forward to two months out of the year. The days are dark and long. Long. The nights are short, tho she sleeps hard, for she is tired, she is still tired when she wakes. She hears there are holidays, she does not know. She cries in her sleep at times, but does not know why. But . . . she has the book . . . no one ever came to get it.

The book was a geography book, already worn, loved and well cared for by the daughter-mother. She read haltingly of Egypt, England, France, Ireland. The world. Her favorite places were Egypt, Africa, the Islands; and in America, she liked the great-sounding names, the oceans and Great Lakes. She could not pronounce them right, but she read about them to her family, even the father, at night. She was their television, you might say, their window to the world. They sat silently, staring at her lips while their minds were thousands of miles away in the lands she read about. A tired, dusty, dreaming group.

Her oldest brother walked off one day, to find one of these lands, and never came back. Her youngest sister died, bitten by something living in the box house that without money could not be gotten rid of . . . you would need a microscope to see it.

That left one brother, younger than she, to help the father. And her, of course, in the house and fields.

As something will grow sometimes even in the darkest of corners . . . love came into her life. Met him at church on Sundays. They dreamed, not with great plans and expectations tho. Her only dream was a house that did not leak or have drafts and loose planks, a few "nice things" and to be cared for by a good husband. She married her father, you might say, except he was her age. He believed he could do these things for his wife. It happened as her mother thought it would. She married young . . . at fifteen. Into her marriage she took the book.

She had her first child at sixteen years of age and one every year til she was nineteen and became sickly from childbearing in very poor conditions, washing and cleaning for white women whose husbands were cheating hers. From working in them fields, rain or shine, with a baby or two pulling on her dress-tail and one on her hip, held in her arm. One thing was different: she could read fairly good and they lived nearer a small town. She had her eye out for a school for her children. She would work hard to send them to school. They would "be SOMETHING . . . anything . . . to get away from here!" People laughed at her publicly and called her a "striver." Then they went home and whipped their own children for not going to school when they could!

She named her children from the book. Her sons, Africa and Pyramid. Her daughters, Egypt and Lake Superior.

The mother thought, or knew, the best jobs her sons could get was driving for somebody or cooking in a big restaurant and she knew they must read to past tests for driving and to read recipes. When they had learned to read, she didn't press them any longer; besides, their father needed them in the fields for longer hours anyway. She noticed that some children just naturally made her sons the leaders in games, and other children didn't like them at all. Especially the white ones they were not allowed to play with.

When Lake Superior and Egypt began school they was about six or seven years old. Superior, the youngest, already knew how to read pretty good, or maybe she just knew the book by heart. She was dark-brown-skinned, big-boned with little meat on her, clear-eyed, quiet but listening to everything around her. Hair kinky, braided and clean. She did not seem to play with the other children much. She seemed older. She would stay in to look at the book. She had common sense, but not much smart school sense.

In school the children laughed at them, making fun of their poor, shabby, patched clothes. Egypt laughed back at them because their clothes were hardly better, but Superior cried. She cried so much the mother took some odd materials and made her a dress with no patch, hand sewn. The day she wore the hand-sewn yellow, purple, orange and green dress was the day of her first fight. The other girl didn't expect it, but of a sudden Superior reached out and grabbed that girl and didn't let go til tears, gravel, blood and snot were well distributed over them both, dress even torn a little. After that the condition of her clothes and bare feet only came up occasionally when someone's enthusiasm bubbled over and bumped into her in some corner studying her books, one foot over the other trying to hide the fact she was still barefoot, teasing her to make their classmates laugh. She never answered, just looked down at her feet. But everyone knew not to touch her, cause she would fight! She wore that dress her mother made her til it wore down to Egypt. Egypt was older, but smaller.

Egypt had an engaging personality. Could and would fight, but rather laugh, so her schoolmates took her as a play thing and sometimes flunky. There were times she even ridiculed her sister for some nonexistent thing, because she wore the same type of clothing Superior did. Her mother would have almost killed her if she mocked Superior for reading and studying.

Egypt was small-boned, slim, pretty; round figure with an easy, ready smile and an ingratiating manner. She liked boys, but all the girls did. Superior paid boys little mind, always going her way with her eyes down or looking straight ahead. Egypt went to school because she knew she had to read and write to get out of town. Superior went because her mother loved it so, counted on it to change her children's life from her own. She was not so smart in her schoolwork, but she worked hard at it and made passing grades. She didn't dream of leaving town, she wanted only to make "Mud Dear" happy.

"Mud Dear" was growing sicker and weaker every day. Superior would hurry home from school to cook and do all the chores for her mother, make her more comfortable. On her way home from school sometimes, if the season was right, she would take an apple, peach or any fruit hanging over a fence. She never thought it was stealing: it was for her mother!

Several years passed.

The mother's sickness was devouring her. She told her husband the children would have to come out of the fields on Sunday and go to church more regularly, that they would help him again when church was over. Since she was so sick, even facing all his problems with money, seasons, time and the landlord, he bade the children go to church. It lasted only a few months fore Mud Dear died.

When the father went to buy the casket and other things needed, of course he had little money. He was told by the white man who owned these necessities that they could be paid for with half of the father's crops for five years. The casket man laughed when he said, "You just haveta pray nobody else don't die fore them five years is up!"

The father looked wearily at the casket and nice robe, thought of his hard work and his children to feed, said, "I'll go home to think about it." Went home to cut a tree, hew it to hold his wife. Paid $3.00 for a blue sheet for his wife's shroud cause that was her favorite color. Then went alone to lay down on the land he worked, to cry because he was her husband and he couldn't take care of her so she wouldn't get sick; couldn't take care of her so she could get well; couldn't bury her decent, now that she was dead. He was not a man! (He said that to himself.)

It was a little tiny church and the funeral was small, the songs quiet, for the grief was deep. Mud Dear looked at peace in her blue shroud and homemade coffin. Superior felt Mud Dear would turn her head any minute and say, "You better come with me, I need you." Superior was ready to follow. But Mud Dear did not turn her head to say anything and Superior's body grew smaller inside her mind while a black hole, right in the middle of her body, just grew and grew and grew, til she gasped the air, trying to fill herself up. She gasped and choked til her father thought she would die. He held her and pulled his other children to him where they stood for a while, til he said "Mud Dear is gone." Then she was taken to be buried.

The day was a hot-cold day. The branches of trees were bare. The sky was clear. The air was crisp to breathe. As they carried the coffin to its resting place at one of the homemade cemeteries where people kept their own, Superior walked behind all the others. She could not stop gasping for breath. She welcomed it, wanted the pain instead of the emptiness, because it came, somehow, from her mother, and anything of her mother's she wanted. Anything, to stay close, to feel her. This way the day passed.

Superior, twelve years old, continued going to school, to church on Sundays, helping in the house and fields the rest of the time. Egypt continued, at thirteen years of age, going to school to keep away from the work at home. Africa, fifteen years old, helped his father and dreamed of being an engineer and building bridges all over the world, even as he fell asleep in school because he was tired and underfed. Pyramid, at fourteen years, helped his father lackadaisically as he looked over the plow toward some girl's house, or set down in an empty field when no one could see him and practiced with his worn deck of cards he had stolen from his girlfriend's house. He had left school far behind in his mind. He was headin out to the Big City as soon as he could win or steal some money. It didn't even have to be enough money, just some. And if one of his friend-girls came up pregnant, he was going to leave without some, even.

The day came when there was not enough food in the house for everyone. Some, but not enough.

The father said, looking down at the floor, "I reckon we just gonna have to let this school stuff go." Superior just looked at him and started sucking her tongue.

The father continued in the slow thick-tongued way Superior had inherited from him, "Mama not here no more. I got to feed you all. We got to eat. To eat, we got to all work."

The children looked at each other (Pyramid wasn't there), the bare stove, the worn, threadbare clothes. Africa didn't have any underwear on, the girls had underwear on but didn't know whose it had been or how it got into the house. Just must have been in one of them bags that sometime came. They looked at the house: the room with a room attached. Clean, but empty, damp and dark.

Egypt asked, "You sure you in the right business work, Daddy? We ain't got nothin!"

Daddy replied, "Don't know nothin else. Ain't nothin wrong with farmin. Just got to have enough help."

Africa thought out loud, "I'm not goin to farm. I'm goin to build bridges and . . . things like that!"

Egypt laughed at Africa, but Daddy just stared at him awhile, then said, "Who gon let you do that, son?"

Africa said, "Ain't nobody gonna let me. Don't want nobody to 'let' me." He frowned and turned his face to the wall.

Everyone looked at their own life in the next moments, in silence, and perhaps Africa caught pieces of their thoughts.

He said, "Goin up the north roads. A man can do what he want to do."

Daddy shook his head and resting his arms on his knees, said, "North, east, west or south . . . it takes money, boy."

With tears in his voice, if not in his eyes, Africa said, "Ain't gonna never get the money on this farm, Dad. Ain't gonna never."

Egypt, wiping her fingers through the bacon grease on the bottom of a cold plate, said, "Sho ain't!"

There were no more answers from anyone, just the sound of the rain and wind outside and the feeling of minds turning, hearts grieving and pounding, grieving and pounding. And wishes being turned this way and that way to see, to find a way to keep them and what piece if any could be made to come true. (You can hear this sometime.) All inside the little house . . . the little dream home of the daughter-mother who had died.

Superior just stared at all of them and sucked her tongue, then said to her father, taking a deep breath, "I'm gonna stay in school. Like Mama said."

The daddy reached over, cupping her neck with his hand, tenderly. He said quietly to the child that reminded him of himself, "I . . . can't . . . take care of you all by myself . . . right now . . . nomore." He pointed to the table. "I can't feed you. I get more behind . . . every day."

Africa looked at his father. "You could take care yourself couldn't you, Daddy? If you was by yourself?"

Daddy leaned on his knees again. "But I ain't by myself."

Superior wanted to go to school not because she was smart or she loved it. She wanted to go because it meant so much to her mother. It was a way she could be close to her mother . . . or know she was doing exactly what her mother wanted her to do. That's what she loved.

The next day after the family meeting, Superior walked to school in the muddy rain without shoes and stood outside because the maintenance man would not let her track the mud from her feet into the school. He made her stand outside the building, in the rain, til chapel was over and somebody could see to her. She was standing there when the children filed out in pairs, heading toward their classes. (It was not a large school but did have three small buildings, which divided some classes.) Most of them laughed at the clay-mud coming up between Superior's toes and her feet sinking in the mud. But one girl hollered out at the others.

"Shut up! I know who used to wear your shoes you got on!"

The girl's cry was unexpected and her shout of anger seemed to sober the children close by and the laughing stopped. They passed on.

Miz Wild, the math teacher, had come out and was telling the maintenance man off. "What's wrong with you, Mr. Reed?! This child could catch her death of pneumonia out here standing in this water with the rain coming down on her!"

Mr. Reed tried to take up for himself; after all, he was the maintenance man. "I just done wiped up this hall for the third time and it ain't even twelve o'clock yet! I don't want that mud tracked up and then I got to hit it again!"

Miz Wild, leading Superior off to the teachers' room–principal's office, threw over her shoulder, "Don't you forget why you are here, Mr. Reed! If these children don't come to school, we wouldn't be needing you!" Mumbling under her breath about all fools.

They cleaned up the muddy feet while Superior answered questions bout how things were at home and told about having to leave school less she could find a job. Miz Wild stood up at that with her hands on her hips and looked down at this dark brown, big-boned, tiny braids glistening with raindrops, wet dress and great, now clean feet with the toes turned under as she stared into Miz Wild's face. Miz Wild saw an angel . . . a child who wanted to stay in school. She knew Superior was a C, sometime D student. Sometime B student in art class. That she was not going to end up being the valedictorian of this school or any other. But, she also knew enough about life to know you don't ever KNOW! So she gave her some shoes to wear and one of her own sweaters, saying, "I'll teach you how to knit these sweaters." Sent her off to her class. The last thing she said was "We will think of something to help you stay in school. Come see me tomorrow." Superior's heart was afraid to smile. But her step in the unfamiliar shoes was lighter. She thought, then turned back to Miz Wild.

"Spose I have to stay home tomorrow?"

"Well . . ." Miz Wild bit her lip. "Come back after school. Maybe I can do something today!"

Superior was looking toward the end of the school day so hard she didn't pay no mind to being hungry at lunchtime. Jewel, the girl who had shouted "Shut up" to the kids, came and stood beside her, taking her hand. Superior didn't say anything because she didn't know nothing to say. She was embarrassed at this demonstration of friendship. It was the first she had had outside her family, but she was happy too! Everyone needs a friend.

After school Superior walked, not ran (she moved slow, talked slow, thought slow, but always with determination), to Miz Wild's class and waited until Miz Wild finished her alternate fussing, threatening, cajoling and ruler waving at the other children around the desk. Some of the children who had never spoke kindly to her before spoke so to her in front of Miz Wild. She nodded her head at them, but kept her eyes on Miz Wild. Finally, when they were alone, Miz Wild handed her a piece of paper and a different sweater, saying, "Keep those shoes til you don't need them and take this blue sweater and give me the red one back. Now this is yours. Keep it. Take this rain jacket; it's old but it still has some fight in it. This is an old oilcloth tablecloth. Take it home and make some hats for you and Egypt, Africa and that old Pyramid!"

Superior thanked her for everything as it came without really looking at them. She knew there must be something else if Miz Wild thought she was gonna be coming to school anymore. Then Miz Wild pointed to the paper.

"You go to that address and apply for a job. They are expecting you." Miz Wild looked thoughtful. "Now . . . these are white people . . . so you don't talk to them like we do to each other. Well, you don't talk much anyway! But . . . with white folks, you listen more. Watch and see how their face goes . . . then you go that way even when you are in front of them. Try to see what they think, but keep what you think to yourself . . . that's your business. And use your manners like your mama taught you to use with everybody no matter what color they are. There is a little girl there and they will pay you to clean up and do a few chores around the house. If they pay you, perhaps your daddy will let you stay in school til the next thing comes up."

Superior smiled that slow smile of hers at the paper and turned toward the door. Miz Wild watched her leaving and stopped her.

"Superior, do you understand me? These are white people. They are not like you, or me or us. They have the power to hurt you . . . and sometimes it's fun to them when they do. Their power is not because they are smart . . . it's because . . . something happened sometime . . . started somewhere and they got on top of the world. They got the power. The only power you got is to learn to live with them, learn to read their minds . . . til you can do better. They don't treat each other right . . . so don't you look to be treated right. You hear me? Sometimes there's good white people . . . but don't you act like that til you know that."

"Yes mam."

"If it works out, you can stay in school and even buy you some clothes . . . and that's what YOU want!"

"Yes mam."

"So give them what they want . . . long as they pay you . . . and get what you want . . . til you can do better. You understand me?"

"Yes mam."

"Okay. Go on then. And hold your head up! You not begging, you are going to work!"

"Yes mam!"

The flash of a big, slow smile caught at Miz Wild's heart as twelve-year-old Superior pulled the door shut, happy to have a job to look for. Lawd, Lawd.

She got the job. It was in a large, old, beautiful home with four people rattling round in it. The father was mostly gone, working at the many places his money came from. The mother was a frail, quiet, apologetic woman who drank periodically, staying in her rooms most of the time. The father's sister, Aunt Sam, a spinster in her fifties, was the true boss of the house. She was mean, tight and narrow-minded. If she had not been there the mother might not have been an alcoholic. The young daughter was Glenellen. Golden-haired, fair-looking, dressed by Aunt Sam, she was reserved, withdrawn or spiteful, whichever the occasion called for.

Aunt Sam was officious, but lazy, so Superior was to clean the bedroom, bathroom, odds and ends for Glenellen. Aunt Sam and Glenellen did not get along. Even at fourteen years of age, Glenellen knew she was really the one nearest the money and saw to it that Aunt Sam never forgot it too long.

The mother could care less and was always trying to keep some kind of peace in the house at the dinner table, which was often the only time she came down from her rooms. Her schedule was to wake up early, reach for a book and her pitcher of gin and ice with lemon slices, called lemonade, left there for her by Aunt Sam. Later Aunt Sam brought her food, which she forced herself to eat, and she then slept again. Waking around dinnertime, she bathed, drank her pitcher of gin (left again by Aunt Sam) til it was time to go down to dinner. She insisted on wine at the dinner table, otherwise she refused to come down to dinner. She loved Glenellen from a blurry distance, sort of because-you-love-your-children way. She grew up almost the same way Glenellen was growing up: never getting to know anything about life. She did not know what to do with it. Her backbone was in her wrist.

She had married for money because her father wanted it, not family. And once the family was acquired she found the possession empty. Her life stood still. Having only one child because of a delicate constitution, she put a tiny foot down and got a separate room and proceeded to pour five or six fifths of gin a week into her delicate constitution. Her parents had done their job well. They had raised her to be genteel, weak and dependent . . . and she was.

With no one really raising Glenellen, she was becoming wary; independent and strong-willed. She was the one who hired Superior. She thought Superior was strong and ugly. She hired her to be her maid, choreperson and playmate. She paid her more than Aunt Sam would have. She gave her $4.00 a week.

Superior took $2.00 home, saved $1.00 (wrapped neatly in tissue paper and placed in a shoe box left in her small room at her job). $1.00 went each week toward clothes and things she needed. She felt her life was MADE! She always ate at work so her father did not have to feed her any longer. She ate in the kitchen until Glenellen discovered Aunt Sam did not like Superior; then she made her eat at the table with them where Aunt Sam glared at them both. Superior learned to look down at her plate the whole time so she could forget they were there. She used the time to think of her new friend, Jewel Bell. It was lucky for Superior that Aunt Sam did not like her, otherwise Glenellen would have disliked her and she would have lost her job or suffered in it.

When Superior was happy she had a droll sense of humor so in time the two girls played and laughed together. Sometime Glenellen was her friend and truly liked her.

They combed each other's hair, tied ribbons, laughing over the shortness of Superior's hair. Played house with Glenellen's dolls. Superior loved to pull out Glenellen's clothes and touching them, dream of having pretty things for herself. But best of all to Superior were the bath salts, bubblebaths, perfumes and plenty water for the deep tubs she liked to sit in for whole hours every day Glenellen let her.

Glenellen gave her two white ruffled pinafores to wear over her patched clothing. Superior bathed everyday, washed one pinafore every night. She used the cream Glenellen gave her for her skin, which was ashy when she started but soon gleamed. She used the perfume given her every day for school. In return she gave Glenellen friendship, honesty, true concern for her, and laughter. They were friends in these ways.

Once returning from a trip, Glenellen brought back a life-size Black doll along with a few white ones. She put her collection of dolls together and added the Black one. The next day she did not like the looks of it, so she gave the Black doll to Superior. The first store-bought doll Superior had ever owned. She loved it always. She kept it all her life and treated it like it was a real baby.

Time passed and life changed for Superior. It grew better and quieter. The quiet was in her heart, above a full stomach and beneath decent clothes. Her school grades became better a little. Especially in her art class. The teacher noted the change in the sad drawings. The barren landscapes turned to filled gardens with rows of bright-colored vegetables and trees filled with full, juicy fruits. The sun was now rising instead of setting. Superior was the happiest she had ever been. She also had her best friend, Jewel.

Jewel was a cinnamon-brown, pretty girl. The small type, cute and sassy. And very fast. She liked boys a lot. Sought them out all the time. They liked her right back. Because she had ready laughter and she let them touch her. Her father had been long gone. Her mother was not a fast woman, she worked, but she kept pretty good company. Wasn't any weeds in her garden! Neither one of them always knew where the other one was. Just knew they'd be home sometime!

Superior being so quiet, shy and all, it seems maybe strange they were friends. But it was the way life seemed exciting to Superior . . . and Jewel wouldn't have let a good-looking girl be around her business!

Her business was following the boys around. If they were playing basketball in some homemade court, Jewel was there, watching and teasing. If they played football in some space on the street, Jewel was there, watchin and teasing.

Jewel always waited til after the games when they all sat around talking, until their attention finally turned to her. There was always someone favorite of the time, which changed regular. Jewel was a girl who 'went all the way' before the way was clear to her. So she was popular in the way those girls are.

Jewel didn't mind Superior because she was no threat to her. Superior liked Jewel no matter what she did because Jewel didn't laugh at her slow ways or talk about her. So they were friends through the years.

Now, around this time I retired from teaching school and was not able to know as much as I need to know to tell you everything important to what I want you to know. My daughter, who I wanted to become a teacher, didn't. She married right out of school. She grew up right along with Superior and Jewel, so she knows more than I do. That's why I want her to tell you as she told me, from now on.

I always liked Superior better than I did Jewel. Jewel was so fast, even for me, and I was not all that slow.

When they was bout sixteen, gettin close to graduation from school, Jewel had escaped gettin pregnant. She really did not want no babies! Superior was still workin and looking forward to graduate as a gift to her mama even tho her mama was dead. They was still friends cept Jewel was gettin testy with Superior cause Superior would not let boys under her dress.

Gossip and the boys shyin away from Jewel made her feel cheap sometimes and she didn't like Superior's virginity. With malice in her heart she tried to laugh and tease Superior into trying "it," but Superior just wouldn't! She wouldn'ta done it anyway. She didn't want no baby messin with her graduation for her mama. Sides, didn't nobody much ask her.

Now, there was a young man, Ruddy, graduated head of them, who Jewel liked a lot. He liked Jewel in the dark, but he liked to stand close to Superior in the day. He loved to smell all the lovely smells she wore. Jewel took to likin Superior less, but didn't tell her. Just treated her more mean . . . playfully.

Superior had some nice, gentle ways. It wasn't long fore that Ruddy thought he liked her. Girls was so easy for him to get, he just knew he could get her. She liked him, but she wouldn't lift that dress up for him like Jewel did.

Now, it's a funny thing. It wasn't cause he really liked her that his ego got next to him and made him think he really liked her more. It was cause he loved hisself and couldn't understand this halfway ugly girl not rollin back when HE asked her to! You know, some men will marry to get what they after! That's what most women used to know. They don't know that so much anymore!

Anyway, Ruddy fancied hisself in love with a woman who would be all his. He got a job as a laborer somewhere and waited til she graduated. He knew she was goin to work cause she already had a job. He courted her all that last month, and the day after her graduation, when she felt real satisfied with herself that she had satisfied her mama, they went to the courthouse and got married!

Now, some other things was happenin at the same time. One, Glenellen had watched the last few months as Superior bloomed in courtship. She was jealous of Superior, not of Ruddy, but that Superior had SOMEONE. Her family didn't allow her to have anyone court her. Said they would be after her money!

She would try to be in the yard when Ruddy walked Superior home from school sometime, or on a Sunday when he walked her home from church. Glenellen would make her presence known and act uppity and cute. She watched Ruddy carefully. She had been told hundreds of times by her family that Negro men lusted after all white flesh. "That they loved white women. Would kill to get one. Might even kill the one they wanted to get. They was animals, with SEX always on their little minds. Negro men were dangerous! Only the very old ones might be safe . . . or the dumb ones like that Percy who worked for them as a handyman sometimes. And then, you couldn't always trust them either!"

When Ruddy would consciously pay her no mind, she would snap at Superior and insist on her goin in the house to do something she would make up on the spot. Ruddy couldn't never go in that house, you see. Ruddy did pay her some mind, but would never let her see him doin it cause his folks had done told him the danger of white women. "That they lusted after Negro men, but the end was almost always death for the Negro man. That the white woman would get her satisfaction and then holler rape! That even if it didn't mean death, it sure meant trouble!" So he did not let her see he paid her any mind. Fact is, Ruddy paid all women some mind. He was a high-sexed man . . . and young!

Jewel took to hating Superior a little. The ugly one had got married first! And . . . to a man Jewel herself wanted. She kept bein her friend to her face tho, cause she planned to borrow some money if she could, to leave this town. She was going somewhere away from the gossip of small-town minds where she could be free! To live . . . have money and dress in the latest styles! Have fun! She was young!

Jewel even started a affair with Ruddy bout a month after he married Superior. She just asked Superior could he come over and help her lift somethin was too heavy for her to lift. He went and when he got there, she was layin cross the bed, naked, with her legs open. So the affair started . . . and continued til Jewel left town, and even picked up every time she came home for a visit or to live awhile.

Meanwhile, Ruddy and Superior moved into a little shotgun house that she kept as warmly homey and neat as a pin. Her little Black babydoll sittin on the bed all day. She was happy. This was HER house. Her mama would be proud. Ruddy was comfortable as hell! Clothes always clean. Stomach always full. A good woman in his bed that he knew wasn't foolin round nowhere!

The first two months or so, Ruddy brought all his pay home. After that, he kept half of it, as he felt a man should. After all, Superior worked! They had aplenty food and furniture at home. Then Superior got in the family way. Of course! She was a fine, strong, healthy woman and he was lusty as hell! She was happy. He was proud of hisself on one side and scared of the responsibility on the other side. He added a few ladies on the side and started drinking more cause he partied more down at the one gambling shack, where men could be men!

Jewel had done got her money some kinda way and was laughin and happy as she made her plans to get on out of town . . . to the Big City! She went by to tell Superior she was goin and see could she get a few extra dollars. She got em. Ain't some people somethin!? Using her husband and now, gonna use her money too! When Superior told her bout the baby, she laughed at her like she was a fool! (Well, maybe she was!)

She say, "Girl! You gonna be stuck up here in this dumb town with that ugly husband of yours! A brat in your belly! Girl, you ought to be shamed! If not shamed, then smarter!"

Superior set a plate of food in front of Jewel, who was always hungry. Said, "Jewel, I always did want a baby. I love little babies!"

With her mouth full, Jewel said, "I shoulda known that by the way you keep that ugly Black doll-baby sittin there on your bed! Well, pretty soon you have a real one. But it ain't gonna lay there quiet like that! It's gonna cry and eat and shit and pee, vomit and walk your ass all night! You a fool!"

Superior shook her head. "If a baby make you a fool, then I won't be the first one."

Jewel set her glass of buttermilk down. "Not the last one either! But you won't catch me catchin no babies up there! Uh-uh! It's better things in life for me and . . . I'm gonna get em!"

Superior smiled. "Of course you ain't gonna have a baby. You ain't married yet."

Jewel quit laughin. "What you mean by that?"

Superior didn't hear the anger. "That when you find the right man and settle down, you'll want to have a baby. Have a family."

Jewel relaxed, "That's what you doin? Having a family, huh? You got you a good husband . . . and now you gonna have you a good child . . . a good family." She leaned her head back and laughed.

Superior smiled. "Well, I want my mama and since I can't have her, I'll be somebody else mama. I want my little baby child."

Jewel picked her teeth, said, "Superior, reach into one of them sacks or teapots and hand me five or ten dollars til I can send it back to you. I don't want to be caught up in no Big City and get broke fore I can strike it rich! I'll send it back to you."

Superior was good-hearted, but not a foolish person. She thought of her child on the way. She did indeed have some hard-earned money in a sack in a pot way back in the cupboard. But she was gonna need her own money, and not for no fun.

"I'll give you a dollar," she offered.

Jewel frowned. "Girl, is that all you got? Marriage ain't done you no good! Just filled your belly up!" She belched.

Superior removed the plates to the sink, saying, "Well, I'm married, that's all. I don't want nothing else." She held the dollar out to Jewel. Jewel took it. They hugged good-bye and good luck. Then Jewel was gone on her happy way. Steppin down the street in her high-heeled shoes with the net stockings and the print dress Superior brought her from Glenellen's. The saucy little hat just abouncing on her head as she busted out of town to her future.

Another thing that happened round that time was Glenellen was going to college. Her parents was planning for her to become a doctor or a teacher. They still did not allow Glenellen to take company. Ain't that somethin! At her age!

She liked a fellow, Drew, was a professor at a small college not too far from this town. Her parents didn't like him cause he was divorced. When she fought her parents to make them at least let her date Drew, they took steps and lied to get him fired or transferred. At the same time she liked another man, friendly like, who was a instructor at the ballet classes she attended. He was married, but his wife was a invalid . . . crippled. Glenellen felt sorry for him. He was goin to leave to take his wife where she could have better doctors and attention. So her two friends were leaving. She had no other men-friends in her close, guarded life. Aunt Sam was like a soldier watchin on a battlefield. Her mama was not about to get in a fight over anything and just stayed in bed with her pitcher of gin. Her daddy stayed gone, leavin everything in Aunt Sam's hands, which Aunt Sam loved! The only other friend she had was Superior and Superior was married to her own man.

The day Drew told her what her family had done to get him transferred, she went home and fought with her family. They screamed, shouted. She cursed and shocked them. Threatened them. Then ran from the house crying. Aunt Sam told them not to worry, she'd be back. She had nowhere else to go. She was not a fool and all such stuff as that.

In the meantime, that same day, Glenellen ran back to Drew. Cried, pleaded, ended up giving him her virginity. Of course, she felt like she loved him, in that emotional upheavel her parents kept her in. She didn't realize that gift to him was only gonna make him leave quicker cause he was scared of her folks. He told her he was still goin!

When she left Drew, all mixed up, confused, she ran to her friend the ballet teacher. In the wanting to be wanted, to love, the need we all have to feel loved, she gave herself to him, too. The love-starved man with the sick wife took her. Her second time that day, on the day of the very first sex in her life.

She went home feelin empty anyway. Lonely, frustrated, guilty yet not guilty. The house was empty; the family off making sure their dirt was done and the young teacher man gone! Mama upstairs sleeping her gin off.

Glenellen cried, off and on, for all her life's worth. She bathed and cleaned herself up. Then she was hungry! She was sittin down to eat, thinking how she hated her family for what they were doin to her, when Percy came in with supplies to be put into the basement. Seeing him, her mind clumped upon the idea of doin somethin to hurt her family like they hurt her. Somethin they would hate like she hated them!

Keeping his eyes off her, Percy went down to he basement. She followed him, took off her robe and scared that poor man to death, nearly. First she coaxed, then she demanded. No matter what you think, it was hard for Percy to do. Cause she was white . . . and he was in her father's house. She was maybe even death. He didn't use his head. But he should have. Anyway . . . he did.

She was satisfied a little in her hatred of her parents.

Then she went upstairs to bathe again and go to bed to cry, even as she slept. I can tell you right now: that day when she had three men was the last day she ever had any man . . . for twenty-one years!

I'll tell you why.

She turned out to be pregnant! And whose was it?! Lawd! There could be no abortion by time the family found out. She had her baby bout two months after Superior had her first son. Her family, followin Aunt Sam's advice, had the baby taken directly from the operatin room to the adoption man to take far away. The doctor, followin advice from the parents followin advice from Aunt Sam, was told to fix her so there would be no more mistakes such as these for a while. He didn't know how to do it for a little while, so he fixed her that way . . . forever.

When Glenellen woke up and asked for her baby, they told her "gone" and that's all. She screamed and threatened, but it didn't do no good. They only put her in a straitjacket and locked her in a room. She turned her head to the wall and you might say she cried for them twenty-one years. She came out, went to college, became a grammar school teacher . . . and taught other people's children. She didn't marry, she didn't court. She just waited . . . for her parents to die. So she could go find her child.

Seem like every time she came home from school, Superior would be pregnant, belly so heavy. Glenellen always pull the upstairs bedroom curtain in her dark room slightly aside and watch Superior struggle with the heavy load inside her and the last baby under her arm as she be comin in to do day work or return washin. She sometime scream at the wall, "That Black bitch is havin another baby! I don't have any!" But still, she criticized her for bein so dumb to load herself up with babies like a fool!

Now all that happened all round the same time.

Back to Superior: she had her baby boy, came home to her house she had left clean, which was now a mess. Ruddy partyin again! She got up cleaning and washin things fore she should have. Holdin on to the table, or a chair, or the sink, as she still worked for Ruddy. Superior smiled when you looked at her even then. She sure loved that baby! Ruddy bragged bout HIS son and hugged his friends round the shoulders as they tracked dirt through the house, leaving. Leaving Superior behind to care for his son.

As you already know, in the next few years she had three more babies. Making two boys and two girls. Then . . . Ruddy brought home syphless and it sterilized both their baby-making powers. Ruddy never would have told her she had it, but the doctor said he would tell the police if he didn't bring Superior in. So he did. But! HE asked HER if she had been foolin round . . . cause he KNEW he hadn't brought this thing they had home to her! She just put her going-out dress on without answering him and went on down to be taken care of. She never did say a word. I'd a killed him just fore I died!

By this time, Superior knew all bout Ruddy and his rovin eyes and ass. But she never talked bout him to anybody. I don't know if she still had sex with him or not, cause I couldn't be everywhere. Wasn't no more babies, so you couldn't tell, and she wasn't the type you ask! I know she still loved him . . . so I guess she did.

Right after that episode Jewel was back in town. She had been back a couple of times, always dolled up in her little cheap, flashy clothes. She had pointed at every child Superior had . . . and laughed. In fact, she say, "You justa putting nails in your coffin, girl!"

Superior would smile and put something on the table for Jewel to eat. Jewel still hungry all the time.

Jewel would point to the Black babydoll sittin on the bed, saying, "And you still got that ole ugly grinnin doll-baby sittin on your bed! Look like you oughta be tired of all these babies layin round here! Throw that thing out, girl! Better still, throw one of these eatin one's out and save yourself some money!" She say all that as she be chewing up Superior's food herself.

This time Jewel was back to stay for a while. Didn't tell none of us what had happened in the city to make her come home for a while. Just came and went back to her mama's house, where they was either partyin, fightin or sleepin. Cept the mama had to work sometime. Jewel didn't. She wasn't no prostitute, but she didn't GIVE nothing away nomore. City taught her that! Them men had to come with somethin in their hands now!

This time, too, Superior knew Jewel and Ruddy was goin together sometime. It did like to break her heart! Seem like she slow down more every time life hit her now.

She didn't feed Jewel nomore when Jewel came by.

She didn't lend-give her a dollar or two nomore.

She just sit and listen to Jewel, didn't talk much.

She never invited Jewel back. But Jewel came anyway. Came pointin and laughin at the children, the load of dirty clothes that Superior took in to feed her babies, the Black babydoll sittin on the bed. Superior didn't say anything, but she didn't smile nomore at Jewel.

Now I had come to be very close to Superior bout this time. I really admired this big, healthy, strong woman. A good mother. Hardworkin woman. She was only workin part time for Glenellen now. She had to have other jobs. She worked hard washin clothes, pickin cotton at cotton-pickin time, cuttin sugarcane, pickin fruit, cookin and cleanin out-work. Whatever she could find to do to feed and clothe them babies of hers, cause she couldn't count on Ruddy now. See, once a person see what you will do if they don't, they let you keep on doin it! All of it! If you let them!

She was a serious, sad-all-the-time woman now. That big smile was almost always missing less she was foolin with her children. She was always lookin off into somewhere she couldn't take you. She talked in such a way folks began to say she was simpleminded. I knew she was hungry. Like any woman, she was hungry for love, affection, honesty. The things that make you proud to be a woman were not in her life, cept them kids.

The perfume had long been gone. Long, long gone. When Glenellen wanted to give her somethin now, Superior asked for food, or money for some doctor or a book for her children. Superior wore a size 11 shoe and you know you don't find them just anywhere. She wore men's shoes or house shoes wrapped up to protect her feet in the fields or on the roads. Superior was dark brownskin, but the insides of her hands was white. White from all the water, soap and lye she always have her hands in. I have found her, late at night, be in the mornin sometimes, sleepin with her arms right in the tin tub on the floor. Just so tired she would fall asleep as she be actually rubbin clothes on that washboard!

If she complained, you did . . . and I don't know you, do I!

Then it look like the devil thought she must be kin to Job.

One night Ruddy was over to Jewel's, drinkin and havin fun! He was in her room makin love to Jewel when he raised up, coughed, grabbed his head, looked into Jewel's face and threw up on her! Well, Jewel don't take things like that! She knocked him off and was cussin him out when she began to see he was havin some kind of attack! She drug him out her room, out the front door—in her slip, mind you! Drug that man to the corner, leaned him on the pole and left that man open to the world with no clothes on! Threw his clothes in his lap. His face was all pulled to the side, spit dribblin down his chin, vomit still there dryin on his chest. He was cryin tears, but couldn't talk!

Jewel went back in the house and peeked out the window at him. Fixed herself another drink and went back to the window to see what was goin to happen to him.

I know the man who sent after Superior, then called for anybody to take them to the hospital. I went and borrowed my mama's car and took em!

Ruddy had had a stroke. He never did get over it. He came home from the hospital and lived in that bed, side that Black doll, for eighteen years without sayin another word and not movin cept to get on or off the bedpan. Superior took care of him. Then the kids helped her as they all got big enough.

She still never complained. Sometime she just sit by the bed, a empty bowl in her tired, white hands cause she just fed Ruddy.

Sit there and stare at him . . . not mean, just sad. The Black doll look at her, smiling.

Years went by, just like that every day.

Superior remembered her mama's dreams. She intended for all her children to go to college! There was nobody to send them but her. For years, I don't know when that woman slept. She worked, and I mean she worked hard! She cared for the house, the children and her useless-for-sure husband . . . and saved something somehow.

Jewel still came over sometime, but not too much. The first time after Ruddy's stroke and he came home from the hospital (another big bill for Superior), Jewel showed up two days later.

She asked, "Girl! I heard the news! How is Ruddy doin? What happened?"

Superior kept on workin on that quilt she was making for somebody. Said in her deep, slow, soft voice, "Don't you know?"

Jewel bent down to brush dust off her shoes, said, "Well, everybody is talkin bout it!"

Superior looked down at her work. "Mm-hmmmmm."

Jewel sniffed as she sat down. "Now, don't worry, he gonna be alright!"

Superior reached for another patch, "Yes . . . doctor say he may make it."

Jewel smiled, "Oh! Good. I'm glad for your sake, chile!"

Superior looked at Jewel. "Won't be doin no more lovin tho. That's over."

Jewel picked up the hem of the quilt. "Sure gonna be hard on you."

Superior slowly leaned back in her chair. "I'll make it like I always did."

Jewel looked toward the bed, where Ruddy lay with that ugly twisted look on his face. His eyes were on her. She looked quickly away. "Ah . . . can he talk any?"

Superior just said, "No," and went back to quiltin.

Jewel asked, "How you gonna manage now, Superior?"

Superior leaned back again, looking at Jewel. "What you care, Jewel? That ain't never bothered you before."

Jewel didn't say nothin for a long time, just got more uncomfortable. "Well . . . I care bout you."

Superior just said, "Mm-hmmmm."

Jewel jumped up, "Well, I got to go."

Superior went, "Mm-hmmm." Didn't look up.

Jewel turned at the door, said "How's the kids? They helpin you? All them kids, ugh! To worry bout, ugh!"

Superior picked up another patch. "Them children are my only pleasure. They don't worry me much as some of my friends do. There's other 'ughs' sides kids."

Jewel, took another step out the door. "I'm . . . I'm leavin again. Goin back to the city!" She tried to smile happy like.

Superior didn't even look up. "Good . . . bye."

Then Jewel was gone.

Far as Ruddy ever got was to sit up in that bed lookin like a broke pretzel layin side that Black babydoll with its eyes wide open lookin to the side at him, with a grin on its face.

Superior labored on. Her times were hard. Her children grew and all of them worked at somethin the minute they was able. She didn't have to ask em! They saw how tired their mama was! She wouldn't let them leave school tho . . . and was still plannin on sendin all of them to college!

They worked at little things. Them boys of her's was sure smart. They could clean that house and fix their father good as the girls could! And did! Superior didn't have to tote that heavy water nomore, stir clothes, empty tubs, wash clothes by herself nomore. Them girls, and boys, helped.

They all was savin their own extra money (extra money?) for the first boy's college bill. And when time came he went! One new shirt and tie, a secondhand suit and new shoes. All the rest of his little things in that cardboard suitcase was old, but clean. And he had his money for them books! He wanted to be a electrical engineer man. His Aunt Egypt was staying in the town where the college was. He was goin to stay with her and work in her little café for his room. So, off he went. Whole family standin by the bus, just agrinnin, as it pulled away with him wavin out the back window! Time is kind sometime.

When Jewel came home, more seldom now, she seemed to be doin so good! All dressed in fine glitter. Even a fur piece or two! No matter what she put on, she always wore them high-heeled shoes. She was just as flip and fast as she had ever been and she was gettin older! She said she had had a husband but now had a boyfriend with a lotta money. Still no babies.

She said, "I am at the best time of my life! The top of my good looks! I don't need no babies! Who needs em? Nothin but work and no pay!"

My mama say Time is like a ocean tide. It just keep rollin on, bringin new things for a person to try to sift through. You don't never know what's comin! Or what ain't comin!

It was soon time for Superior's second child, a daughter to leave for college. Money was low, low. She didn't get any new clothes to wear but she had book money. She wanted to be a dentist. The first son, already in college, sent every spare dime home for her, and I know there was not too many spare ones. She worked for her room and board. The grins at the bus station when she left were different. They were still happy grins, but they also knew how hard it was goin to be. The worry showed through the grins of good-bye.

They all went that way, except her third child, a son. As each one got out of college, and even while they were still there, they sent money back for the next one to go.

The third boy didn't want to go to college. Already could build a house all by hisself! He wanted to be a contractor. He had done been working with a white builder since time he could tote a box of nails. By time he was grown, Superior's house had lots of nice little things done to it. Even made some things for his daddy's bed that made things more convenient.

Ruddy was still layin up in that bed stiff as a board. Sometime, when Superior feed him, his eyes don't never leave her face. She look back in his eyes, hard. The tears might come in his eyes and he try to say something, but . . . just can't. She wipe his mouth and say, "We got some good children, Ruddy." Sometime when she bathe him, she hold that little dried-up part and look at him. She say, "Yes sir . . . I blive this gave you most all your troubles . . . long with that whiskey." Then she dry him off and cover him up in a clean bed. Eighteen years passed that way.

Superior's daddy had been doin well by hisself. He had worked hard on the land and finally been able to buy a little ole dry, hard piece of his own. He might have fooled around a little, but he never did marry again. Round bout this time, he died. Superior buried him, long with Egypt, who came back for the first time, to grieve.

Now, Superior wanted to move back to the farm, but it was just too far for her to walk back and forth to some job every day. Her son, the builder, had his own little jalopy now. He told her, "Let's move if you want to! I'll drive you where you got to go. I'm kinda my own boss now!"

The last girl home didn't want to go. She was bout ready to graduate and wanted to stay close to her school and friends. Then Superior splained to her they could grow some little things to use and sell that would help with the college money for her and medicine for Ruddy.

They moved.

And was gettin on alright! That builder son fixed that ole farmhouse up! They grew lots of what they needed. Got along! Ruddy had his own room now. Sure bet it was lonely and quiet in there all by hisself. Even the Black babydoll was gone to Superior's room.

Then the first boy graduated from college. The girl dentist graduated a few years later. They both want to stay and work in the bigger city so they didn't come home to stay. The builder son was still at home, but was thinkin of gettin married. He finally did. He built him a house on his own piece of land he had bought! Now! But still . . . he helped his mama right on. Went by there or called every day God sent! When she had to get to town for some work, he was right there!

Then the last daughter was going to be a doctor. The other three sent her! Superior didn't have nothin much to do with her money now, but save it!

Superior had more time of her own too. To use any way she wanted. She was kind of artistic in strange ways. What I mean is, one time when her children were very young and her birthday came, they could only buy her a large box of 5¢ matches. After she hugged them kids and thanked them with tears in her eyes, she put them matches away like they were gold or something. Next day she bought some glue, already had some dye. Took this flat board she found somewhere and glued them matches in a kind of design, all dyed up pretty, and hung it on the wall. It really was pretty!

She could take soda-pop tops, paint em and all, and make things out of them too! So now the kids sent her all kinds of things! Beads, seashells, colored sand, things like that. To play with and make things with. She still loved that Black doll best tho!

As time went on by, them kids also bought her a freezer . . . a refrigerator, new stove, nice bedroom set for that Black doll to sit on and roll her eyes, grinnin!

Then Ruddy died one day. Just died. Well, most of him had been dead a long time anyway. She gave him a nice little funeral like everybody expected her to. The people really came just for Superior, didn't nobody care much bout Ruddy. Just glad he was off her back. She didn't say nothin one way or the other. Just cried at first, then dried her eyes and didn't cry no more. Now, seem like I remember Glenellen coming to that funeral too.

Now, I don't have the time all clear in my mind, but I know round that time soon after I saw her at the funeral, Glenellen's mama died. Her daddy had been already passed on a few years before. Superior went to those funerals, too, standin way in the back til Glenellen beckoned her up beside her. Glenellen didn't care too much for them friends of her family! She didn't like Aunt Sam at all!

When her mama died Glenellen inherited the money. Aunt Sam was worried lest Glenellen put her out of the house or in a old folks home! When she found out Glenellen wasn't thinkin of doing those things, she worried bout how Glenellen was spending the money. Cause first thing Glenellen did when she came home from the last funeral, where she did not shed a tear, was call a lawyer and a detective agency to find her lost, given-away child who was grown now! That's what she had been waitin for all those years!

Glenellen had had three men in one day and far as anybody could see, no other man since! Bout twenty-one years or so! A couple of men might have tried, but they didn't get nowhere. Musta not! Cause Glenellen never was seen with a man. That Percy, the Black man, had moved away from here with his family even before the baby was born, so she wasn't gettin nothing on the sneak.

We looked up one day and Superior was goin over to help her pack to go to New York! New York!

Round that time Jewel came back . . . to stay. She was sure older now . . . and showed how she had been livin. She hadn't got fat. She was thin . . . brittle. Teeth missing. Hair thinnin. Trouble with a knee and a hip.

Then her mama died one night, peacefully in her gin and her sleep. Jewel went over to borrow money from Superior to bury her. Superior let her have the money cause it was the mama she needed it for.

Jewel had the house, but she had to take a job to keep herself and that house up. Day work. She wore a uniform . . . with no fur piece . . . and she left them high heels at home! She did have a little ole car tho.

Jewel was alone most of the time now. When she did have company and they drank that ole cheap liquor, her voice was so hard you could hear it way down the block! She be puttin some man out . . . or crying. Even a fight now and then! They had to bring money so most them ole loose men stopped going by her house. So . . . she was alone. Sometimes she went by Superior's house. Drove out there when she be high sometimes. Superior let her come sit on the porch with her, but she don't feed her or lend her no money nomore. Jewel just look around at all that nice stuff Superior had. Stead of Superior buildin a coffin with kids for nails, Superior had a better home than a whole lotta people! Jewel just sat and looked confused and mad . . . like she was tryin to think of something and was mad cause she couldn't!

Then. Glenellen had found her child! A daughter.

The daughter had grown up in a orphan house cause people don't adopt Black children very much. The girl had white skin, but, nappy, nappy hair. When her mama found her, that hair was standing out from her head in a big, wide afro style. I wished I had of been a fly on the wall when they first saw each other! After all those years! I know both of them was surprised at who the other one was!

Now, here's something! Glenellen was raised against Black people, but was not really against the ones she liked, like Superior. But her house was empty cept for Aunt Sam, who she did not like. She had kept her life empty cept for teachin other people's children. Her heart was empty. The most important thing in her mind was searching for her child, her love, through all these twenty-somethin years! Prayed for it. Dreamed of it. Searched for it. Now . . . it was a Black child! Part of her family. Part of her flesh. Most all of her heart and could be the rest of her life!

Superior did tell me this, they were both stunned! Cause the girl, Victoria, had thought her mama was Black and her daddy white. She was a militant young woman with race pride. Marchin and all! The first time they met each other, their minds almost flew away!

I don't know all the particulars, but I know that child, Victoria, acted like she hated her mama for bein white, at first. Glenellen had to come home from New York without her. (That's where the adoption place had sent her when she was a baby. Far away.) Glenellen didn't know whether to be glad or sad cause she was confused bout how Victoria would fit in this place we live in. But she did want her child. Couldn't have no more! Don't you see? She was always goin out to Superior's house to sit, talk and cry.

Glenellen say, "She wants me to be Black and I want her to be white."

Superior tell her, "Seem like wantin a mother and wantin a daughter is more important than wantin a color, to me."

Glenellen scream, "But she's a NIGGER!"

Superior would stop rocking. "Ain't no such thing as a nigger like you talkin bout! No such thing at all."

Glenellen would wipe her tears. "You know what I mean. Her daddy . . . was Black! A Negro!"

Superior start rockin again. "It don't make no difference who the daddy was. You the mama. That's your child."

Glenellen cry again. "Oh, what must I do? What must I do?"

Superior say, "Do what your heart tell you to do. That's your child."

Then Glenellen be quiet for a minute, then, "She didn't want me to be her mother. She doesn't like white people."

Superior say, "Well . . . look all what they done to her. She been livin all her life alone cause of white people."

Glenellen say, "She talks about what white people have done to HER people! HER people! She is white!"

Superior say, "She is both."

Glenellen say, "She is my daughter . . . and I love her."

Superior turn to Glenellen saying, "I'm glad to hear you say that, cause if you didn't, then I know you don't like me at all. Cause I'm ALL Black and she half Black. And if you don't like your own flesh and blood cause they got some Black, I would know sure and well you can't like me at all and I would not be able to be your friend nomore in this life. Nor work for you no-more either, cause I don't have to. Nomore. Cause of my Black children."

Glenellen say, "You and your children are different."

Superior say, "Children are children whatever anything is. And that's your child."

Then Glenellen got up to go, slowly, draggin herself to her car. Superior just sit and watch her, then she had a thought. She leaned forward from the rockin chair and said, "When a Black Negro woman have a white baby, by rape or not, we keep it; we raise it and love it. Cause that's our baby."

Glenellen try one more time. "This town would never stand for—"

Superior cut her off, "That ain't this town's baby! Right is right! She done already been given away oncet! You find you some way, then do it! That's your child." Then she go back to rockin and Glenellen drive slowly away, hollering back, "It ain't all up to me! It's up to her too!" Then she be gone.

Old Aunt Sam was still hanging on, and she was glad the child hadn't come back with Glenellen. Old folks, if they are dumb, hate to get used to new things. Glenellen had told her that Victoria was Blackish . . . and she sure didn't want to have to get used to livin with that!

Superior's builder son's wife had had one child with that cesarean-type birth, now she was having another one and it killed her. He was left with two children to raise, one a day-old baby. Superior took them right in and tried to comfort her son. He had truly loved his wife. Superior never missed a step! She loved them babies! Well, you know that, cause she loved that Black doll-baby so much and it couldn't love you back! She had other grandbabies too, but these were home with her!

Strangest thing, Glenellen would come out and try to help her with the babies. Tryin to get used to Black children I guess.

Anyway, that daughter of Glenellen's, Victoria, must have thought about her mama cause she had spent more than twenty years dreaming and searchin too! She came home to her mama. Glenellen tried to make her wear a straight wig. Victoria tried to make her mama wear a afro wig. Neither would wear it. But somewhere in their hearts they made it past these things and got to be close.

The problem, or whatever you want to call it, came when both Superior and Glenellen came to see that Victoria was fallin in love with them two children and that builder son of Superior's! Now, one white-Black could be got used to for Glenellen, but to go all the way Black was another story! She loved Superior, in her way, but there was a line somewhere! Couldn't they see it?

Victoria couldn't.

Her heart went out to them orphan children of that man's and since he really was a good man, kind, steady, young and kind of handsome, her heart went out to him too! He missed his wife, but he needed a mother for his children and a woman for hisself! Victoria was good-lookin . . . and smart. And loved his babies! Now! Plus . . . now that she had a real home, her real home, for the first time, that girl just blossomed on out into a love child. And now with that man havin his own home and land, she could have TWO homes! Ain't life something? Go all your young life with NO home and then you got the possibility of two homes! Now! Victoria was happy! Glenellen didn't know what to be, but she was gettin used to things!

Aunt Sam was like in a cauldron of hate . . . and fear. It boiled over one night when everybody was sleeping. Aunt Sam couldn't take that visit of a Black man in her home so she started a fire in the part of the house Victoria slept in, upstairs.

You know, that house burnt to the ground? But nobody died in it but Aunt Sam. See, she was hiding. They couldn't find her . . . and they had to get out! They went to Superior's house. They stayed there the whole time the new house was bein built. Built by Superior's son exactly to the specifications of Glenellen's daughter. That's when, after all these years—thirty-five—or so they had known each other, Superior and Glenellen really got to be really friends. Superior is a good superior person. Glenellen was learnin about love . . . and likin it. Victoria grew to love them both. White and Black.

Them kids got married. The Black folks fell out and the white folks fell out flat! But they did it. But Glenellen had a heap of money and that money carried a heap of power. She lost some friends, but she had done got to that place in life where you don't give a damn, so she didn't. She even grew to love them grandchildren of hers. She go off sometimes on trips and travel cross the ocean where she can be white all to herself. But once she told Superior bout the time she forgot and showed some people her grandchildren! She laughed and said, "Them's my babies!"

Oh! It gets touchy sometimes . . . but what don't!?

Three or four years passed and things seemed to roll along peacefully. Superior's kids was so good to her, their mama. The woman had everything . . . and it was all brand new. She kept it like that! Clean, clean. She even had a TV in every room (she tried to stop them from that, but each one wanted to do more), a record player and plenty gospel records, a tape machine they sent them gospel tapes for, washer and dryer, big ole storage house just full of foods and meats in that freezer. She had clothes she never would wear and . . . all kinds of size 11 shoes! Now! And a fur piece or two!

Them now-city kids come down to see their mama, stay awhile, then go on back to the city. She got four grandchildren come stay with her sometime. She go away with one of them city kids when she a little lonely for them. They keep her a room ready! "That's my mama!" They say. "She done already worked hard enough for us! It's our turn!" they say.

The last time Jewel rode out there, she sat and looked at all that stuff. She needed Superior's son to check something on her car; it was tryin to stop runnin. While she was sittin there, she said, "Superior, ain't you over doin things a lot? You must be in a right big debt for all this junk you got!"

Superior smiled in her slow way. "I don't buy this 'junk,' them children of mine buy me these nice things. It's all paid for already. I tell em I don't need all these things, but they just keep doin it."

Jewel sniffed. "They must be makin a pile of money. Piles of it!"

Superior said, "I don't know and never ask. They send me more than I need. My son keeps this house up. Don't let nothin break down."

Jewel sniffed. "They seem to give you all things to work with. Betcha they ain't gonna send you no fur or diamonds like every woman should have . . . once, anyway! I did!"

Superior got up heavily, age and work had slowed her a little more. She went into the bedroom, opened her closet and pulled out a box, sitting on her beautiful ruffled spread. "These here are things I told them not to bother for me with, but that girl of mine, Nile, she don't pay me no mind." Superior looked proud as she smoothed the fine hair of the silver fox stole. "I wear it to church sometime."

Jewel had followed her into the room, naturally. That's how come she to be in there to see that Black doll-baby again.

"You still got that ole Black doll, even after havin all the real one's you got?"

Superior smiled, fluffing the dress of the doll. She makes all the dresses as each one get old. "This my real baby. Always gonna be my baby cause it was the first and it ain't never gonna leave me." She patted it lovingly and went back to the living room.

Jewel followed, saying, "I guess it's too late for me to have any children now."

Superior frowned. "Way too late. It takes time . . . and work to raise a child."

Jewel sniffed. "How come you don't never invite me to eat with you nomore? It's been years since we set down and ate like real friends!"

Superior answered after a moment, "It's against my own laws to feed you anymore in my life."

Jewel turned her head to the side and looked surprised. "You could come eat with me!"

Superior said slowly, "I never have taken anything from you. You never had anything and I didn't have anything then, so I couldn't take nothin from you . . . then. There ain't noways nothing to take from you now."

Jewel came back with, "I got a home."

Superior came too. "We all got homes, now."

Jewel smiled. "You welcome in my house."

Superior didn't. "That's cause I ain't never taken nothin from you . . . or your house."

Jewel sniffed. "Well, we friends for all these years . . ."

Superior just looked at her, finally saying, "Jewel . . . We both women. We been grown a long time. We both gettin old. Ain't no sense in lyin over things or even talkin bout them. I liked you . . . a heap. You was my friend, til you wasn't my friend. You hurt me . . . but Ruddy hurt me more."

Jewel interrupted her. "That Ruddy! He wasn't nothin! He wasn't no good! I tried to tell you in the beginin!"

Superior interrupted her. "Who are you? To show me? To tell me? Don't show me with my own husband. MAYBE . . . tell me if you just have to do somethin. Don't show me nothin with my husband!" Superior got angry, for once! "You always talkin bout my children, too . . . and how I was a fool! Well . . ." She waved her hands to include all her house and everything in it. "Well . . . you can see what a big fool I was! I don't have to hit a lick at nothin no day God sends nomore! On account of them kids you said I ought to try to get rid of! Now! What you got? You ain't got nothin but your mama's ole house what needs fixin! Seems your head always been empty! Now your house is too! And probly your bed . . . cause you ain't what you use to be! Now!"

Jewel broke in, "Ain't nobody what they use to be!"

Superior sat back and smiled. "That's right! I'm more! Four times me is in this world. Loving me! And four times them is growin up calling me Big Mama. Loving me. That's what I am . . . a big mama. A Mud Dear."

Jewel started to say somethin but Superior cut her off. "Don't let's talk like this no more. We can't talk like this. We gettin old. Ain't nothin we can be for each other now but be nice. So let's be nice. And leave the past where it went . . . gone!" She got up and put on a gospel record; "Help Me Over This, Jesus."

Very soon Jewel went to the bathroom, came out, and left. When Superior went to bed that night, she finally noticed her

Black doll-baby was gone. Her first thought was, Jewel done took somethin else I love.

Superior walked slowly back out to the porch and stood there lookin toward Jewel's house a long time . . . thinking. She wanted to go flyin over the land and houses to get her baby, but we know she couldn't. She did not want to bother her son in his evenin homelife, so she waited.

Early next morning she called him and he came. Together they drove to Jewel's little shotgun shack. Superior walked right in, for the first time in many years without knockin. She found Jewel standin at the foot of her little rickety bed, with the baby-doll not on it but in it. All covered up to be nice and warm.

Jewel had not put her wig on or her teeth in yet, so she stood there with tangled gray hair and a almost empty mouth with the gums showin, grinnin at the babydoll, while at the same time the babydoll was grinnin and rollin its eyes toward Superior. It musta looked mighty strange like with the early mornin light coming through that little window in that dusty, junky room with the rageddy quilt covering that doll, and everybody grinnin!

Superior must have felt what was happening long before her mind understood it. She shook her head slowly, sadly; then she raised her scarred, strong but tired, arms to God and said, "She's yours . . . this babydoll is mine. It's mine, Lord." She dropped her arms and moved, slowly, to pick the doll up. Said, "It ain't just a doll, Lord, it lived my whole life with me. It's mine, Lord. You got my mama . . . you gonna have me . . . I want this babydoll now, Lord." The babydoll just grinned and waited.

Superior leaned down to take the doll, then Jewel spoke, said softly, "This is my baby. They still sell em. Buy one."

It seemed they stood in midair, just lookin in each other's eyes for a long time. When Superior took the doll up, seem like it left a big empty spot in Jewel's bed. Then Superior was gone, her babydoll held tightly in her arms.

This was a ending, or a beginning to somethin . . . I don't know what.

But, do you know what? Superior was waitin when the store opened that morning. She went and bought a doll for Jewel! Took it straight back to her, handed it to her, but Jewel wouldn't take it!

Jewel said, head thrown back, "I don't want that baby! I want your baby!" Now!

Superior didn't say a word. Just laid that new babydoll down on the steps of Jewel's house and went on home. Jewel slammed her door and left it out there. The doll smiled at nothin all that day. But I know Jewel creeped out there and finally took it in, cause she had it when she died, layin in her bed.

I think it's like rain and rainbows. It rains in everybody's life. And some people don't never get a rainbow, but some people do.

Jewel, and a lot of other people, look for the pot of gold at the end of the rainbow. They don't find it cause it just ain't there! The rainbow is a gift from God and He ain't never cared nothin for gold.

Glenellen, like a lot of people, wanted her rainbow to be a special color at first. But she finally saw there was more value to the rainbow than the color. So she is doing alright now!

I have found out, too, sometimes you got to have the rain in order to get to the rainbow. It's like my mama being unhappy when I didn't go to college to become a teacher like my brother did. Well, I knew I was the marrying type. I loved my husband and I wanted to be his wife . . . then! My brother went and never did come back here to stay. I listen to mama talk bout my uneducated butt most all my life, but I am here for my mama. And her rainbow is my children callin her Grandmother, runnin in and out of her house and talkin bout going to college. My rainbow is her and the husband I still love and my children.

Superior was able to reach back to her great-grandmother, grandma and mama . . . to grab their dream and bring it on down to her children. They graduated not only from school, but from college too! Now! And they make rainbows for her! Still makin them!

Anyway, it was years fore Jewel ever came, hesitant like, out to Superior's house again. When she did, they would just sit lookin out at the land and sky from the porch. From the emptiness of Jewel's heart. From the fullness of Superior's life.

When Jewel died, Superior had to bury her. She buried her with that doll she had bought her. It was laying in Jewel's bed, just asmiling.

Superior don't have nothing she got to do now but sit on her porch, go to church and go visitin. With me, almost always. With Glenellen sometimes, and they got a couple of the same grandchildren now. But almost always with one, two, or four or five of her grandchildren with her.

Never alone . . . even when no-one is there but her Black babydoll.

Yes, some people search for the pot of gold at the end of the rainbow. They don't even think of the rainbow. But Superior has beautiful rainbows in her life.

And you know when the rainbow comes, don't you? Why . . . after the rain!

THE LIFE YOU LIVE
(MAY NOT BE YOUR OWN)

Love, marriage and friendship are some of the most important things in your life . . . if you ain't sick or dyin! And, Lord knows, you gotta be careful, careful cause you sometimes don't know you been wrong bout one of them til after the mistake shows up! Sometimes it takes years to find out, and all them years are out of your own life! It's like you got to be careful what life you live, cause it may not be your own! Some love, marriage or friend done led you to the wrong road, cause you trusted em!

Of course, I'm talkin bout myself, but I'm talkin bout my friend and neighbor, Isobel, too. Maybe you too! Anyway, if the shoe don't fit, don't put it on!

I might as well start at the beginning. See, Isobel and I went to school together, only I lived in town and she came in from the country. Whenever she came. Her daddy was always keepin her home from school to do work on that ole broke-down farm of his. He was a real rude, stocky, solid, bearlike, gray-haired man with red-rimmed eyes. Can't lie about him, he worked all the time hisself. But that's what he wanted to do with his life. His kids, they didn't mind workin, but not ALL the time! He never gave them any money to spend on pleasure things like everybody need if they gonna keep workin all the time.

He was even stingy at the dinner table. Grow it or don't get it! Even his horses and cows was thin. Everything on his farm didn't like him. All his kids he hadn't put out for not workin left soon as they could, whether they was out of school yet or not! That finally left only Isobel. She did farm work and all the housework, small as she was. Her mother was sickly. I magine I'd get sick too if I knew that man was comin home to me everyday!

He ran all the boys off who came out to see Isobel. He either put them to work on some odd job or told em not to come back. I know, cause when we was bout sixteen and still in high school I rode out there with one boy who was scared to go by hisself. I wasn't scared of nothin . . . then!

I saw that ole man watchin and waitin for us to reach the house. Isobel was standing in the doorway, a pot in her hands and a apron on, getting ready to go slop some pigs. She looked . . . her face was all cracked, it seemed. Not cause she liked that boy so much, but because she wanted to be young, stead of old like her father. We left.

Now me, I grew up any which way in my parents' house, full of kids and everybody building their own world right there inside that house. We had the kind of family that when Mama and Daddy was gone off on some business or other and we sposed to clean the house? we would slop soapy water all over the kitchen floor, put our skates on and have a skating rink party. Oh! That was fun, fun! Then as soon as Mama and Daddy drive up, them skates be off! We could mop, dust, wash dishes, make beds, whatever, before they got in the house! There! Poor, for sure, but happy!

Well, you know you grow up and forget everybody and everything cept your own special business. That's what I did. I was grown and married twelve years when Isobel came back into my life. She had been married bout seven years then herself.

Tolly was her husband's name and he had done got to be a good friend of my husband. Tolly was a travelin salesman, for true. He had traveled right on Isobel's daddy's farm and stole that girl right out from under her daddy's time-clock she was still punching at. She was twenty-four years old then, still not ever married. We was both thirty-one or so when they moved next door to me and Gravy.

I was very glad to have a old school chum for a neighbor. I had just at that time left one of them ladies clubs that ain't nothing but fussing, gossip and keepin up with the Joneses type of thing. Not doin nothin important! Just getting together to go to each other's houses to see how everybody else was livin! Stuff like that. My usual best friend had moved away from this town and I didn't have a new one I trusted. My mama had told me that I would look up one day and could count my friends on one hand and sometimes, one finger! She was right . . . again.

One day, just before Tolly and Isobel moved in their new house, he was over to see Gravy, and I told him, "You all have dinner over here with us on your movin day. Tell Isobel don't bother with no cookin!"

He looked at me like I was in space. "Better not do that, Molly. I been puttin off telling you that for some reason Isobel won't tell me, she does not like you . . . at all!"

I was honestly shocked. "Not like me? Why?"

He frowned and shook his head. "Won't tell me why. Just got awful upset when I told her you was going to be our neighbor."

I never heard of such a thing! "Upset?"

He nodded his head. "I mean she was! Almost didn't want to move here! There just ain't nowhere else I like right now, and the price is right."

I thought a minute. "Well, when you all move in, I'll find out what's wrong! I can't remember nothing I ever did to her. I was lookin forward to havin you two close—"

He cut me off. "Don't count on it! Isobel is kinda sickly and it makes her awful mean to get along with! Sometimes I want to give up, but we married and I'm gonna make it work, single-handed if I have to!"

I sat down, wondering. In all the time we knew him I never had guessed they had a problem marriage.

He turned to my husband. "Man, you lucky havin a wife like Molly. Molly got sense. My woman think everybody always lyin to her!" He turned to me. "If you ever run into her accidently don't mention nothin bout my name! She blives every woman is after me! Anyway, she say you already done told all kinda lies on her when you all was in school."

I gasped, cause it wasn't true!

He kept talkin. "She told me some terrible things about you! But I know how she lies, so I didn't pay them no mind."

Gravy was looking at him with a funny-lookin frown on his face. I looked like I was being pushed out of a airplane.

Tolly ended up telling us, as he shook his head sadly, "She goes to bed . . . and every mornin when she gets up, the pillowcase be just full of blood. Her mouth bleeds from rotten teeth. Her breath stinks! Bad! She don't never bathe. I have to make her! We don't have kids like you all cause she hates em! Hates sex!" He looked at Gravy. "I have to *fight* her to get a little lovin!"

Oh, he told us so many bad things about his own wife!

When they moved in, I pulled the shades down on that side

of the house. And don't this sound dumb? we never hardly spoke for twelve years! Twelve years!

If I happen to come out to empty garbage or do something and see her over the hedge, we just did nod and sometimes we pretended we didn't see each other. At the market either, or . . . or anywhere!

Sometimes at some holiday gatherings when we all happen to be there I'd see Isobel. She'd be in a corner somewhere. Sad eyes, mouth always closed, and when she did talk, she put her hand over it. Which made what Tolly said seem true.

Sometimes when I had problems, I'd look over there and wish we were friends. Tolly was gone bout four days out of every week. Even when he was home they never went anywhere nor had any company. So I knew she had to get lonely, sometime. But when Tolly would come over, he always reminded me by some word or other that Isobel did not like me . . . at all.

The twelve years passed without us ever getting together. Ain't that dumb?

You remember I mentioned my problems? They didn't seem to be big ones. All the ladies said I was lucky to have a husband like Gravy. The fact is I got so many things to tell you that happened all at the same time, I don't know how to start.

Now, Gravy was a good husband, good provider. We raised our kids right. One went to college, one got married. Now we were home alone together.

All down through our married years, he always liked me lookin kinda messy. Said it made me look homey and woman-warm. He urged me to eat to get meat on my bones til you couldn't tell I had any bones! He liked gray hair, so when mine started turning, he wouldn't let me dye it. He didn't like makeup, so I didn't hardly wear none. Just liked my cooking, so we never went out to dinner, I always cooked! He liked me in comfortable clothes, so I had a lot of baggy dresses. Didn't want me to worry my "pretty head," so he took care of all the money.

I looked, by accident, in the mirror one day . . . and I cried! I was a fat, sloppy-dressed, house-shoe wearin, gray-haired, old-lookin woman! I was forty-three and looked fifty-five! Now, ain't nothin wrong with bein fifty-five years old if that's where you are. But I wasn't there yet! I had been lookin in mirrors through the years and I could see myself then. I felt bad, but I could take it, if it made my husband happy. That last day tho, I couldn't take it!

That was the day I saw Gravy in the park. A Sunday. He had gone out to do somethin. Hadn't said what. I was sitting in the park, on a cold bench, by myself. THEY was walkin, laughin and holding hands. He even peck-kissed her every once in a while, throwing his arm round her shoulders and pulling her to his old slim body. Not a gray hair on his head cause he said his job might think he was gettin old. He dyed his hair. He just liked mine gray.

Let me tell you, PLEASE! She was slim. Wasn't no potatoes, biscuits and pork chops sittin on her hips! She had plenty makeup on. I'd say a whole servin! Black hair without a spot of gray in it! High-heeled shoes and a dress that kept bouncing up so you could see that pretty underwear she had on. She was half his age! Why, she wasn't his type at all! And I could tell by lookin at her, she didn't know how to cook . . . he took her out!

Big as I was, I jumped behind the bushes and watched em slowly pass by, all my weight on my poor little bended knees. Cramped. By the time he got in front of me, I could have yelled a Tarzan holler and leaped on him and beat him into a ass pate.

But . . . I let them pass. I didn't want HER to see how bad I looked! I know I looked crazy, too, as well as ugly.

When they was well past me, I walked like a ape out of them bushes cause I couldn't stand up straight too fast! Some kids saw me come out them bushes and musta thought I had gone to the bathroom in there, cause they said something about a "swamp" and ran off laughin . . . at me! I cried all the way home.

I'm telling you, I was hurt. Now, you hurt when somebody meets you and loves you up and in a few days you don't hear from them nomore. But . . . this man been lovin me up twenty-four years! Settin my life, my looks and my thoughts! I let him! Well, that hurt filled my whole body and drug my heart down past my toes and I had to drag it home, forcin one foot at a time. Going home? Wasn't no home nomore. Chile, I hurt! You hear me!?

Now, I'm going to tell you somethin. If you ain't ready to leave or lose your husband . . . don't get in his face and tell him nothin! You wait til you got yourself together in your mind! You wait til you have made your heart understand . . . you can and will do without him! Otherwise, you may tell him you know what he's doin, thinking YOU smart and he's caught! And HE may say, "Well since you know, now you know! I ain't giving her up!" Then what you gonna do?

Tell you what I did. But wait, let me tell you first things first. Gravy came home, sat in his favorite chair lookin at TV, smokin his pipe. I stared at him, waiting for him to see that I knew. He didn't see me so I got up, put my hands on my fat hips, nose flaring wide open, and I told him I KNEW!

Gravy put his pipe down, just as calm as I ever seen him in my life, turned off the TV, sat back down, put his hands on his knee's and told me . . . he wanted a divorce.

A DIVORCE!?

I felt like someone had dipped me in cement. I couldn't move.

I couldn't speak. I couldn't do nothin but stare at Gravy. My mind was rushin back over our years together. Over the last months . . . looking for signs.

We had been so . . . comfortable.

He said to me, "You have let yourself go. You make me feel old. You ARE old."

I thought of answers but my mouth wouldn't act right. He went on and on.

"I ain't got but one life, it ain't over! I got some good years left!"—he pat his chest—"I need someone can move on with me. You don't and can't compete with nobody. You don't know how to do nothin but cook and eat! You ain't healthy! All that fat! Look at your clothes! Look at your head! A lazy woman can't spect to keep a man! You been alright . . . but . . . I GOT to GO! You tell the kids."

My heart was twistin round in my breast. I was struck!

He went on and on. "We'll sell this house and each get a new fresh start."

At last, my lips moved. "Sell this house? My house? My home?"

His lips moved, "Ain't no home nomore. Just a house." He got up talking, putting his foot down. "We gonna sell it and split the money and go each our own way."

I said to myself, This m——f——!

Then I said to him, "You m——f——!"

He walked away, "Ain't no sense in all that. It's too late for sweet names now!"

Now, at first I had been feelin smart, but that flew out the window. Chile, I lost all my pride, my good sense. Tell you what I did.

I fell out on the couch, cryin, beggin him to think of our

years together, our children, our home, our future, his promises, our dreams. I cried and I begged. Got on my knees, chile! Tears running down, nose running, mouth running, heart stopping. I fought in every way, using everything I could think of to say to hold that man! That man who did not want me! If I had waited til my sense was about me, I'd maybe begin to think of the fact of why was he so much I had to want him? After all, he wasn't no better, no younger than me! I had already had him twenty-four years . . . maybe that was enough! For him AND for me! But I didn't stop to think that. I just cried and begged.

I had heard some old woman say, "If your man bout to fight you or leave you, go somewhere, take your drawers off, go back where he is and fall out on the floor and kick your legs open when you fall back! That'll stop him!" Welllll, it don't always work! It don't always stop him as long as you want it to! Gravy stopped for bout thirty minutes, then that was over. I was back where I started.

He left, GOING SOMEWHERE. While I sat in my house that would soon be not mine.

Then I fought for that house like I had fought for him. Why, it stood for my whole life! It's all I had, sides my grown children, and they was gone on to live their own lives, have their own children, their own husband and wife.

I was alone.

Just yesterday I had a family. A home. I thought it was the worse moment in my life! But, you see, you never know everything til everything happens!

Then all this stuff started happenin at the same time! Before my house was sold, when Isobel and Tolly had lived next door twelve years, Tolly died. Had a heart attack. A young man too! Prove that by the fact that he had that attack in bed with a seventeen-year-old girl! Isobel was forty-three, like me. Now she was alone, I was half dead.

I decided to just go on over there, whether she liked me or not! I baked a cake and went to the wake. She was lookin like a nervous wreck before Tolly died. Now she still looked a wreck but not so nervous. She looked like she was holdin up quite well. So well, I wished Gravy had died stead of getting a divorce. Anyway! She looked at me, her lip dropped, her eyes popped. I slammed the cake down as easy as I could, not to hurt that cake, you know, and said, "Yes, it's me! I'm doin the neighborly thing whether you like me or not, and whether you eat it or not!" Then I turned to go and she grabbed my arm.

"Whether I like YOU?" she asked.

I turned to her. "Yeah! I don't care if you don't like me. I think all this mess is foolishness! I ain't never done nothin to you!"

She looked kinda shocked. "Why . . . you're the one who does not like me! You didn't want to be friends with me! Tolly told me all those bad things you said about me!"

It was my turn to look shocked . . . again! You might say I was at the time of life where ever which way I turned, I got shocked.

I gasped. "I never said anything bad about you! I wanted to be your friend."

Her eyes opened wide. "I wanted to be your friend. I needed a friend! I didn't never have nobody but Tolly."

We looked in each other's eyes til we understood that Tolly had planned all this no friendship stuff.

Well, we became friends again. She told me her new name was Belle, said, "Who wants to be named Is-so-bel!?" Said, "Now that I am free, I can change my name if I want to! Change my whole life if I want to!" Now!

I learned a lot I did not know, just on account of my not

stopping to think for myself. Listenin to others, taking their words. Trusting them to THINK for me!

Tolly had told Belle the same thing he had told me. PLUS, he ruined that girl's mind! Just shit in it! Told her things like when she talked and opened her mouth, spit stretched from some teeth to some other teeth and just hung there. So she tried never to talk to people.

Told her all kinds of mean, violent things. Every time he went to the store alone, he would tell her stories, like someone was beatin his wife bout tellin lies. Or someone had killed his wife for lying! Sneaking out on the side! Everyday he had things like these to tell her. He would slide out of bed and tell her she was the one left streaks of shit on it, cause she didn't wipe herself right! She got where she almost bathed when she went to the bathroom.

He had her believing nobody liked her! Everybody told lies on her! She was weak-minded. A fool about life. Was even ugly. Had a odor. Was very dumb and helpless. That she lost things.

He had taken her wedding rings once, for two years. Hid them. She found them in the bottom of a jar of cold cream. He told her she put them there. She knew she hadn't.

He told her she needed therapy and made her take—GAVE her—hot, hot baths, let the water run out and then he ran cold, cold water on her, holdin her down in the tub. He threw her food out, said she was tryin to poison him. Him! Complained he was sick after he would eat somethin of hers. Whenever they was gettin along alright and she wanted to go somewhere, he would dress, get to the door, then get very ill. If it was the show, he'd wait til he was in the line almost at the ticket window, then he'd get sick. If they went to the market together, he'd accuse her of talkin and huggin a man who had never even been there. He didn't allow her to spend any money except for the house note, food and insurance. She bought plenty food, paid the house notes and bought lots of insurance, cause that's all she could do!

Wouldn't let her join any clubs. Well, that mighta been good. I was in one at the time I needed to get out of. Tell you about that later!

He kept her up hundreds, thousands of nights, wouldn't let her sleep! Makin her tell him about her past, and she really didn't have any. From her daddy to him. He had to know that. He did know that! He was sick, crazy. The kind of crazy that can walk round lookin like everybody else and get away with it! I bet he told Gravy about all them ugly bleeding teeth, bad breath, oh all them things to keep Gravy away from her when he was out of town!

I never did see her cry.

The slick bastard!

Well, you know. You know all about things like that.

We became friends again. I helped her settle her affairs and all. She said, "I'm gonna sell this prison."

I said, "Sell your only home?" Aghast.

She said, "Money buys another home."

I thought about that!

She said, "Some of the worst times of my life was spent here! First I was glad to leave my daddy's house. Now I'm glad to leave Tolly's! The next house I get is gonna be mine. MINE! I'll live in that one in peace."

I thought about that.

I went to the bank with her to get all the matters set straight. The lady at the desk heard the word *deceased* and looked up in sympathy. But Belle was smiling, a bright, happy smile. She was the happiest woman in the bank!

She sat there in front of that lady, a little ragged, hair undone but neat. Nervous breakdown just leavin, but still showing round the edges. Nails bit off. Lips bit up. Graying hair saying she was older, but bright future-lookin eyes saying she was ready! MY friend!

That woman really had bought a lot of insurance! Over a hundred thousand dollars worth! And insurance to pay the house off, the car she couldn't drive yet, off, and any furniture they owed for, off. That's one thing he did for her, he let her buy insurance. And she sure did!

Belle was gaining weight, lookin way better as time went by. And she was going to the hairdresser, buying clothes, going to shows, nightclubs and restaurants. I went with her most times. I was still in my clubs, a reading club and a social club. I left the reading club cause they wanted us to make reports on what we read. I didn't want to make no report! I just wanted to read in peace . . . exchange books, eat, things like that. I dropped out that club and just started buying my own books.

Both Belle and me was lookin better, healthier and was more peaceful every day. She was taking painting lessons now and music appreciation. Tolly hadn't liked her to go to school; she might meet somebody. He always told her as he laughed at her, "What kinda thing you goin over there to waste time doin? Showing them people how clumsy and dumb you are! Girl, throw that mess out of your mind!" He put little holes in her plans and her confidence just leaked out. The desire to go had stayed tho. She was the busiest widow I ever did see! Some people might turn over in their graves, but I knew if Tolly could see her he was spinning in his!

I looked at her livin her life and I began to really like what I saw. Stead of staying home in case Gravy called, I started goin to a class to lose weight cause Belle said it was healthier and I would look better too! I started goin to the hairdresser. Not to dye my hair, that's too much work to keep up, but a natural ain't nothin but a nappy if you don't take care of it! It's shaped and highlighted now. Belle was learning and showed me how to use a little makeup right. Don't try to hide nothin, just bring out what you got!

She gardened a lot and I began to help her. We ate fresh vegetables and bought fresh fruit. Dropped them ham hocks and short ribs, chile, less we had a special taste for em sometime. I didn't miss em! Found out all that rice and gravy and meat was really for Gravy. Wondered how he was eatin lately, but threw that out my mind cause I had to get to my financial planning class or my jewelry-making class or my self-awareness class. The only one I dropped out of was self-awareness. I knew myself. I was learnin my strength every day. I already was over my weakness.

I missed a man beside me at night, but I was so busy when I looked up six months had passed and I hadn't cried once.

I didn't fight for the house nomore. I wanted it to be sold. I didn't fight for Gravy nomore. I was glad he was gone. Mostly. He had done me a big favor by giving me MY life back. You hear me? He handed my life to me and I had fought him! Fought him to take it back! Keep it! Use me some more! Chile, chile, chile.

Gravy noticed when he dropped by to check on the house. He noticed a lot bout the new me. He slapped me on my behind. I didn't say nothin; after all, he had been my husband. I sashayed it in front of him as I walked him to the door. I put him out cause I had to get to school or somethin. Or maybe just lay down in peace and think of my new future. Or take a bath and oil and cream my skin for the next man in my life who I might love . . . anything! Whatever I want to do! Now!

I prayed for the house to sell. I wanted MY money! Cause I had plans.

Belle's house was sold. She moved in my spare rooms while she looked for somethin she wanted to buy.

I asked her, "You gonna buy a smaller house this time? You don't need much room."

She looked at me, thoughtfully. "You know, I been thinking. A house just sits you in one spot and you have to hold your life into that space and around the town its in. I don't need much room in a house, but I need a lotta space round me."

I thought about that.

Soon after that, she told me she had bought five acres on the edge of a lake. She was goin to buy a mobile home, nice, roomy and comfortable. Live there with the lake on one side, the trees on the other, and the town where she could reach it if she wanted to.

I thought about that, liked it, but I couldn't afford that. I told her, "I like that. That's really gonna be nice."

She answered, "Well, come on with me then!"

I know I looked sad. "Girl, my money ain't that heavy. Not for land AND a mobile home. You got over a hundred thousand dollars; I MAY get twenty thousand."

She say, "I can't live all over my five acres. Get you a mobile home and live on my land!" I know I smiled big as she went on talkin. "Better still, I'll buy your mobile home cause you gonna need your money to live on. You buy the landfill I want for the garden cause I want to grow my own food."

I thought, only a minute; I wanted this to be MY life. So I told her, "The land is yours. If I buy landfill, if I ever leave, I ain't gonna take it with me so it will still be yours too. Tell you what, I'll buy my mobile home and pay you rent for use of the land. Then if I ever move, you can buy my home, cheap."

She laughed. "Girl, the land is paid for. I don't need no rent for land that's gonna sit there anyway! You my friend! The only one I got now."

I was happy, said "You my only friend too!" I was happy cause friends are so hard to find. People count their money fore they count friends.

Then she was serious. "I want to be alone. Don't want no man, woman, chick or child tellin me what to do nomore!"

I shook my head. "Me neither! Lord no!"

She went on. "But everybody need some company sometime. You keep me from gettin lonely enough to run out there in them silly streets and bring somethin home I don't want!"

I spoke. "You got me started on my new life . . . school and everything!"

She was still serious. "I trust you."

I got more serious. "I trust you."

She kept talkin. "I'm goin to try to pay for everything in cash. Pay it off! Don't want to owe nobody nothin!"

I added, "And grow our own food."

She nodded. "Come into town for whatever we need or want."

I was eager. "Don't need no fancy clothes."

She smiled. "We can live on a little of nothin . . . and be fine! Don't have to go to work or kiss nobody's behind for nothing!"

I laughed out loud. "NOTHIN!"

You know what we did? We went downtown and bought cowboy jeans, hats, boots and shirts! We was dressin for our country life. We was sharp!

It was finally time for her to go, everything ready for her. She drove off with a car full of paints and canvases. I forgot to tell you, she had learned how to drive and had a little red sports car! She wore dark goggles and a long scarf round her neck, just aflyin in the wind.

One day, for a minute, just for a minute, she looked sad to me. I looked sad to me. Two older ladies lookin for a future. Goin round acting like we was happy. I felt like crying. Belle saw me and asked why and I told her. Then I did cry.

She put her hands on my shoulders, "Molly? You bout forty-five years old."

I corrected her—"Forty-four"—as I sobbed.

She didn't laugh at me. "Well, spose you live to be eighty?"

Somethin in my breast lifted.

She went on. "What you gonna do with them other thirty-five years? What you gonna call em if not your future?"

The tears stopped.

But she didn't. "Now, Molly, you my friend. But don't you move out there, away from all your clubs and people, if you gonna be sad. I don't want no sad, depressed, killjoy for a neighbor, messin up my beautiful days! Don't move!"

I could see she meant it. I thought of my clubs where I couldn't stand nobody hardly. I thought of my empty days of food with Gravy. I even thought of my kids who had their own families now. I shook my head so hard. Clearin it! Shit!

She looked at me steady. "If you even THINK you might want to stay here, PLEASE stay! Til you get all of what you need. Cause if you get out there and you got a complaint, I don't want to hear it! Less it's cause you sick or somethin!"

She left.

At last my house sold. I went and told the mobile-home man I was ready, gave him a check with no signature on it but mine!

Then I gave my last club meeting, cause I knew I was never gonna have to be bothered with them again!

One woman specially, Viola Prunebrough, always was talking bout me and laughin at me. This meeting was specially for her, but the others deserved it too.

In my reading class we had read Omar Khayyám and I learned about wrapping food in grape leaves. At the last meeting before this one, I had served them, thinkin it was some high-class stuff. I didn't know what to put in them, so I stuffed them with chitterlings. It was good to me! Viola had talked about me and laughed all over town. Made me look like a fool in front of everybody. Now you know why I wanted to pay her back. It's ugly, but it's true.

I let everybody in the club know the date for comin. Then I went to try to find me some mariwanna. It was hard to get! Didn't nobody know me that sells the stuff! But I finally got some. A quarter pound! When I prepared the food for that meetin, I mixed that stuff in everything I cooked. I put on a big pot of red beans. No meat, no salt, no onions, no nothin! Just cooked. I had a plan, see?

When them ladies, all dressed up so nice to show off, got to eatin all my good food, they went to talkin loud, laughin and jumpin all over the place, saying stupid things. Eatin and drinkin everything in sight! I had to snatch some things right off the trays and hurry up and replace em cause them ladies was gonna eat my dishes and furniture if I didn't! Dainty, painted lips just guzzled the wine.

Then I just happen to put on some records by Bobby Blubland. Chile! Them ladies was snapping their fingers, movin round, shaking their behinds and everythin else. Dancin like they hadn't moved in years! Some was singing so loud they drowned Bobby Blubland out. They'd have got me put out if it wasn't my own house. We hadn't had no meeting yet either!

Then all the food was gone cept the beans. Them women musta been still starved cause B. B. King was singing when I looked up and ALL them ladies was bearing down, coming on me in the kitchen, lookin for anything they could get their hands on to eat. That mariwanna must be something!!

They got hold of them beans and ate them all. Gobbled them, smacking their lips and ohhhhhing and ahhhhhing till every bean was gone. I laughed til I cried. Why, these were ladies! Beans were in their clothes, in their shoes, even in one lady's hair. I shoulda felt shamed, but I didn't. I didn't eat anything myself! Some of them was getting sleepy. Well, they sure were full! Lou Rawls couldn't keep them up anymore. I told them they better go and then I fixed something for Viola's stomach: a cup of hot tea with a little Black Draught in it. I rushed her out then. I know when she got home, she didn't get no rest! I played music for her exit, she wanted to stay and talk and hug and cry between belches. She danced out the door with her fat self, cramps only beginnin to hit them beans in her belly. Then they were all gone. When they came to their-selves, to ask me what I had cooked, I was gone too!

I picked up all the supplies I would need for my jewelry makin. I had found out I was very good at it. People always wanted to buy whatever I made. I was goin to make a little livin on the side!

I moved into my new two-bedroom mobile home with the little fireplace. I always wanted one. As I drove over there for the first time the smile on my face liked to stretched from here to yonder! I laughed out loud, several times . . . and wasn't nobody in the car but me!

We each had a little sun porch built facing the lake. Just listen! Most every morning we wave to each other as we sit on that porch and watch the sun finish coming up, while we have coffee or tea or whatever! If it's warm, after the sun is up good, I always go for a swim. Belle usually comes out and sets up her painting stuff. Then maybe I fish and catch my lunch. I take her some, or if her sign is out that says don't, then I don't!

Next, maybe I either put on some music I have learned to appreciate or go in my extra bedroom that is my workroom, less my kids are here visiting, and make jewelry to sell when I want to. Or I work in the garden, which is full and beautiful. Or I read. The main thing is I do whatever I want to, whenever I want to.

Sometimes I don't see Belle for days. I see her in the distance. We wave, but we don't talk. We ain't had a argument yet, except on where to plant the onions, tomatoes or potatoes. Something like that.

I'm telling you, life can be beautiful! Peace don't cost as much as people think it does! It depends on what you want. Not money. People with plenty money don't get peace just cause they have money. I get lonely but I never get sad or depressed.

We both got lonely for a man sometime. But we didn't know any that wouldn't come out here and mess things up . . . in some way.

Then the generator broke down and we had to call in a repairman. He came. A little, thin, bowlegged, slow-walkin, half ugly man. He was the sweet kind. Anything you need, he wants to fix it for you. Well, there is always something that needs a little fixin.

He would work, but he wouldn't talk bout nothin but sex while he worked. He talked bout how many women loved him. Loved him makin love to them. What a lover he was. That kinda stuff. He would stop and look for a wrench or screwdriver or hammer, look off in space and tell you bout that last beautiful woman who wanted to leave her husband for him, but he don't take nobody's wife! Or the sister who said, as she took off her clothes, "My sister told me how you make her feel. Now you ain't leavin here til you make me feel thataway too!"

I don't know was he lyin all the time, but he did put stuff on your mind.

One day he came back by when everything had been done (and nobody had taken their clothes off once). He went to Belle's. She showed him her shotgun and told him, "If I don't send for you, don't come! I bought this to use and I know how! Don't bring no clouds round here, cause I will make it rain!" He left, wavin his hand telling her he didn't mean nothin wrong. She thanked him and shut her door.

Now, it had been raining all night and the leaves was dripping over my roof. I could hear the steam sizzle as some of em hit my fireplace stack. I had awakened and instead of putting on Percy Faith or somebody, I had put on B. B. King. When Mr. Repairman passed my house I told him, through the window, I had somethin needed fixin! He came on in.

The big LIAR! He couldn't do nothin he bragged about!

He wanted to lay round in my bed and smoke a cigarette, drink a little wine and talk. I told him, "You got to go!"

He left saying, "All you women are crazy! That's why you ain't got no man!" I just laughed.

He still comes to fix the generator when we need him. But that's all!

At that time, Belle's loneliness came out in another way. See, when you have all this space and beauty, it seems to bring you closer to God. Belle decided she ought to know Him better.

This is what she said: "I know the human race ain't no accident. Be bout three billion accidents now! And ain't no new kinda accident happenin all by itself! Nowhere!"

I started to give my opinion, but she wasn't through.

"And another thing," she went on. "There has got to be some truth somewhere! Some of this stuff got to be lies! If we die and rush up to heaven right away, what is the resurrection for? What is judgment day gonna be if everybody is already gone on to heaven? And if everybody returns to God, then who is on that big, wide road Jesus said would be so packed full of people?"

She made good sense and it felt warm talking bout it. She got some books and pretty soon she had a Bible study man coming out here. They'd sit on that porch of hers and study, argue and talk for two or three hours every week. Then she would teach me what she learned. Show it to me in the Bible even! I enjoyed it and was reading the books myself.

On one of Belle's trips to town in her little red sports car she ran into Gravy. He said he needed to see me. She called me and let him talk, cause it was my business to give out my own number. I told him he could come out and talk.

He came. He drove up early one morning in a very big, nice blue car. I know he came that early cause he wanted to see was anybody there with me. There was only me . . . and peace. I thought I'd be nervous but I wasn't.

He stepped in the door, head way out in front of him, looking in and around. His shiny pointy-toe shoe slipped on one of my small steps and he went down on one knee. I know it hurt and he wanted to holler, but he held hisself together and limped on in.

Said, "Hot damn, Molly, you got to do somethin bout that step! Shit!"

I told him, "I ain't never slipped on it. Come on in, sit down. Want some coffee?"

He set. "Yea, bring me some of that good coffee of yours. You make the best coffee in the world!"

While I got everything together I was lookin at him lookin at my place, my home. I really looked at him tryin to see my twenty-four years. I ain't gonna talk about him. He didn't make me do nothin. I let everything that happened happen. Other than Mala, his girl. Maybe that too. Remember, I begged to stay with him even when I knew he had her!

He had changed, naturally, a couple of years had gone by. I looked at his hair. He was letting it go and it was pretty damn near all gray now. He saw me lookin and patted his head, sayin "Mala like this ole gray hair, say it makes me look mature." He laughed a low, empty, scratchy laugh.

My eyes happen to look down at his stomach when I handed him the napkin. He saw that too, and said, "Mala say she like a round, cozy stomach. Say it's a sign of satisfaction!"

I thought to myself, Or constipation.

He stirred his coffee. "She like all them hamburgers and hot dogs, boxes of candy, jelly rolls from the bakery. Say all that meat and gravy is too heavy to be healthy." His voice was tryin to sound happy and young, but it still came out disgusted. He looked at me. I was a slim-plump. Meat all where it ought to be, and healthy!

I sat and crossed my legs, the one's he hadn't seen in twenty-four years. He looked, and took a swallow of hot coffee. It was too hot, but he couldn't spit it out. He finally got it down.

I asked, "How is Mala?"

He put the cup down. Said with a surprised look, "You know, I came down a little sick and she got mad at me for it! Like I could help it! One little ole operation!"

I said, "For heaven's sake!"

He said, "Yeah!" He started to take another swallow of the coffee, but put the cup back down.

I asked, "Well, things are better now since you up and all."

He pursed his lips and rubbed that sore knee. Said, "I don't rightly know. She left me bout two months ago." He looked outraged. "Do you know, the judge ain't gonna make her sell that house I bought? Cause she got two kids!? Them kids ain't mine! Mine is grown and got they own homes! Them some other man's children livin in my house that she won't let me live in!"

I sat up. "Well, what happened, for God's sake?"

He looked like he could cry. "She told me she like this gray hair . . . this . . . this belly and my . . . my . . . scuse me, Molly—my lovin! Then she got tired of my gray hair, my cozy belly and my gas and the way I cough in the bathroom in the mornings! Have you ever heard of such a thing!? You got to cough in the mornings to clear your throat! She crazy! That's what! Crazy!"

I sat back. "Well, I'll be damned!"

He was ready to really talk. "Ain't it a damn shame! And I have seen that man—that boy! She got him coming to MY house after dark! Nothin but a kid! I could tell him somethin bout what he is gettin into! She ain't shit! She is a lyin cracked-butt bitch!"

I sat up. "Don't talk like that in my house, Gravy. I got a special kind of vibration and atmosphere in my house. PEACE. I won't allow it to be disturbed."

He looked at me like I had just said, "Let's get in my flyin saucer and go to Jupiter today!"

Well, I'm not goin to bore you with what all he said. He added up to him and me goin back together, "like we always shoulda been in the first place." After all, I was the mother of his children. He missed me. When he got to the part where he had always thought of me, even in her arms, I gave him a look that he understood to mean "You are really killin it!"

I didn't tell him, but I thought clearly, He don't have nothin to show for twenty-six years of livin now, cept gray hair, potbelly and a blue car. I had a home . . . with atmosphere. I had a place where my children and grandchildren come spend the summer. I looked good. Because I was healthy. I ate right. Wasn't gonna go back to cookin all that shit again!

I didn't need to say all those things. I didn't WANT him. Nomore, ever again, in this life, or no other life. I didn't love him.

I loved me.

Trying to hug me, he left, saying he'd be back bringing me something pretty. I told him, "Call first. I may be busy." As he drove away, he was the most sad, confused-lookin man I had seen in a long, long time.

I never let him come back. He had done been free to pick and he had picked.

Belle got married to the Bible study man. She said to me, "Ain't it funny? People go to bars, be round purple-headed, shaved-headed or even normal-lookin people, lookin for a mate. Why do they cry when things go wrong? What did they expect to find in a place like that? Moses?" That's the way she talks. Then she say, "How you doin, girl? Need anything?" That's what she says to me. My friend!

As a matter of fact, I'm doin alright! I got a couple of fellows I go out with sometime. My jewelry makin is so good, I sell it fast as I can make it.

To think I fought this! Well, I don't know.

I don't have anyone I want to marry. Well, hell, I'm only goin on fifty. I got a future if I live right. I got dreams. Now, I swim in the lake. Maybe someday I'll try a ocean!

I get lonely sometime. But not loooooonely.

I might even get married again someday. That'd be nice too. Only this time I know what kind of man I'd be lookin for! Cause I have done found ME!

I love myself now . . . and everything around me . . . so much.

I know if I got a man there would be just that much more to love. But believe me, I'm doing alright!

You hear me?

RED-WINGED BLACKBIRDS

I just don't know how to tell things. Bout myself nor other people neither. But today, looking back over my life, I see how strange life can be. Sometime, very sad-strange. But sometime, very wonderful-strange. Sometime just mean! Strange or not, I know! Cause I'm a sister to hard times! A sister to the rain.

This story is not about me. It's about another sister to the rain, Reva. I just have to tell about me to get you to understand bout her. She is my child.

I'm goin to tell this fast and in a hurry, cause I don't like to dwell on it too long!

I was a only surviving child and lived a good life with both my parents til I was twelve. My mama was a happy person, liked to laugh. She could help you laugh your sore fingers and cut knees, or fusses with your friends, away. She always told me, "If you laugh at things, they get lighter and you can bear em better!" She loved all living creatures. Birds specially. She was always whistling, marking them. She named me Birdie.

We had a nice small house my daddy and his friends built fore

I was born. Nice, clean, warm house. Plenty food, cause Daddy worked full time and Mama worked part time. Had nice clothes cause my mama sewed.

My daddy worked for a white man who we all knew was a KKK . . . and this ain't in the South either. But he didn't cheat Daddy too much, so that had to be alright. Jobs was scarce.

I'm the one made the mistake. I took a ride home from school in the truck with the boss's grown son one evening. I really coulda walked, cause it wasn't far. Shorter if I cut cross the fields. But I wanted to walk on the road that day.

I'll remember that day til I die. I can see it clear as ever. I remember lookin off through the truck window to the green hills over the tops of houses that looked real small, far away. Seeing some cattle, black and white, every once in a while a red one. And big red barns what looked better than some houses. Lots of fields was showing their richness with the wheat things blowin in the wind, or ripe red tomatoes and green peas, ready to be picked.

But that man, that grown boy, turned to me with a snaggle-brown-tooth grin, like he had a secret or something, and reached over to me, pullin one of my legs toward him and diggin his fingers at my personal body. The day just shattered like a big puzzle breakin apart, flying everywhere.

He didn't get to do nothin to me! I wasn't scared cause I knew my daddy would back me up! I was a fool! I struggled and slapped, and since the truck was still movin, he didn't have but one hand. I had two! He stopped the truck as I gave him that last hard slap. I jumped out the truck and ran the rest of the way home. To TELL! I was a fool. That boy hadn't got to do nothin to me!

My next mistake was to tell my daddy fore I told my mama! But he was outside feedin the two hogs their last slop for the day; Mama was inside the house. I blive if I had told her first, she would have stopped me from telling him cause it wasn't nothin I couldn't handle just by stayin away from that boy and all rides home in any truck but my daddy's. Even walkin home with groups stead of strayin off like I sometimes did. I liked being alone . . . then.

Anyway . . . I told him. He jumped in his little homemade kinda truck and drove off to see his boss bout the boss's son and my daddy's daughter! I can see right now, to this day, them little thin wheels carrying that black truck off down our homemade road, hearing the rattles we listened for when he was due home.

I went in then, and told my mama. Well, I was outraged! But the look on my mama's face blew that all away . . . and I got scared. She had tensed up and her face was full of fear. She almost knocked me over gettin to the door to look after Daddy! Then she hugged me, told me, "You did right to fight, baby. But you should have told me first! Now I got to get on over there to that lumberyard, quick, fore your daddy get himself killed! Oh, Lord!"

She was grabbing her coat, just arunning through the house as she talked to me.

"Stay here! Lock the windows and doors! Be quiet if anybody comes!" Then she was gone, walkin, runnin, stumbling after that truck!

It seemed like hours before they came back. I sat in the dark, peeping out the window. Oh God! I was glad to see them! So glad. Daddy was fussing, Mama was pleading. They even looked like they was still moving and talkin when they finally sat down and was silent.

Once Mama said, "You shoulda waited! That man coulda killed you for talkin bout his son and the police! Police is his friend! Lawyer's his friend! He got money!"

Daddy said, "She my daughter. My only daughter! Ain't no

grown-ass . . ." He banged his fist down on the empty table. Dinner still sitting on the stove, gone cold.

Mama looked at me, said, "Go outside and bring the clothes in off the line!" I went, even tho it was dark and I'm usually scared of too much dark.

I was outside pulling them clothes down when I felt the strangeness . . . and knew something or somebody was out there. I stood still, listening. My skin started to itch and move, it seemed. My heart started pounding even harder than it already was . . . and I hadn't even seen nothin yet! Then I did. Because the sky was lighting up. It was some white men with that grown boy who had grabbed me. I ran in the house, throwing them clothes aside. My daddy was loading his gun.

My mama's eyes were opened big and scared, but her mouth was set like it wasn't nothin to do now but fight! She said to me, "Run baby, run! Hide!"

I held on to her. Lord knows, I should have held tighter! I said, "You come too, Mama!" She looked behind her at my daddy.

I cried, "Pleassssssse!"

She pushed me away. "I got to stay here with your daddy! You go! Run!" She was reaching for a gun and her purse at the same time.

Her head snapped round to all the places in our little house where we could hear the fire cracklin, eatin up our home. She grabbed her purse and shoved it to me. Grabbed me. Hugged me so hard I thought I would break. I wish I had!

She screamed, "Go to your teacher's house, baby! Run!" as she shoved me out. Then pushed me out the back door and slammed it shut!

I ran, but not to my teacher's. I heard more shots as I ran to the woods nearby. Near . . . so I could watch and wait for them to come out. My mama and my daddy.

I could feel the heat of the fire that was glaring up the night. Just eatin our house, sound like, and laughing. But I was cold, cold, cold. I watched and waited, but my mama and daddy never came out. The shots died away, the house died away. I wanted to die away. I just stood there, screaming. But my fear of them white men was so great that even as I screamed, mouth opened wide, no sound came out. I cried and made that soundless scream, standing there clutchin my mama's purse with the worn brown cloth and the peeling brass clasp, til there was nothing left but smoke comin up from the ashes, drifting up to the fresh morning air. Lazily smiling at me cause it had done its job so well.

I cried, I cried. All through that darkness that was left and all through that morning while I waited. For what? I don't know. It's just that I was where my home was sposed to be. Where my mama and daddy made everything alright for me. I tried laughin to make things lighter, like my mama had told me, but no sound came out.

I was scared to go to the teacher's house. Scared THEY would come lookin for me!

When the dew fell on me, I realized I was shivering like a earthquake. My face felt tight from the dried snot, spit and tears. My head was heavy . . . heavy, and so tired.

The only place I could think to go to was the schoolhouse. I had forgotten it was Saturday and no one would be there. It was a four-room building with a little office. It didn't have a basement but had a crawl space. I crawled under there, closing the little door behind me. I was too tired to be scared of rats or snakes, but I couldn't sleep for thinking bout all that had happened.

I got up and went back home again. It was still very early. In all that quiet, alone, darkness, I wasn't scared of snakes or nothin else cept them white men.

I searched over them warm ashes for my mama and daddy. Found what looked like two people holdin on to each other near a twisted gun barrel. I went and found a jar and filled it with all the ashes it could hold, from both forms. Found a small piece of twisted, melted gold that musta been my mama's weddin ring. Put that in the jar. Got the clothes and sheets off the line, cryin so hard I couldn't see nothing. Went back to the schoolhouse and moved into the crawl space with my jar of ashes, clothes off the line and my mama's purse. When I finally looked in that purse, there was a handkerchief, some safety pins, a stub pencil, a little metal heart, broken, and $3.78.

I lived under that schoolhouse two years, til I was a little over fourteen years old.

I got food from the trash cans and stuff left over in the school by kids. I got in when the janitor went in. Sometimes he had company over and I was free to roam round in every room but the one he was in. I got leftover sweaters and jackets, and once, a pair of rubber overshoes that was too small unless I wore them with no shoes on.

I was warm, cause I made my bed where the stove was right over me. I got lessons, cause I could hear most things under there. I could get the book they was using when the janitor came in. When I got tired of one class I could move to another without nobody bein bothered.

I must say this tho, after about six months, my own usta-be teacher, the one my mama told me to run to, always left big sandwitches and milk *by* the garbage can when she left for the day. Sometimes knocking gainst the building "accidently" as she did it. I never forgot that, either.

I made it. I survived.

I survived, but I lost everything was important to me on account of that little thing down there I was born with. I never was able to use it on account of that. Still a virgin at forty-six years of age!

By time I was goin on fifteen years, I had done got tired of that space I lived in and I was too big and awkward to be able to keep livin on my knees. I stole—had to steal—a jacket with a little knotted-up, false fur collar, a run-down pair of teacher's comfortable shoes, and $10.00 from the janitor's pants he hung up when he had company one night.

I didn't have no watch, but I waited til it was as black and quiet outside as it could be then I started out walking up that road to somewhere else. Them shoes had little heels, run over, and I stumbled along, carrying my mama's purse and my ashes jar in a paper bag. I left and kept going for five days.

I passed through some places, but they didn't look like the right place to me, so I kept goin! I finally came to a pretty big place that I could be lost in. I came in on the poor side of town, seen a Help Wanted sign, went in, had a cup of hot coffee, and asked for the job.

The white man—his named turned out to be Joe—looked at me for a long time. From my muddy, sure nuff turned-over-now shoes; dirty, twisted, wrinkled skirt; up to that fake fur collar on my too small jacket, on up to my kinky, smoothed back but uncombed hair and my mama's little ole purse in my hands. I made myself stand up straight.

Then he looked in my eyes.

"Mister. I am not a liar. I need a job, awful bad."

He just looked at me. The few customers in the little diner giggled. I didn't even turn to look at them.

I looked in his eyes. "Mister, sir. I need any job. If I can't do the one in the window, can I do some other one?"

He just looked in my eyes.

I kept looking in his, didn't blink even, and I knew I was going to cry any minute. "I'm clean. I just been travlin . . . walkin. But I'm a good worker. I work hard. And long."

He just kept looking in my eyes.

I didn't look away either, the tears backed up. "Please . . . sir." I wanted to show him I had manners, too!

He smiled a sad smile, his eyes was talkin to me. Then he gave me a job washing dishes. Then I cried.

I kept that job three years. Then I was promoted to waitress for him for five more years. Til that man died he could count on me. God bless that man for seeing into my heart. I don't know what all he mighta saved me from in this big town I didn't know nothin about. Maybe something better . . . maybe something worse. The main thing is, I survived.

This seems like it's my story don't it? But I got to tell you all this so you will understand about Reva.

Through the eight years I worked, I saved every dime I could . . . put it in my mama's purse. I never had touched that $3.78 of her's. I'd rather starve!

Since I was saving all I could, I always shared a room or a apartment with another girl. Most of em were nice, clean, hard-working women. Some of em was lazy, sloppy, and always late with their half of the rent money.

It was one of them lazy, sex-hungry women who drank, screwed and played all month and never had her part of the rent, Lolrita, who changed my life for me.

Now, I have to tell you this. Usually, I hoped that one of the screwing types would get pregnant and give me the baby, but I didn't even want hers. See, I just couldn't—didn't want to—have sex, so this was my only way to have a baby, of course. I had met men on my job. Black men who were hardworking and very nice. Mannerable. I'd go out with them a couple of times. Even kiss and hug. I liked that part. But when it came to that thing under my dress . . . I just froze. Couldn't do it, that's all. Couldn't!

Anyway, Lolrita had more men friends than you could shake a skirt at. Always keepin me up nights. And not just the noise either! It affected me . . . them squeaks, squeals, and moans! Made my body want to do what my mind wouldn't let it do! But all that lovemakin and still she had no rent money when it was due. She was always crying "Broke! Carry me."

One night, when John or Jack or Sam, one, came by, I stood at the door and told him she needed some money for the rent. He gave me $10.00. I was only half serious, not believing he would give me nothin! When he handed me the money, my mind said, "Uh-huh!" and flew right on in to the next plan.

Every time a man came after that, he had to give me some money. I divided it with her and soon I had the rent every month and she had extra money. When I took to washing sheets and towels for her, I took to keepin more of the money. Pretty soon, I was saving all my money, still payin the rent and saving some extra! Before I knew it, I was in business. She had a girlfriend who used her room sometime. I charged her, too.

To make a long, hard, no-plan story short; pretty soon I had to rent a house, a large one. I was in business. I called myself the maid and collected the money. Soon hired another maid to help me serve drinks, clean up and play records.

Joe, my boss at work, seeing how tired I was all the time, asked me why. I told him the truth. He looked at me a long time again, and asked if I was sure that's what I wanted to get into.

I said, "I'm in it!"

You know what that man did? My friend? Took me to a appointment with the mayor, his friend some kinda way. Told the mayor he had known me a long time, since I was a child. That I had been misused and had five kids to take care of. That I had no education and needed to open a house. That I would run a good, clean, no-robbin house. That he didn't see why I should have to pay any graft as long as I didn't make no trouble. And that I was a virgin!

Now I don't know how the mayor took all that. Five kids and still a virgin. But he didn't say nothing. Shook hands with both of us. Asked for my address and showed me out. He never came to my house. But I never had any trouble and I never paid no money to anybody as long as I was there. Lots of people use to vote out of my house tho. That's all.

I stayed open thirteen years. Saving plenty money. Plenty money. I still had my mama's ole brown purse with the metal clasp, but it wouldn't hold all my money now. I still had her $3.78, too. Cause it was hers and I needed everything she had ever touched. I had been hungry and wouldn't spend that money!

After thirteen years I had done been sick and tired a long time of them low women. I got to say, a few of em came through there that was doing the only thing they could think of to do to get out of the fist of poverty that was crushin their lives out. They saved. Didn't give none of their money to no man! Stayed to themselves and didn't socialize when they wasn't gonna get paid for socializing. Dressed clean and neat and went off by themselves on their days off.

I remember one wouldn't take a day off less she was really sick. She got her own business now and it ain't no whorehouse.

Another one went on over to Europe once a year for two or

three years. Then she come back with beautiful clothes she put in storage. She had a whole line of nightgowns. Beautiful. Them men went with her sometime just to be with the nightgown! One year when she left, I got a letter saying she was gettin married and wouldn't be back nomore. And she didn't come back either. I'm glad for them. But there ain't many like that! To me, ain't nothin but a fool do that kinda work! And to do that kinda work AND give your money away is a double fool!

BUT, I know a prostitute, or a whore, as they say, ain't sposed to be nothin! And usually they ain't. But to me, and I mean this, they worth five times as much as the woman who lays down at the drop of a hat or a whiskey bottle for a "feelin." When she gets up she ain't got nothin but dirty drawers! She got to pay for the drawers, the soap, perfume, clothes, hairdo, toothpaste and cleanup equipment! Whatever she uses! Sometimes, most times, it's on her own bed! So he ain't paid for nothin! Nothin! It don't make a man like her no better either. He don't hardly like nothin he don't invest nothin for. So if he don't pay you no money, make him pay you some respect! Get you some respect and usually you will get you some real love! Not the fancy-passing kind . . . or the passin-fancy kind. If you think everybody should be free to "do their own thing," well, that's what Hitler and Jack the Ripper thought! Did that make it right?

Anyway, back to me getting to Reva. After thirteen years I just packed up and walked off. I didn't want nomore of that. I was feelin dirty even tho no one was touching me. Smoke, liquor, cuss words, dirty minds, dirty fingers and dirty thoughts rub off on you, or they soak into the walls, and you feel it. I was tired of it. I was also pretty well off!

I got in my good ole car and just drove off. Then I put my car in storage and took a little ocean tour to let the wind blow the smell of my life away. Some of my frown lines went away. I didn't mix too well. Mostly stayed alone cause I had plenty thinkin to do. About my life. I still had no one but me. And . . . I was getting older. I didn't want to be old and alone. I wanted a child.

I had remembered my mother's advice. I had tried laughing in life, and at life, to make it lighter, more bearable. I couldn't laugh. Most times, I opened my mouth and no sound came out. No laughter to lighten my heart. That's why I had to have a child. A child would lighten my life.

After the trip I drove back to my place of birth. Time had taken care of whatever the fire had left. My old schoolteacher, old now, had been paying the little taxes all those years. She was the principal now. I thought of all I had done, been and seen, just by walkin bout two hundred miles away. She had stayed here and was the same. Had moved from the classroom to the little office. Bout a hundred feet in all. She was content tho. I wasn't.

I gave her back her money for the taxes. Built a house of stone that would not burn down, on the edge of my land closest to the school. Put a small theater in it, two rooms for art, one small library, a music room with a piano and several instruments. Turned it over to my teacher friend, in her name and mine.

I built another four rooms of stone right on the old foundation my daddy had used. My home. Then I did what I had been dreaming of. I buried that jar of ashes I had been carrying around. Buried it where I had stood and watched the house burn down. Put two markers on the grave. One for Daddy and one for Mama. You know, I didn't know their first names? Or where they came from? My teacher looked in my records and told me their names. All I knew was Mama and Daddy and our last name.

I lived there for a couple of years and watched the community house grow. Watched kids pick up the books, them instruments. Draw pictures, paint and play-act on the little stage. It was not the start of no college. It was just a community house! But, the start of new kinds of knowledge for some. And it was paying the school back for being my home, even such as it was, for those two years.

Then I drove off again. Looking for a home? My child? I don't know. I just had to go! My car was old but it still ran. And I don't blive when you carry money, big money, you need to be in no fancy car . . . if you a lone woman. That's just my way.

Now. I get to Reva. But I wanted you to know HOW I got to Reva.

To Reva . . .

My car had done got to stopping and starting when it felt like it. For some reason I didn't want to spend all that money on no new one. One night I was driving along another road in my life. It was black dark. Blue dark. Hazy like, with fog and a little drizzle of rain. The land outside was a dead, flat land and the road was mostly mud and gravel. I could see dim lights in houses off in the distance. I had just passed a few dark stores and a closed gas station, so I musta been on the main street of some town, I thought. But you couldn't rightly call this no town. I could see the small steeple of a church outlined in the dark against the sky and that's when my car stopped and wouldn't start again.

I got out and walked over to the church, pickin my way. Lucky it had white stones on the walk paths. The church was dimly lit, and, it was my luck, several people were sitting in there at a wake. I went in and sat in the back. The people kept turning to see who I was, so the preacher finally interrupted himself to ask me if I was a friend of the dead woman. I said, "No, my car broke down." I felt like a fool. All them sad people and I'm cryin cause my car broke down. They all frowned, which made them all look alike.

The preacher said, "Well, when we finished here, maybe we can help." They went back to wakin and I sat and waited.

When they did get to me, the preacher and a few men just pushed the car over to the side of the road, near a small shotgun house. As he took me to that house, he told me a lady named Miz Wilks lived there with her two daughters, twins. He thought they would have room for me for the night, til I could get my car fixed.

Miz Wilks was a small, wiry, squeaky-voiced, brown-skin woman. She wore a big cotton dress, apron and a bandana. One daughter stood beside her, leaning on the door—that was Jewel. The other daughter was in the kitchen washing clothes, that was . . . Reva.

The house was dark cept for a coal-oil lamp in the kitchen so Reva could see to work by.

Miz Wilks said, "I ain't got no room here, Why you bring somebody over here and you know I ain't got no room!?"

The preacher said, "Well, you was the closest, Miz Wilks. This lady don't look like she be any trouble so I—"

She cut him off, lookin at me. "Take her to your house if she ain't no trouble! I ain't no Red Cross!"

I spoke up. "I can pay you." I opened my purse. "I would like to stay close to my car."

She looked at my purse. "You can have Reva's bed; she can sleep on the floor just for tonight." She held her hand out. I moved into the room. The preacher left.

She took the $5.00 I gave her. Said, "I hope you already ate. We don't have much food!"

I spoke up, "I can pay you. I am hungry."

Then she thought of some food. She stopped Reva from washin clothes and had her fix it.

I saw this tired, thin, child wipe her brow and her little arms, look at me sadly, fold the towel, put it away, then start outside. Her mama stopped her, saying, "No meat. Just eggs, bread and jam." She spoke in a hard, steely voice people use when they talk to someone they don't like. I rubbed my brow.

Miz Wilks sat and so did Jewel, lounging and leanin on her mama. They smiled. Reva worked.

The dinner was much better than nothing. The bed was clean. Reva did all the washin, so it was fresh.

The twins were about fifteen years old. They did not look alike. Reva was thin, light-skinned, with kinky hair. Jewel was plump, brown-skinned, with long curly hair. Jewel was snotty, spoiled, selfish and lazy. Reva was reserved, shy, always ducking from some slap, fearful, but very sweet.

In the morning Reva fixed all our breakfasts. Jewel went to school after she had eaten.

Miz Wilks said, "Jewel is the smart one, so she goes to school." Her voice hardened. "Reva . . . she the dumb one, she don't need to go nowhere! But the school makes me send her, mindin my business for me!"—to Reva—"Hurry up, Reva, clean that kitchen, then get on out of here!"

Now, I know girls and women pretty good. Intelligence was in Reva's face. I know dumb when I see it! Dumb was in Miz Wilks's face.

My car took a week to fix. Parts to get and all. At the end of that week I had paid Miz Wilks at least $100 just to keep staying in her house.

I knew . . . Miz Wilks had given birth to my child. Reva was my child, my daughter. Lost here in this shotgun shack. Away from her real mother. Me!

I bought the only empty house in town. The haunted one! Just up the road from Reva. It wasn't really haunted. Just cost a lot to fix up! I fixed it up. Got a dog, a rockin chair and sat back to wait til I could become friends with my daughter.

I could see, anybody could, Miz Wilks loved money. So I hired Reva to keep my house for me. We became friends. I bought her things. She was a sweet, sweet child who loved that woman she thought was her mama. She loved her! I tell you it's some amazin things in life. I've seen girls hate their mamas for much less!

Why, Reva was run one way and another all day at her mama's. She was slapped, kicked even. I couldn't blive it! Miz Wilks always said what was wrong with Reva to explain the treatment. Reva's braids were pulled to jerk her around to see something she had missed cleaning. Her face was knocked into her plate as she was eating to make some point about manners. Many things, many things.

Now, usually, a sister would take up for a sister. But not Jewel. She didn't. She just smiled slyly. The devil must have been in Miz Wilks's womb to make playthings out of its fruit. Reva was snatched out of bed and struck in the mornings if Miz Wilks woke first or Jewel overslept. I've seen her nose bleed. I've seen my child weep quiet tears. I've seen her pushed out the door into the cold to reach into cold well-water for bacon for their breakfast. I have read Cinderella. Now, I have seen one.

When Reva worked for me, I gave her some little nothing to do. I would comb her hair with loving hands. Smooth her serious brow with loving fingers. I put ribbons in her hair and smiles on her face. When I laughed with her, the sound came. I loved her.

Her mama liked the money but not the good treatment Reva was getting, so she tried to stop her workin for me. Told me she was a thief and Jewel would be better for me.

But I said, "No. Reva knows how to work. Jewel does not."

She answered, "Then save all your work for one day and Reva can do it then." She thought then there would be no time for the loving.

I answered, "Miz Wilks, I don't spend my money to let people tell me how to run my business. I know how I want my work done! I'll just find someone else if you don't need the money!" She mumbled on out of my face then. She wasn't going to let that money go!

The love kept going on in my heart. I learned to keep it out of my voice and my eyes when Miz Wilks was around.

I was idle waiting for my child those few hours every day. So I decided to open a café and bar. The bar for the money, the café so Reva could work there.

I had another car now; not old, not new, just good. I kept the old one in my back yard. It was mine and had served me well. Me and Reva rode all over into different towns lookin for things for my new business. Reva was workin. She had learned not to be happy when she went home. Her mama was makin a liar out of her!

When we was out riding we ate at the best places and even went to picture shows. Reva not bein home to work, Miz Wilks had Jewel cook. Jewel couldn't cook, hated to work! Her food was lousy! But Miz Wilks raved bout her cookin while she forced herself to chew. Saying in her squeaky voice, "Mm-mmm-hmmm! Now, this is real food! Not that mess of shit that Reva cooks!" It made Reva sadder, but she wasn't such a fool as to miss doin all that cookin!

My café and bar was a huge success in a small-town way. The factory close by gave me plenty customers for lunch and dinner and the little bar always had men in it drinking beer.

Three years passed. Reva graduated from school.

I told Miz Wilks I needed Reva for more things, so she could make more money. She, Reva, was supportin that house already. Miz Wilks had quit her part-time job at the factory and stayed home, sittin sippin on beer all day and night. Her eyes was bad, she said.

Because of the money, Miz Wilks let me send Reva to school in the city, what wasn't far away. I paid for everything. Reva had told me she wanted to be a nurse. Miz Wilks didn't know what she was studying. Didn't care. Told me I was wastin my money. But the money, she wanted.

I missed that child of mine. But I was proud. Sure nuff nursing, not that cleanup stuff.

Jewel got out of school by quittin. Got engaged, got quit. Screwed round with my customers and got pregnant. She didn't let her mama know, but she had Reva's address in the city. She went where Reva was, had them babies . . . two. Twins. Left them with Reva, came home and told Miz Wilks Reva had two bastard children. Reva dropped out of school to care for them babies and came home. Her mama cussed her out for bein a bitch and a whore. Reva didn't tell her mama the truth cause she thought it would hurt her too much to find out Jewel was the mama, the bitch, the whore.

Reva's old life started again, only worse. Cause this time Miz Wilks thought she was also takin care of Reva's bastards. Reva worked for me, hard, in the café and supported herself, the kids, her mama and even Jewel. Cause Jewel wouldn't work and didn't much like her kids, not as her own anyway. Devil in her womb too.

Miz Wilk's eyes was gettin worse. She needed more help at home. To keep from doin that, Jewel went to work for me in the bar. If there had been prostitutes there, she would have put them out of business, she gave so much away. As it was, the men flocked round her like flies for a while. When one flock was through, another flock would take over.

Bout this time, Reva was at last getting tired of bein used, misused, abused by her family. Then Miz Wilks came home from the doctor's, just torn apart. Found out she was goin blind! Reva kept on helping her. Jewel had been going with most everybody. One of them somebodies had a wife. Wife came to see who had given her husband a case of the gonorrhea. She cut Jewel comin and goin, before and after. Jewel died. The dumb woman who killed her, didn't do nothin to her husband who brought that stuff home to her! And didn't do no time, cause nobody cared enough to tell the law who did it.

Reva now went crazy trying to think of a way to tell her going-blind mama that her best-loved daughter was dead. In the end, she decided not to tell her. She hushed it up, had her buried and pretended to her mama Jewel was still alive.

Miz Wilks's vision was awful dim now. Reva bought a wig just like Jewel's hair. She wore it to her mama's in the afternoon, when Jewel had always come. She pretended she was Jewel for four years! I was outdone.

Reva didn't go back to school. She mothered two children who were not hers, was her own sister half the time and herself the other half. She always came to me when she could be herself. Put her elbows on her knees, chin in hands, stare off into space and cry them silent tears. I cried too, cause I couldn't change her from doing these things.

If she cooked without the wig, (her mama use to reach up and feel the hair) the food was lousy. Mama would throw it against the wall, out the door, spit in it! If she cooked with the wig, the food was good. Mama ate everything, saying, "Honey, Reva can't beat you doin nothin! I can eat this. I can't eat that slop of Reva's!"

If she brought a present or cleaned up the house without the wig, Mama cussed and complained. If she brought the same present and cleaned up with the wig, Mama said, "Baby, Oh darlin, my child. Protect me from your sister. She does me bad on purpose when you not here! She hits me! She hates me! And I hate her! I'm lucky God blessed me with you! Lord, I don't know what I'd do without you!"

The kids began to take on like Miz Wilks did. The ungrateful brats!

Reva grew old, tired, frustrated, lonely, and began to drink to keep goin. I talked to her, but she didn't know I was her mother.

The old lady, Miz Wilks, got down pretty serious. She was dying. I remember it was round the time my dog was havin puppies. She had a cat and it had kittens bout the same time. I watch everything that lives round me. Especially mothers. I watched my dog nurse and love those fat little pups. I watched that lean cat shake her kittens off when they tried to eat.

I watched Miz Wilks as she sank toward death. I watched Reva, how she worked hard to do her mama right. Wearin that wig all the time now, answering to the name of Jewel. I watched the children demand more and more in the voice their gramma used. Their price for not tellin Gramma was Reva do almost everything they asked!

Their cat finally threw them babies off and walked away to get a new set, no doubt, or just on about its business.

My dog followed me over to their house one day just about

then and saw them kittens mewling and hungry. She laid down and fed them. They didn't know it wasn't their mama. My dog had a good heart. Better than the heart this witch had I was going to see! Miz Wilks!

I went in and sat by Miz Wilks' bed. She was dyin. She held my hand and cried to me all her daughter Jewel had done for her. She cried out of them blind unseeing eyes. Even as she cried, I looked for a reason to grieve for her. There was none. There was nothing bout her, her eyes, or her heart that could touch your heart. She was a ugly, twisted, bird-body without love, cause she had never put anything in the love bank. Yet . . . she looked so sad and lorn . . . I wanted to feel somethin for her, but I could NOT! I knew her as one of the ones without any love for others, only themselves. She didn't even love Jewel. She just wanted her cause Jewel didn't remind her of that man who musta got away. She had a secret so deep in her heart that when she choose to forget it, she did. She only hated the result! Two men made them babies . . . not one!

She slowly said, "If I only had one child, I could be happy."

I leaned over to her. "Who have you made happy? You know why you ain't happy?"

She tried to raise up. Raised them blank eyes to me and frowned.

I held her hand tightly, leaned over more and said in my sweetest voice, "Why don't you hurry up and die, you low, stinkin, motherless bitch!"

She opened her unseeing eyes wide, wider.

I said in a whisper, "Die, DIE! There ain't one reason you should live, less your god, the devil, knows one! Go ON, do what your body is tellin you to do . . . DIE!"

She sank back on the bed, "Who is this? Who are you?" She couldn't hardly breathe.

I breathed in her ear, "I am Reva's mother."

She gasped for air. "Who . . . what? Who are you?"

I went on. "Thank you for having her for me."

The old lady began to spasm.

I went on, God help me. "Jewel been dead seven years. Reva been takin care you. You ain't good enough to die not knowing that!"

The old lady got foam on her lips. "LIAR!" she almost shouted in a hoarse squeal.

I spoke low. "You lived a lie when you called yourself Mother, you old evil bitch. Now . . . do something right! DIE!"

She did what I told her.

I gently pulled the sheet over her, walked out and told Reva. Hugged her. Said, "I'm your mama when you need one and always will be."

She hugged me back. "I want a mama."

I kissed her hair. "You got one. You got me."

I went and made all the arrangements and buried that woman, Jewel's mama, Miz Wilks.

Life settled down again. Reva lived in the little house and continued takin care of her niece and nephew just like they was hers. They were selfish, mean little kids. Cause they had been trained by their gramma.

Reva worked for me but wanted to get back to nursing school and on with her own life. I wanted her to do that so I said I would watch them kids . . . like a mother should help her daughter, you know.

She was getting things together. Done wrote the school and all. I gave her the money she needed. She was almost set to go. Had to wait a couple months for the term to start right.

Now! I have to tell you this.

In my café and bar, I had noticed mongst the others, two men in particular. One, Wallace, because he had a angel's face, sorrowful voice, beauty of the kind sure to be weak. He could tell the most real-soundin lies you ever heard. He didn't work nowhere, cept beggin or beatin people out of their hard-made money. Women was pretty good to him, too. You already know that. He would do anything for money. Had already killed a man or two. He had a albino friend was always with him, named Pink—I didn't like to look at. They was a strange-lookin pair to see coming at you. Wally always joked with Reva a lot, but I could see the evil glint in his eyes, even if she couldn't.

The other one I noticed was Eagle. He was made kinda ugly by a scar cross his face he had got fighting for his sister. The scar was just so fixed it gave him a look like a devil or a very evil man. He was as nice a person as you ever want to meet. Kind, considerate, generous. He stayed alone most of the time. He loved Reva and was very nice to her. Little presents and things. Tried to do her heavy work. Mine too. But people laughed at him and that embarrassed her, so she shied away from him. He worked at the factory.

It hurts my heart to think of this so I'm just gonna jump right in and tell you and get it over with.

Wallace set up a celebration with Reva in the bar one evenin when I was home resting my mind. He got her drunk. She didn't never hardly drink much anymore. When she closed the bar without cleaning up, he and his albino friend talked her into goin to what they said was a real groovy joint for one last drink. She said no, but they walked and talked her to the car at the same time. I don't know where Eagle was, cause he loved Reva and would have seen that setup.

Wallace raped my Reva. The albino settled for the money

in her little purse, cause Wallace must didn't want him to have what he had had. Then they brought her home.

I found her the next morning crying and feeling guilty.

I held her and told her, "Don't you feel guilty. He the one did the rapin! You only guilty of drinkin and bein dumb, which is two big guilts. But take it as a lesson you didn't pay for with your life! You got the rest of your life not to let that happen again!"

Then everybody knew, so Eagle knew. I had to talk to him, hard, cause he loved Reva even if she didn't love him. He wanted to kill Wallace, who was laughin at what he called a "joke" on Reva.

I told Eagle, "That piece is gone! Don't go to jail for something that is gone. She ain't dead! She's smarter! If you want to do something for her, stay round her. Work for me part time and look after her. She ain't dumb, she just trusting. Not so much nomore, but we need to see don't no more mistakes happen."

He did what I asked. That couple of months before Reva was to leave, we both got to know him much better. That scar covered up a wonderful, good and kind man. Do anything for you anytime. Didn't lie. Didn't carry on with foolish women. I grew to love that man myself. Reva did too, but looked on him as a friend only.

That's what made me decide to spend some of my money what was just layin there . . . on him. I called a friend I knew who knew everything about beauty. I found a doctor who could take your face and beat it on the ground and it would come up beautiful. So you know he could fix a scar! Now, I didn't think Eagle should be beautiful, cause pretty is as pretty does. But I wanted that false evil look off his face. That block between him and Reva. When I set my mind, I can do anything, almost. I talked him into goin to that doctor . . . I'd pay! He went. He was gone two months.

In them two months, something else happened.

One day, sitting in my café eating a piece of good, juicy, crispy fish, I heard a commotion goin on up the street. Several of us went out and there was Reva. Running, cryin and throwing rocks at them two kids that were now hers. I caught up with her, grabbed her and she snatched away. She's a strong little thing. She was cryin and blubberin, say, "I ain't never gonna have no life! Every time I get a hold on somethin, somethin else bring me down!"

I cried, "Oh, baby."

She screamed at life. "I kept my mama; she didn't love me. I'm keepin my sister's kids; they don't love me! I'm tryin to do myself something to make my life somethin, and now . . . I'm pregnant! Gonna have a baby by a man I don't love and he don't love me!"

She grabbed another handful of rocks and commenced to throwing them at them scared, big-eyed kids again. Just arunning! She ran on cross the road, into the fields. I heard her sobs growing fainter. Them hard, deeper than sad, sorrowful sobs of rage. After I got the kids settled somewhere, I went and sat on Reva's porch and waited for her to get tired and come home.

Reva didn't come back for a long time. I had put the kids to bed. She was exhausted. She hugged me and apologized, then threw herself across her bed. I went home thinking I could talk to her the next day. I had all this money and didn't know what to do to help her. I'll tell you somethin else too! I'm not a cussin woman less I'm really mad. But I was gettin really sick of all this shit! I was ready to leave!

When Reva didn't come knocking on my door, calling my name the next morning, I went to see her. She was still in her bed . . . blood everywhere. I don't even know what she done or where she went to do it, but she was losing that baby.

I tried talking to her as I rushed round cleaning and fixing her up. I could see I needed a doctor. She stopped me from talking.

She looked me dead in my eyes and said, "This is my life. I'm the one got to live it! What I have done, I have done! That's over! I don't want to talk about it nomore in life!" It was over then.

I was scared for her, but I was proud of her! I like people who take control over their own life! Don't just let life happen to them . . . but fight back to have some say-so of their own, bout their own life! Now!

Reva was mighty sick for a long time. Eagle was back lookin after my place and sure lookin after Reva. And the kids. I was everywhere helping all I could, you know that. She was my daughter.

Reva was sure nuff falling in love with the new Eagle. Lord Jesus! He was happy with his face restored to its kind look. He looked good! The main thing tho, is somebody was loving her for herself. Doing things for her. Being kind to her. I figured they'd get married, settle down and live in that house and run the café I was gonna give them. I was thinkin bout getting away for a while. I was sick of that café and bar. Sick of this dried-out, mealy-minded, small-butt town. I didn't want to leave Reva tho.

But luck came . . . at last.

Her first mama's relatives came to live with her in that little house. They took it over! Treated Reva just like she wasn't nothin!

Reva said, "My life just ain't gonna get off the ground and fly! I'm buried in shit!"

Anyway, something happened in that house one day and Reva came out cryin and shoutin again. Relatives standing in that crooked doorway, shoutin back! Reva was holding a suitcase together, spilling clothes, crying and walkin, all at the same time. She started on down the road, staggering from tired nerves, worn wishes and that suitcase.

I waited for the kids to run out and follow her. They didn't! I ran and got my coat. Ran got Eagle. Ran got the preacher, told him take over the café, keep half the money, run it, close the bar if he want to, or serve orange juice. I didn't care!

I ran down that road after Reva til Eagle picked me up in my car. Then we picked her up, threw that suitcase in the back seat and took off!

For a minute we was all serious. Reva frowned up and sniffling. Eagle looking confused, but ready to do whatever we wanted him to. Me, thinking very seriously. Then I laughed! A happy, free, open laugh . . . and couldn't stop! I like to tore up my dashboard slapping it, I was so happy! Then Reva started smiling . . . then laughing. Then Eagle started laughing.

We all felt the past slip off our shoulders. We was free! We was together and we was goin somewhere where the future was! Hey now!

I took them home. Where my mama and daddy's grave was. Where my house stood waiting. HOME! My daughter, my soon-to-be-son-in-law (I knew). WITH me. I was home at last! With a family! I cried, and they got sad til I told them I was crying cause I was happy.

Didn't take no time to settle in. Reva and Eagle got married with the condition she could still go on and be a nurse.

I got work started on another little house for them cause I think newlyweds should be alone to make babies for a family. Soon Reva was gone off to school. She was pregnant but was going as long as she could, when she could, til she was through. She had two babies that way. Me and Eagle loved em and took care of em while she was away fulfilling her other personal life. It worked.

Eagle wanted to go in business to make his own money. He borrowed from me, (actually I gave it to him, but if he want to pay it back, so what? It'll all be theirs someday). He went into the homemade-ice-cream-parlor business with selling gospel records on the side. He makes good ice cream so he sure makes good money. Open in the summer only, unless a special order comes in. The rest of the time he takes care of cows, pigs, chickens and the garden with me.

That community center I had built, the teachers had other teachers now. They have added a Black History room. Me and Eagle are over there a lot, doing things for them and learning.

When Reva got to be a graduated nurse, she just stayed home and take care of anybody who needs her. She love that uniform! She gets up, bathes, dresses in those pretty white clothes and makes her rounds; the school, community center and anybody who's sick. She even tends animals sometimes.

They were happy, so you know I was! And two grandchildren too! Chile, chile, chile.

I'd stand over there by my mama and daddy's grave sometime and talk to em. Tell em, "I'm making a home where you wanted one to be."

I thought life was full and I could live like this til I died. I was getting old after all. Then . . . life chucked another piece to me.

Eagle's father and sister came to visit Eagle to see the children. I understood why Eagle had fought about his sister. She was sweet, ready to jump up and help you do anything you had to do. Not lazy at all. Clean. She was married, so couldn't stay long, but I enjoyed her while she was here.

The father, Davis, was a solid-looking, medium-tall man. You could tell he had worked hard in his life. His face was open and honest with a kind of question on it. His hands were large and scarred, but the fingernails were clean, always. He had most his teeth and a smile always ready. I watched him a lot til I noticed he was watching me a lot, then I stopped. Least when he could see me. See, he might think I was thinkin of him in a man-woman way. That stuff wasn't on my mind! I was already forty-six years old. I was goin to die a virgin!

He always seemed to be there when I needed a hand for something. He had a lotta good ideas for fixing things up. He could even tell the kids over at the center how things were when he was a kid . . . in person! He liked that! He liked his grandchildren too. I watched him.

He started out spending time sitting on the porch with Eagle and Reva, in the cool of a evening. Then I looked up one day and he was spending all his evenings on my porch . . . sitting. We didn't talk much. He talked mostly. And did things! Always doing things round my house, or in my yard weeding the garden. He made me laugh . . . too. Without thinkin of it.

Pretty soon, without thinking, I was fixing little nice things for us to eat and drink when we sat on the porch. Pretty soon I was gettin ready, dressed and all, for the evening sittings.

Once or twice he didn't come . . . on purpose. But I'm wise to things like that. So, a couple of times when he did come . . . I didn't fix nothin for him and went in early and left him out there! Now!

I knew it was coming tho.

One night, birds settling in the trees, pig's squealing lightly in the distance, somewhere some cow hollering for its milk time, he turned to me in the dark.

He said, "Birdie? Where you get that name?"

"My mama. She liked all birds."

He asked, "Where is your mama . . . and your daddy?"

"Dead."

He rocked the chair he sat in. "How long?"

"A long time. A lonnnng time."

He asked, "Was this their home place?"

"Yes. Right here where we sittin."

He wouldn't shut up but somehow I didn't mind. "Is that the tombstone, over there?" He pointed in the dark.

I sighed. "Yes, that's the tombstone."

He asked, "Was that all the family you had?"

I smiled. "Yes, at that time."

He smiled. "Where your husband?"

Softly I laughed. "Ain't been born yet."

Softly he laughed. "Never been married?"

I was tired of this game. "No, never . . . been married."

He stayed on it. "Then . . . we your only family?"

See, he had put himself as part of my family! But, you know what? Some foolishness got in my head on that dark night and I told him all about what had happened to Mama and Daddy and me. He just set there quiet, shaking his head. (I didn't tell him bout that whorehouse cause it wasn't none of his business!)

Anyway, I was so deep in my memories when he left, I didn't notice he put his arms around me and held me for a time. I knew only that for a moment I was at peace and my mind was quiet . . . and it was two other legs holdin me up and I didn't have to stand all on my own . . . all by myself . . . for a minute. That's some feeling!

After he left, I got mad at myself . . . a little. How he gonna come over here and step into my life and even hug me?! I went to sleep planning to tell him bout hisself the next day!

Before I could say anything to him the next day, he grabbed my hand, rubbed my arm to the shoulder before I could snatch it away! (It felt good.) Asked me to help him do something. I have forgot what it was, cause my mind went blank.

The man just could make me laugh. I was happy when I was with him. At last my heart and mind was quiet.

That evening he brought something over he wanted me to taste. After we was through tasting and was sitting back in the dark, he asked me, "Birdie, do you get lonely?"

I told him, "I got the kids over there do I get lonely."

"Nawwwww, I mean lonely for someone of your own. When they go to bed to sleep, that's them kids own private life. Where is your private life, Birdie?"

I got mad, a little. "None of your business, Mr. Man! Just none of your business bout my private nothing!"

He reached for my hand; I moved it, a little. He told me, "Everyday . . . I want you to remember . . . you are now my business, far as I'm concerned. I don't want no other business but yours."

My heart jumped and I could have slapped it.

He went on talking, "You know, Birdie, we ain't got a lot of time to be dancing and playin with each other. We got some life to live, do we know how to go on and live it."

He spoke so quietly and gentle. But he was still in MY business and I hadn't invited him!

I asked him, "Who do you think you are, comin over here tellin me *I* am your business?! I didn't send for you! You think cause you a single man every woman wants you? You crazy!"

He got up and stood over me, "I think I am a man and you are a beautiful woman."

I waved him off, but he went on talkin, only he leaned over

me and put his hands on the arms of my rocking chair, stopped me from rocking, and looked into my nervous eyes. Told me, "I think I am falling in love with you and want you for myself the rest of my life."

I tried to get up, he gently pushed me back and kept talking, "I know I love this place and the . . . peace and love you ALL seem to have. I never had that before."

Now I am going to tell you the truth. My blood was pounding in my throat. I heard my heart beatin in my ears! I thought it was nerves! I shook a little like I was cold. I wanted to pee-pee. My hands got wet as I looked in this good man's face and didn't know what to say.

But I said, "I have never had a man in my life. I don't see no reason for a man in my life now!"

He leaned on, "I'm gonna splain all the reasons to you." Then he thought. Then he said, "What you mean, you NEVER had a man in your life? You musta had SOME man! Did he do you wrong? Hurt you?"

I got my head together, my strength, and pushed him away and stood up. "I am a virgin! They lied when they said you can't take it with you! I'm going to take this to my grave with me!"

Can you imagine? He laughed, softly tho. "Oh Birdie. Oh, Birdie."

Without my letting him, he gently put his arms around me and . . . I held still. Scared to death. Cause you see, my body was answering him. He was putting words in my body's mouth!

We didn't do nothin . . . then. Time went by. He was patient . . . and gentle. We walked a lot, talked a lot. Sat and smiled a lot. Laughed a lot. We moved in off the porch in winter. At first, I had wondered when he was going home. Wanted him to go home where his daughter and her husband kept his house. Now I was scared he WAS goin home and . . .

I got that foolish TV put in and it went in my bedroom. We started laying in there, watching it. Wellll.

Now, I'ma tell you. That man started slow. He held my hand and stroked my arm, just one, for bout two days. Then he rested his arm under my head and stroked my arm for bout a week. All the time looking at TV. Those old, tough, scarred hands were soft and gentle on me.

One night when the people on TV kissed, he leaned over and kissed me. Just lips together softly. The third time, his tongue slipped through my lips cause I had relaxed them. I felt a new wonder at this smooth, tender feeling in my breast for him and his kisses.

It took about another week, and that man was under my cover, between my sheets and, mercy me, my legs. Didn't nothin really happen tho, it took two more days and some Dixie Peach. Then it happened!

I love Davis. I love Davis.

He raised his head, looked into my eyes and said, "Birdie, we are ONE!"

I thought quietly, "We are somethin, for sure!" Then I laughed softly and held him with my arms, while my heart just flew away over them trees, circled that house and gently floated down back to me . . . and him.

At my age! I'm in love! I have more family!

Lovemaking is something tho. When people call me, I can't yell back, "I'm comin!" anymore. I get embarrassed. Cause I know what it means.

Davis is my husband now.

I got my daughter. I got my son-in-law who is also my son now.

Sometimes I walk over by my mama and daddy's grave. I sit and smile and even laugh out loud. I tell my mama, "Oh Mama, laugh with me, laugh for me. I am happy. I got a family again. And you . . . you got a family too."

Then Davis comes over. He always knows where I am. He takes my hands, hugs me, and love, laughter and happiness just pour over my little ole full heart.

You know, I thought this was Reva's story. But, it's really mine, isn't it?

Ours.

ABOUT LOVE AND MONEY
OR
LOVE'S LORE AND MONEY'S MYTH

Seems like a long time ago I was born and grew up in a little ole town ain't nobody ever hardly heard of. For another long time I was afraid it was going to be the whole world for me and I thought I'd live without anything nice or good happening to me in my whole life! I found out it was silly to think like that but it wasn't crazy, cause a whole lot of people live poor, in one spot, all the days of their life.

Already you know we was poor. The house we lived in seemed held together by the newspapers glued on the walls and taped over cracked windows. We wasn't always unhappy or nothing, but everybody in our house seemed to like somebody living outside our house. Daddy and Mama too! Daddy killed Mama when I was eleven.

Now, I had heard my daddy and mama say they loved each other. I wondered how could this thing happen . . . if they loved each other. How can you kill somebody you love? I decided then that love better be watched closely. So I did just that. Watched to see how everybody did their loving. I have been doing it now all my life, and I can tell you . . . it is a lesson and a education to watch the way different people love, or don't love, other people. In families, between men and women, parents and children, everybody. I studied them all. I watch life.

I had a older sister and brother. My sister took over when Daddy went to prison, but she wasn't one of them good-hearted, do-everything-fore-she-go-to-school, long-suffering mother-sisters that raised us. Course, she was only sixteen, but you don't have to always get old to be kind and good to people. She worked me like a dog while she laid up and read magazines. My brother just stayed gone! I had a littler sister who was kind of sickly, so I did all her work for her, and any food I got hold to, I shared with her.

I could tell you how much I missed my mama and daddy, but I don't feel like crying nomore. If you had a mama then you already know, and I ain't got to say a damn word. Course I miss my mama. Even if she wasn't hardly never home, she was somewhere! And she use to talk to me all the time, telling me about life. Her favorite saying was "In life, you can go as silly as you want to, but don't go crazy!" I wish she'd listened to her own self . . . then she might be alive.

Anyway, the county did something for us, neighbors did something too, but once it came in the house, it didn't seem like enough . . . like nothing. You had to hustle inside our house to survive!

I liked school but didn't like school, cause I didn't have nothing to wear. My shoes was always too big or too small, or boys' shoes. Somebody had always wore em first. The soles flapped . . . or the newspaper was ragged and left a trail of scraps behind me. I ain't even going to mention my clothes! I don't even want to think of it anymore! Cept to thank God that's past!

One thing I can thank my sister for, she taught me how to

really clean up a house and do things that need to be done! She didn't have no stranger-boys running in and out either . . . til later. She protected us, but sometimes we needed protection from her. She got the best of every secondhand thing that came in the house! Clothes and food. First choice of everything! She wasn't bad tho, just lazy. I don't want to think about her anymore either. Don't know why I did.

This the kind of world, if you don't die, you just keep on growing up and living through everything that comes. That's what I did. When I was fifteen I got a job where I could get paid for all that cleaning a house. I dropped out of school cause money was more important. I'd get my pay and hide it so I could save it. I planned to get my own house someday, not knowing how long it really would take me. But it didn't matter noway. Cause it got so my sister and brother would look for and find my money and spend my hard work and sweat on some little nothing they wanted, then lie on each other bout who had done it. Since I couldn't save it, I took to spending it myself. I was, in the end, just working like a fool for nothing! Wasn't getting nowhere! But always, running through my mind, was the words my mama had left with me: "Go silly as you want to, but don't never go crazy!" I knew working every day, every week, and never having no money was too silly to keep doing and was headin into crazy.

I thought up asking a old lady who lived in the next block in a better neighborhood, Mama Phyllis, if she would keep my money for me. She did. So I saved a little. Bout $30.00 a year. Cause people don't like to pay young women nothing even if we do the same work them old ones do. Like we don't need everything they need! It was slow. I was tired and disgusted when I was nineteen years old.

I turned to a little ole church for solace and serenity. I found it for a while . . . then the preacher found me. That man could talk anybody into anything! And usually did! He was older and he was married, but he came to be my lover. In one way, I was lucky. He was gentle. It was my first time with a man. In the way I was unlucky . . . he was somebody else's man. He wasn't mine (maybe I was lucky). Ever which way you look at it, he wasn't the Lord's! Being the Lord's means you live under and die for God's words. He shoulda been satisfied with the wife he had, stead of the women the devil dangled in his face! He didn't really pay the Lord no heed and he didn't help me to either! He was a awful good lover tho! A good lover!

I had heard people holler when they made love. I expected that! But he made me sing opera! I mean it was that good to me! He didn't never holler cause he was too busy trying to cover up my mouth. See, we always went to this blind lady's house so we could "talk," he told her. But she could hear so he tried to keep me from singing OPERA too loud. He always told her, "the spirit came upon us."

Time passed. I looked up one day and I was going on thirty years old. Sounded like I was ancient age. Never married yet. Still poor. Going nowhere. Well, one day I sat down at Mama Phyllis' and cried. She sat there rocking awhile, then said, "Why don't you go on back to school?" Her own daughter had gone to college for a year or something, then gotten married.

I cried, "I'm too old!"

She grunted. "Never too old for nothing but crawling!"

I sniffled. "How I'm going to go to school? I got to work or don't eat and sleep!"

She rocked another little while, then said, "Would you go to school did you have the chanct?"

I thought awhile, "Ain't never going to get no chance."

She stopped rocking. "Don't kill yourself off before you die!"

I stopped crying, "I got bout eighty dollars saved. Where that gonna take me? I'm in the tenth grade . . . I think."

She thought another little while, while I thought she must be crazy thinking there was some way I could do something good for myself.

She finally said, "You know, my daughter Mavis done married a man is a dentist. Four, five years ago. She dropped college and is making a home. She always complaining bout her maids. You a good housekeeper and you sure ain't ugly, but you sure ain't pretty so much you a threat to her. She a beautiful woman." She paused to think a minute. "If she say so, would you take a home in exchange for work?"

I say, "I got a home already."

She say, "Pshew! You could go to school . . . live and eat free . . . cept for housework."

I say, "A nice house, huh?"

She say, "Ain't never seen it. But knowing my highfalutin daughter . . . it's a nice one! Them dentist charge pretty good!"

I smiled. "Yes . . . yes. I'd go and work so I could go to school, cause I ain't going nowhere here. Black woman with education can sometime do something now! Better themselves. Have something! Yes! I'll go!"

She smiled a small smile. "We got to wait and see what she say. I'll write today. You buy the stamp and mail it."

She wrote:

I got a woman here is a good worker and a good person. Needs a job and will work for a little nothing and live in so she can go to school. I blive she what you need for your problems. I don't blive you'll be sorry. When am I gonna get to visit you?

Love, Me.

Your mother.

p.s. Her name is Bessy.

I got that stamp and mailed that letter that day! I was ready to get out and into a new life.

A couple weeks passed, then we heard from the daughter, Mavis. She said I could come. I went. I had to pay my own way tho. I told my little sister where I was going so I could keep feeling like I had a family. She was the only one who had got married. None of us older ones had. Remembering Mama and Daddy, I guess. Also nobody had asked my older sister. You could see lazy on her a mile away. My brother was in and out of every thing.

My little sister had met someone at a Saturday night dance. She was still sickly but he musta been kind, cause he wanted to take care of her. You know, some people are sickly, but they are strong as steel. They had three babies now. Both worked; her, part time. They was buying their own little shotgun shack they had fixed up real nice. I didn't have to worry bout her, she was alright. I wanted to get married. Have somebody love me. Have some help in this life. Sing opera again. But nobody asked me and I didn't really know nobody I wanted. They was all doing bad as I was. So I went to the future. School and . . . another job. Come to think of it, as I look back, I know there are some good Christians but I had found a devil at church and my little sister had found a angel at the Saturday night dance. Anyway, I left.

I arrived in the city and called Mavis to let her know I was at the bus station when nobody showed up to meet me. She gave me directions how to get to her house on the city bus. Now, this city was big and I was very nervous! All them people and cars and buildings and all that noise, Jesus! After a many questions, I got there. To my new home. My future. I was surprised as the bus rode on through the streets where people lived, to see everything get bigger and better and better and it still wasn't my get-off spot! I said, "This woman, Mavis, is really living! Or is she working up here?!" When I did finally get off, mostly domestics and kids were getting off. The houses were large and the yards well cared for. I found my house and, I have to tell you . . . it is a fine, solid, huge house. Very nice! Uh-huh!

I had to ring the bell a couple of times between waits, but finally Mavis came to the door in a negligee-type gown. Her first words were, "Use the back door. I'll have to give you a key." I followed her through the house to the kitchen, behind which was my room. She kept on talking. "How is my mother?" I thought to myself, She is your mother, you ought to know!

Then she asked, "Where did you live? Do I know your family?" I didn't get to answer because she said, "We don't need to talk about our hometown here, Bessy. I never discuss my family or my hometown." Then she became businesslike. "I hope you work out. I need someone I can trust to be here and work right. What did Mama say I would pay you?" Right away, I skipped from "exchange" to a "little something" plus room and board so I could go to school. She looked at me then, starting at my feet, size six and a half going over my hundred thirty pounds to the full head of hair I had. I am not a bad-looking woman, I just need a little fixin up. She said, "Mmmm-hmmmm. Well, that's smart to go to school. Find yourself a husband. Anyway, I hope you will be here a long time. You will, if you work well. You cook, of course?" I nodded yes. She went on, "I lead a very busy life so you will have to cook for the Doctor. I usually eat out." I nodded. She kept on talking while I looked her over. I could see through that gown she had on. She was indeed beautiful. Beautiful hair, color, skin, body. Her face looked a little hard tho, like a carpenter had taken a plane tool and sculpted her face. I seen pictures like that. Abstract or something.

She showed me my room and before I could set my cardboard suitcase down, she had me in the kitchen showing me the cupboards, where drinks and food were. Then the rest of the house, as I carried her champagne, caviar and crackers behind her. When she got to her room she got in bed and I gave her the tray of wine and fish eggs for her breakfast.

She smiled beautifully up at me. "You can call me Mavis, since you are from my hometown and know my mother," she begrudged. But I said "Miz Mavis" as long as I worked for her. Cause I know people who feel one thing one day, sometimes feel another thing the next day. People may seem to give you something but don't like you if you take it. I might be silly, but I ain't crazy. I needed this job so I could better my condition, and it depended on Miz Mavis.

She stretched out in her bed, sipping her champagne. Leaned back on satin pillows, wiggling her red-painted toenail's between satin sheets. Smiled up at me, saying, "You can go get started. Do whatever you see that needs to be done. I have a club meeting this evening at seven. I'll probably sleep til four o'clock. You better cook something that can be heated up around seven thirty because the Doctor will be home then." The phone rang at that time. She snatched it up, smiling, saying "Helllloooo." Then she frowned and said, "Oh, hello, Harvey. Well, I had the phone turned off! I was very tired when I got home last night . . . Alright! this morning! Sometimes it takes all night to iron out all the problems to give a benefit, Harvey!" She listened, then said, "No, you don't have to eat out again. Your dinner will be ready when you get home! Honey, don't give me a headache, dear." She listened, then said, "I'm talking to the new maid, Harvey. I'll talk to you later." She hung up. Picking up her champagne glass she explained, "My husband, Harvey, the Doctor. You can call him Doctor. You can also go now . . . I'm tired."

I was a little worried. I was in a Black family's home, talkin to a Black woman. I had thought I could relax and feel a *little* at home. But I could see I had better tend to my business.

So I did. "How much money am I going to be paid, Miz Mavis?"

She frowned. "Oh! Well, let's see, after you do some work, how it looks! You won't be cheated, dear! What is your name again?"

"Bessy," I answered. "How do I find the school I'm going to go to?"

She lay back. "Bess, I'll run all that down to you Saturday afternoon."

But I wanted to know. "Is it far? Will I have to take a bus?"

She made a disgusted sigh. "I'll tell you all that Saturday! I'm tired!" Then the phone rang and she perked right up and snatched it. I left and went downstairs to my work.

I can't tell you how I felt. All of a sudden! in this big, fine house, a sadness came down on me. An aloneness. And I felt so insecure. Either it came from me and went through the walls of the house or it came from the house to me. I felt not settled, not secure and . . . sad, sad, sad. I am not a crybaby! I'm a woman! But I sat on my little bed and put my head down on my new cardboard suitcase I paid $2.98 for . . . and cried. I knew I had work to do tho, so I decided to cry later. I got up from there and went on taking care my business.

I really cleaned that house! Everything was so pretty it didn't seem to look like it needed cleaning, but that house was some dirty, chile. That house was dusty, grimy, sooty, spotty, smelly and what all. Not as clean as that raggedy house I left behind me, but you couldn't tell it cause it was so pretty.

I started in the kitchen when it got to be round three thirty to see what to cook for the Doctor. Ran her bath at four, woke her so she could turn it off herself. I ain't crazy! I called her Miz Mavis. Putting that distance between us that I needed as much as she did. I looked around upstairs while I was up there this time. They had separate rooms. His wasn't made up. I left it. Hell! I was tired! And still had to cook and serve.

I was cooking when Miz Mavis came down. Dressed to the T! Diamonds, furs, silk dress. I know the shoes was expensive cause I never seen a shoe look like your foot was poured in it before! Perfume trailed her as she came through the house, not noticing the dirt was gone. She looked in the pots, grunted and went out to the garage, got into what I now know is a Mercedes-Benz, then she was gone! She wasn't my best friend but she was, in a way, my sister. I said, "Get on, girl!" Other people may come from the halls of Montezuma, but we came from the fields of poverty! "Get on, sister! Get on!"

The Doctor came home bout seven thirty. I don't know what he expected, but he found me . . . and a hot dinner. I wasn't sure what to cook for him—she hadn't mentioned nothing he special wanted—but I guessed if they had bought it, they liked it, so I cooked what I found in the freezer. Steak. Added baked potato, asparagus and hot biscuits for me, which he ate almost all of, and a apple cobbler. He told me to sit with him and eat but I took a tray into my room and ate by myself. I didn't know enough bout things round there yet! I'd mind my business til I found out more bout this other business.

I finally got in school. Junior college, night classes. Business course. Doctor helped me. I took some kind of test, GED, and passed right on over high school. It was all up to me now! I studied hard . . . for myself! Miz Mavis had said I could find a husband in college, but all I found there was people as poor and searching as me. I found out later from her she was in college when she found Doctor. When they married she dropped out to make a home for him. She was about thirty-three years old now, and he was eight years older than her. She confided in me once, before I could stop her, cause I don't like people to tell me too much of their business. They get mad at you later because you know what they done told you! Anyway, she told me Doctor wanted children very badly and had been trying for five years to get one, but every time he made one she got rid of it before he found out he had made one! She say if she had a baby for Doctor, he would make a prisoner of her staying home with that baby! And that he would surely try for another one! I liked the Doctor bout that time cause he was very nice to me, so I felt sorry for him. I almost liked Miz Mavis too, so I felt something for her, hoping she didn't hurt herself getting rid of babies. You know? Going so far past silly it's crazy? Another reason she didn't have them babies, she didn't mention. I knew she wouldn't know just exactly whose baby it would be! I mean, she spoke very proper, dressed very proper and all like that, but she laid very loose. Very properly discreet, of course.

Now, I do not mean that just cause she came from a ghetto she was not as good as them women who did not come from the ghetto or a underprivileged family. (I love learning these big words, they save so much time.) She was better than some I seen round that time. I mean in that highfalutin neighborhood, within them beautiful houses, was the same alcoholics, same families that argued, same people that lived on dope. They wasn't shooting heroin but they was dropping them pills their doctors kept them supplied with. A child molester lived just down the block! He was caught at the school he was a principal at! Now! I came to understand that people was the same all over. Money don't change your mind none too much, just makes things easier to get at! Sometime a beautiful house don't hide nothing but the same ole shit inside. The outside might fool you, but they could be livin in a cave for all the good it makes them do!

Anyway, my future was moving along. I was learning a lot from her just by watching. I learned a lot from him by talking. I ate in the kitchen and as time passed he came to join me, eat what I ate. We had some sure nuff good suppers! Basically what it was, he just liked home cooking! Everything! He didn't ask me to, but I took to getting up early enough to fix his breakfast before he left for work and I left for school. It gave the man such a pleasure to think somebody did something for him special. Just making his homelife more homelike.

Miz Mavis gave me $50.00 a month for twenty-four-hour-a-day service and thousands of dollars worth of work! Doctor added $100.00 more with his finger cross his lips . . . like, "Quiet." I saved almost all of it in my room. Nobody bothered it now. I didn't have to be ashamed of my clothes at college now. I had nice new ones.

Miz Mavis was always buying something new and giving me things she didn't want anymore. But I didn't take them for myself, and if I did, I changed the design so much it didn't look the same. I slept in the nightgowns she gave me tho! They were pretty! And she didn't get to see me in them. See . . . I didn't want her to think she was taking care of too many of my needs. People will begin to think they own you! See . . . I support myself!

As the months passed, Miz Mavis begin to talk on the phone

around me. Miz Mavis had several men friends, close. She made love with some of them. Now, the true fact of life is if you have some personal business you really need to keep that to yourself! Miz Mavis explained to ME one day that she "had never had a orgasm!" Why tell me? There wasn't nothing I could do about it! I said, "What?"

She explained, "A climax in sex!"

I shook my head sadly.

She went on, "Doctor is so boring. It's like making love to a rabbit anyway! So I guess that's what I am searching for."

I didn't want to go into no kinda personal consultation bout her business with her. I didn't want her mad with me cause she had told me. I felt a little sorry for her tho. All that for nothing! I mean, there is nothing in the world like a beautiful end to lovemaking. I loved singing opera. Singing opera played a big part in my future plans for myself. Miz Mavis was only singing the blues! She hadn't found the right bandleader yet, I guess!

It got to the place that when I was serving one of her luncheons or club meetings, I began to notice things. When things were over and most everyone gone except Miz Mavis' close two or three friends, they would talk dirt and laugh at the quiet women who were happily married or in love with their own husbands. Talk about them behind their backs! They would drink Scotch or champagne and talk about lovemaking, sex, having a strange new man or what so-and-so did in the bed! And laugh and laugh. They never seem to go home and cook or do nothing for their own husbands and children. Just go out to eat! They drank a lot, too. It didn't look like fun to me. I didn't really know their husbands. Had only seen them at parties I served. Pinching some other man's wife on the behind or making plans to meet some woman later, then going over to grin in her husband's face!

This little tight group, all professional they bragged; always held tight to each other tho. The regulars at the parties had almost all made love to each other over the years! Chile, it was something! Their mama didn't tell them bout being silly but not crazy!

I really liked Doctor tho. He was one of the nice ones. Just a dumb, nice man, who sighed over the bills as he paid them.

Anyway. My living went on, my future kept coming. I watched wintertime come, for the first time in my life, with ease. I didn't dread it cause I knew I wouldn't have any of those nights when I'd lay in bed and shiver, trying to get warm, with the drafts coming in hard enough to blow you out the bed! I slept warm and cozy all winter. I would never even have known it was winter if I hadn't had to go outside. I didn't have to worry bout food. I KNEW I was going to eat. Just that was worth all the money in the world to me. I found out winter was pretty. Snow was beautiful. Oh, I rested easy.

When spring came, I actually noticed the change in things. The trees, flowers, the sky. My mind was alive, blossoming, feeding me as I fed it. My head was turned up . . . stead of bent down. In summer and fall, I saw more changes, different changes, beautiful changes. I now knew the seasons in a new way. I knew their advantages instead of just their *dis*advantages. Oh, I rested easy.

I was sitting in the library one day when my mind began to think. Yes, chile, I was thinking! Thought about the alphabet. Twenty-six little letters. I looked at all those books surrounding me and realized they had ALL been done and made with twenty-six little marks. Then my mind stretched out! I realized that all the books in England, France, Germany, Switzerland, all the white countries, were written with these same little twenty-six marks!

You could take one typewriter and write millions of books . . . all the tools you needed were in these little twenty-six letters. That's really something to me!

Then I thought of music. Seven notes, take em up higher or bring em down lower, and every song written, ever, since the beginning of time could be done with these notes on five little lines. Ain't things sometimes a miracle?! I mean music in ANY country in the world! You may not think that is so much to think about, but let me tell you . . . for me the joy of thought was filling me up with love for what life could be like. How it could be if a person had the time, the money, the way to go to school with ease. I started piano lessons!

I kept to my English class so I could enjoy saying my words. Oh! Beauty! You know that Shakespeare really was right when he said "To be or not to be!" Let me tell you, that's the most important question in the world! It even takes in religion, and that's as big as you can get! I had done decided . . . I was going to BE!

Now, I thought about love . . . sometimes. I surely did, deep down in my heart, want to sing OPERA again. I was not even getting a hummmm. But I still did not know nobody I wanted. Or nobody that wanted me!

Do you know what I mean, when I say singing opera? Well, let me tell you. Some people love you and make you sigh til they through. Some people love you and make you hum. Some people make you sing the blues, before, during and after. Some people make you lie, like you swinging along with them. Some people, like prostitutes maybe, sing popular . . . like whatever is happening that day. But when you find a real bandleader lover, chile, you sing opera. Least *I* think so.

Now, Doctor and me always talked a lot. We was friends. One

of them days he got through paying some bills, he sighed and said to me, "I neither smell, taste, see, hear nor touch all these things I pay for. I just pay."

Now, I didn't think of Doctor in no special way for me. I just felt sorry for him. Like sometimes, thinking bout love, I felt sorry for me. I wanted somebody to watch over me, make love to me. Love me. Say, "Bessy, you is my woman!" But I felt sorry for Doctor. So I began to put on some of Miz Mavis' perfume, so he could smell it in the mornings when he came in for breakfast while she was sleeping. He smelled it and he liked it. I liked it too! It was nice to be able to get up and cook breakfast wearing that beautiful $50.00 or $100.00 a ounce perfume. Not a lot, just lightly, cause I didn't want Miz Mavis to miss it. But Doctor soon took care of that.

One evening I turned my covers back and under my pillow was a bottle of Joy! And what a joy it was! Every week he added a new bottle. A different kind. Then I started finding pretty robes to cook in. Pretty gowns. Pretty morning dresses. It was like a game we played every morning. We both had a family and a home. Them kitchen walls started throwing back warmth to us and it stretched into other parts of the house, downstairs. Now this was all innocent pleasure to us. He never touched me nor asked to. He helped me with my homework sometimes and we talked about all the wonderful thoughts in the world. He taught me little scientific things. He had me down to his office to fix my teeth. He didn't make me pay cause he knew I was saving money to buy me some kind of house someday.

He took to making appointments at the hairdresser for me. Having my nails done and my feet too! Chile, I was feeling too good. I hadn't never been so happy before. I felt I paid for it with all that work I did and I was glad to do that work. It was my home where I lived and was happy. I did everything Miz Mavis asked me and ran her bath and turned it off too!

Miz Mavis was still running steady. Soon as she get up and bathe, she be gone. Shopping, to lunch, club meetings, to dinner, benefits, fund-raisers and all kinds of things. If she was happy I was happy for her too.

One Sunday, on my way to church, I went upstairs to let them know I was going. I heard them making love. Well, he was trying to, anyway. He sounded like he had been begging for a long time and she had dreaded to let him do it.

He said, "Good grief, Mavis, it's been three weeks!"

She gave her big sigh and said, "Well . . . hurry up then! You know I have to get up and get down to the Willing Wives meeting! You make me sick! You always want to screw! That's all you think of! Watch out—your knee is on my gown! Damm it! Hurry up! Shit!"

Well. I could see why she thought he was like a rabbit! That kinda talk would make a rabbit out of Godzilla! And him taking that kinda talk made her lose respect for him and you can't have no love without respect for somebody. And I do believe you got to have a little love mixed in there if you ever gonna sing opera!

I sure hate to sound like I was listening, but then I heard the bed squeaking as all that talk went on! He breathed heavy, then the squeaking stopped. I heard her say, "Move. Don't get anything on my gown!" The last groans of the bed, then I heard him going in his room. I also heard her say, "Shit!" softly. Then I left. I didn't mean to listen, I just couldn't move. I also couldn't believe he would want any if it was give to him like that! He never would get to sing opera. I went on to church.

The next morning when he came down for breakfast I put on

extra perfume for him, but I couldn't look at him. He chewed awhile, looking off into space over the sink, then he asked me, "Bessy, was that you I heard going down the stairs yesterday morning?"

I sighed and said, "Yes."

He was quiet a long time, drinking his coffee and looking over by the window. Then he said, "You know . . . I buy the house, the furniture, pay all the bills, buy all the clothes, food, sheets, beds and perfumes. Keep the water running, the house warm and the lights on. Pay the hairdresser, the masseuse, doctor bills, give the money for donations and benefits. Give some type of security, you might say, the only security this house has." He shoved his coffee cup away. "And I can't even get screwed in my own house!"

I looked at him awhile. Then he laughed a disgusted, sad and useless kind of laugh, saying, "But you could say I am getting greatly screwed in my own house, couldn't you?" Then he left for his office. I left for school. Miz Mavis just kept sleeping, getting her rest after spending the last evening into the early morning with other people who didn't pay her bills!

He told me they argued sometime later that day and he had told her I was nicer to him then she was. Oh Lord! He say, when he buys something for me, he gets to enjoy it . . . a little! When he buys something for her . . . only other folks enjoy it! Oh Lord!

She asked, "Are you sleeping with . . . the maid?"

He told her we "wasn't nothing to each other!" Still, when I got home from school I was surprised to see her still home. She was in my room and the four bottles of perfume was on my dresser and the dresser drawer with the new robes was open.

Miz Mavis asked, "Bessy? Did you buy these bottles of perfume yourself?"

I didn't say nothing, just looked at her.

Handling the bottles, she went on, "This is Joy, Shalimar, Chanel Number Five and Bal à Versailles! You didn't buy these with what I pay you."

I had no real reason to be feeling caught, but I felt caught right on. "No mam, I didn't."

"Doctor bought them?"

I nodded yes, and I said, "But . . ."

She was suddenly mad. She reached for them bottles. "Well, they are mine then!"

I reached for them bottles too. My womanly nerve-strength, I guess. "No mam, these are mine. They are a honest gift. Ain't no funny stuff going on here. But these are mine!"

She let go and looked at me strangely, saying, "I have given you a home and this is what you do behind my back! Don't you even have sense enough to look out for the one who is looking out for you? We are both women! I gave you a home!"

I moved slowly. "Miz Mavis, I don't mean you no harm and I am grateful. . . . But, it's the Doctor who needs a home. Not meaning no disrespect . . . that's the only reason he is friendly to me. Cause I'm here, in you all's home, cooking for him and talking to him."

She snarled (like a lady, of course), "I don't need you to tell me how to keep my husband!"

I nodded, yes mam, no mam.

She went on. "Perhaps you don't understand. We are both women. You are suppose to protect me more than you protect a man!"

I had to answer what I felt. "Miz Mavis, if the devil was a human woman, just cause she was a woman don't mean I would protect the devil while the devil do wrong."

She gasped.

I thought I better clean that up a little, so I said, "I never . . . Ain't none of this my business. I'm just trying to do what we agreed for me to do. Just doing my job, Miz Mavis. How I got caught up in this I—"

She interrupted. "Perhaps you better find another place!"

"Yes mam," I said as I went crazy in my mind trying to think of what I was going to do. Damn the Doctor and her and all this business that I didn't want nothing to do with that was interfering with my own life.

She looked me over again and musta thought of all that work I was doing there. Then she said, "Well . . . I'll think about it. I'll let you know later. You better stop involving yourself in the affairs of this house. Fix dinner as usual."

I did, gladly. That night she stayed home and ate with him in the dining room. I ate in the kitchen, alone, and didn't mind at all. I was eating . . . and wearing my perfume. He was grinning as he looked across the table at his wife. Maybe he even got a better piece that night. I hope so, but that ain't my business to worry bout!

I don't know what she would have decided later about whether to keep me or not, but the emergency came up and she had to think about other things.

Miz Mavis' sister and sister's husband were killed in a automobile accident and she had to travel to their house in a little town bout fifty-five miles away to take care of things that always have to be taken care of in these situations. Also, you know, her sister's interest and all. After a little thought she told me I better pack up and go with her, I could take a few days off from school. She said, "You're very smart . . . you'll catch up!"

Doctor took us to the airport, cause she didn't feel like driving. She talked about money all the way there. He finally gave her all he had on him, and when she was turned another way he tried to slip me some, but I pushed it back in his hand. He seemed to be enjoying all this undercover stuff. But I had a home to hold on to!

Well, we got there. It was a nice little house. Her sister hadn't married a well-to-doer. He was an ordinary working man. The house was nice tho, and well kept. The sister's husband had a brother, Quint, who lived near. He was there, all heartbroken over his brother. Miz Mavis looked at him in his work clothes and him needing a haircut and a shave. Her nose went up and turned away like he was smellin or something. She didn't even act like he was there. She took over. Called the mortician and the lawyer, then went through all the papers she could find. I just did whatever was to be done. After we had eaten and was getting ready for bed, Quint asked if she would like him to stay over, you know, in case anything happened. She told him, "No! Bessy is here!" I wondered what that meant, cause I knew I wasn't there for no protection unless she meant my opening the door for her as I left!

Miz Mavis didn't seem to like Quint much. Well, he did act like a fool sometime. Always making rhymes . . . and little dumb jokes. Trying to make her feel better, I guess. Anyway, we got through everything. People brought the usual stuff to eat at the wake and asked the usual nosy questions of Miz Mavis' business, but her nose turned up at them too. Quint could have been invisible for all the notice she gave him.

As the days passed, tho, we both noticed how many ladies called Quint and came by to see how he was and bring things, good things, to eat. He had plenty, plenty women! He was a divorced man, so wasn't nothing to stop them. I noticed Miz Mavis begin to watch him with a wonder in her eyes. One day she asked him, "Why do all these women run after you? Call you all day and all night?"

He laughed, threw an orange in the air, caught it, said, "I don't know! You know womens is crazy. Who knows why women do anything!?"

Miz Mavis looked at me with a lot of meaning. I knew we both knew why women call a man day and night. She started treating him a little different. Smiling at him, laughing with him more.

After the funeral we was supposed to finish the business, put the house up for sale and go home. Then Miz Mavis came down with a pain in her legs and we had to stay longer. Now, Miz Mavis and Quint had taken to talking deep into the nights, laughing in corners and running to the store together, so when her pain came down on her, he felt concern, naturally. He said he had a special athlete's oil he would rub on her legs and all that pain would go away.

She looked aghast (like a lady) and said, "I can't let you rub my legs! What would all your women say?" They laughed. I thought more to the point is what would Doctor say? He was the doctor!

Quint said, "This is a good medicine deed. Can't nobody say nothin bout that! Besides, we related! Besides, I don't blong to them women! Besides, you won't hate it!" See, he was always trying to rhyme things. They laughed, but he went home and got his oil, came back and later that evening when the pain in Miz Mavis' legs got worse, much worser, he rubbed that oil on them pretty legs. I know he did a good job cause I was cleaning up the kitchen and could hear her "ohhhhhhhhhs" and "ahhhhhhhhhhs" and little crys of pain. He rubbed them a long time. Then as I was finishing up and all, I heard him say, "You know, your legs is connected to your back. You better let me get that!"

She said, in a nice, soft, sleepy, hesitant voice, "You think so? Can you rub on top of my gown?" She knew he couldn't.

He quit rhyming. "Turn over, woman. I seen a woman's body before!"

I heard her voice dwindle away, saying, "You are like a brother, Quint. Your hands are so strong."

I went in my room and closed the door. I hadn't made any love in so long. I mean, sang any kinda song of love. I couldn't stand to hear and imagine what no man's hands felt like. I got in bed and my legs started to hurt. I mean really! I had almost talked myself into going to sleep stead of laying there awake thinking, when I heard Miz Mavis singing. Singing! Opera! She was in there singing opera, chile, and he was leading the band! I covered up my head and went on to sleep. My whole body ached!

Now, after two weeks we still hadn't left there. I had to get back to school. I told Miz Mavis, and she said, "Well, Bessy, I have so much left to do here. There is much more than I thought. You go on back." She looked at her fingernails. "Go to school . . . and take care of the Doctor. Give him my love and tell him I'll be home . . . soon."

I went on home to sing the blues and left her there singing opera!

Things got back to normal. I got back to wearing my perfume and cooking breakfast and he was grateful as usual. Everything was still clean and innocent tho. We didn't do nothing! I wanted to sing opera, but I don't just sing along with everybody!

Two more weeks passed without Miz Mavis. Finally Doctor called her on the phone and asked, "Just exactly how much business is left to take care of down there?" I don't know what she said.

Another week later he told her, "You better come on home. We need you here. A lawyer can take care of the sale when you get one. Come home!" His voice said he meant it! Another week later, she was home. But he had to beg harder than ever cause she said she was "tired."

She went to going out again to all her meetings. She was often on the phone talking softly into the speaker part. Three weeks passed and that woman got too hard to get along with. She couldn't sit still! Didn't sleep good, she said. She screamed at everybody. The Doctor, her friends, everybody. But for some reason, not too much at me. One day she said she had to go see about her business and she left, going back to her sister's house. Well, I understood. You understand. Only Doctor didn't understand.

She took the house off the sale market, saying, "After all, it is a good investment and the brother, what's-his-name, is going to watch over it til I get it ready to rent . . . or whatever." She was always gone now. Well . . . I do know opera singing will go to your head. Can make you go farther than silly! Make you go crazy!

Life went on through these ins and outs. I stayed home taking care the house, going to school. Things were peaceful. Doctor and I got on well. He enjoyed teaching me little scientific things in the kitchen and helping me with my homework. For the first time in my life I had what you might call a family life. I know he liked me like a family cause I wasn't in his league at all for him to like me personally. I might be silly but I ain't crazy. That's why, one night, when I was lying in bed thinking about my life and he came in my room in the dark and sat on the bed, I didn't get alarmed or nervous or nothing. I knew what I was gonna do with my life!

He whispered, "Bessy?"

I whispered back, "Yes, Doctor?"

He whispered back, "I want to make love."

"What?"

"I want to make love."

I couldn't believe it. "With me? Or with somebody? Or any-body?"

He waited a minute. . . . "With . . . you."

I wasn't crazy, I held on to my mind. "I can't make love with you."

"Why?"

I told him, "Not in this house that blongs to you and your wife." It was hard, because I did like him and we did have a kinda personal understanding of our own and he had been so nice to me. But I had to remember . . . I worked there . . . as a maid and cook. Nothing else. And I was poor . . . while they were rich like. He had bought his wife a house and everything else she had. All I had was a room, and that belonged to her too! Her house, her husband, her room and her bed! I would have been stone out of my mind! When he got through making love with me she would still have HER house and the money. I would then have her job, my little room and my job. See what I mean?

He just sat there. I finally said, "I like to feel at home when I make love, Doctor. This ain't even my bed, much less my home."

He said, "This is your home!"

I said, "I LIVE here. This ain't MY home."

He thought a minute. "Well . . . what . . ."

I didn't want to go too far . . . yet. See, crazy works in both directions. I said, "This ain't my bed, it's yours and your wife's. At least I should make love in my own bed!"

He looked at me. I looked at him. Through the dark. He left after patting me on the breast, which I covered up then.

The next day when I got home from school, my old bedroom set was in the back yard waiting for the cleanup man to pick up.

In my room was a beautiful new white bedroom set. A card on my new dresser said, "To Bessy. This is all YOURS. May it be enjoyed!" Well, now!

I am not going to take you through all the different changes in my mind, but I let him make love to me because I felt sorry for him, always having to buy everything he got. I made love to him in the perfume he bought, the gown he paid for, the hair he had had fixed. Rubbed his back with the hands he had had manicured and tickled his feet with the toes he had had pedicured . . . in MY bed. I could sleep in that bed by myself and not feel alone anymore. Things is things . . . when they are yours!

The realization came to me after that first time why Miz Mavis was always rushing him. Doctor just absolutely could not make love. He couldn't even make you hum . . . much less sing opera! The size of life ain't got nothing to do with it! It's another way to say this: quantity ain't got nothing to do with quality! See, I'm learning how to talk better, also.

Now, since I am his friend first, the next time he came in my room, I stopped him. I said, gently, "Doctor, listen here; Let's talk."

He was trying to get on in my bed, but I stopped him again. "Sit down, Doctor, I want to talk to you." So he sat, looking impatient. I still spoke gently. "Doctor, you a doctor who is supposed to know all about the human body."

He said, "I'm a dentist." And reached for my hip.

I held his hand and went on talking. "But you don't pay no tention to the body when you get ready for sex. You act like it's a tunnel and you trying to get through to the other side."

He stopped patting and rubbing and frowned.

I went on. "Now, I'm your friend, so listen to me. You gonna always have a little trouble with women til you learn about this loving business." I waited to see how he was taking it. He was looking at me, hard. I told him, "Don't you know you supposed to feeeel what you doing? Not just at the end . . . but all along the way?"

He looked confused, cause see, he made love like he was rushing to the end of it. I went on, "You ain't galloping through no wild jungle. You supposed to stroll through a beautiful garden."

He said, hurt, "No one has ever told me that before."

I said, "I didn't think so."

He asked, "Why are you telling me this?"

I answered, "Cause I am your friend. And you are missing a lot."

He thought awhile. "You mean I am inadequate?!"

I nodded, painfully. "Yes. Lousy."

It's hard to hurt someone, but you got to remember this was for his good. Mine too, if I was going to let him make love to me. I don't like to be messed over. Makes me nervous.

He finally asked, "Well, what can I do? What can I change?"

I was ready. I answered, "Well, you went where they have all that medical business information to get to be a doctor, didn't you?"

He answered, "Yes, but where would I learn, unless you . . ."

I went on. "Well you go where making sex is the business and learn from that school!"

He looked at me with darkness in his eyes.

I said, "A professional woman who that's all she does!"

He looked at me with a little light in the darkness of his eyes.

I said, "A good older one, a clean one. Not a street woman, cause ain't no telling what else you get instead of a lesson."

Twilight was shining in his eyes as he looked off in space.

I smoothed the covers, saying, "You . . . ah . . . know somebody?"

He patted me again. "I'm trying to think." He paused. "Why can't you teach me?"

Well, I ain't crazy. Let him bring his learning to me . . . not from me to somebody else. I shook my head no, saying, "I don't know how to teach it. I just know when it ain't there." As he slowly left I said, gently, "Get about six lessons, then you can practice on me." Anyway, I wouldn't let him that night. He went on to his own bed. Things on his mind. He is a quick mover. I can see why he gets so much accomplished. He gets right on things. That's what he did in his love lessons.

Miz Mavis was sending home for money all the time and in between times she would come home looking all fresh and bloomy, full of energy and restless to get away again. She always checked my room to see if there was any addition to the perfume bottles. There wasn't. I got better sense than that! She looked shocked at my bedroom set. "What is this!?"

I smiled. "Well, Miz Mavis, I thought I been away from home over a year now and it's time I made some progress, so I started with a bedroom set."

She looked at me kinda funny, saying, "That's where a lot of progress seems to get started!" Then she shook it off and rushed through the house, going off somewhere. Soon she was gone back to the country again. Doctor and I were alone, together, again.

He had learned. Doctor might never be no champion band-leader but he could get a song out of you now. Then, what I didn't expect, he looked around for his wife so he could prove to her what a new man he was. His wife was still gone taking care of her business. He called her home, proud of his new stuff. She didn't want to come home just then, so he went there, to surprise her. That's another time I realized what a difference a day can make. He came back, full of his feeling of being a new man with new confidence . . . and filed for divorce. Miz Mavis came back screaming and shouting, then later, begging and pleading. But the divorce came and she went. She looked at me with hate when she was leaving, but I hadn't told that man nothing! It was not my business, was it?! She runs her own life! I try to run mine. She fired me, but Doctor told her she must be crazy! He said, "This is not your house to run any longer! Go run that hut where I found your butt!" (Lord, *he* was making rhymes now.) She spit fire but finally she was gone. Back to her opera stage.

Later on, when I learned she was marrying Quint, I thought she had gone past silly to crazy. But I don't know everything. Do I?

Doctor missed his wife a little during the divorce, but it seemed to pass. After a while I could see he was settling in. My bed was warm and I admit I encouraged him to lay and rest "after." Finally he would fall asleep and wake up in my arms all cozy. He didn't really want to get up and go get in that cold bed of his. He urged me to move up to the rooms upstairs, but I wouldn't. I ain't crazy. This might not be *her* house anymore, but it was his, and that still wasn't mine. I like my own, so I stayed in my bed.

The doctor was full of good food, living in a clean house, making good love that was all his. I lay in bed and thought about that all night one night.

Doctor was taking me for granted. He expected me to be there . . . all the time. Well, all that does not need no explanation, you know what I mean? So after thinking about what I wanted out of life, I made a few decisions. I told Doctor I was taking a trip home. I left, saying I'd be gone two days, had already planned to be gone at least a week.

It was the hardest thing I had done in a long, long time to stay in that little crampy, poor house. I managed two days, then went to a hotel with my own savings. I couldn't live poor like that no more! I just couldn't. My sister fingered my clothes. I know she took some. My brother borrowed my money; I knew I'd never get it back. I know he stole some when I left my purse laying around. I had to always keep my purse beside me where I could see it. That ain't no kind of home! They ate on the run. No fine dishes. No candles, no nice silver. Not even cheap matching sets. The sheets was some of the same ones were there when I left, only with more holes. My baby sister's house was much better, but she had a family and I didn't want to bother them. I took her out to lunch tho. She had NEVER been out to a nice restaurant. I enjoyed doing that! But I was still glad when it came time to go.

For my plan, I bought a little ole diamond ring from the pawn-shop, an engagement ring. Polished it up and wore it home. I stopped at the florist before I got home.

Doctor was really glad to see me. Acted like he had missed me or something. I cooked and everything, as usual, but it wasn't until we sat down to eat dinner, candles and everything, you know, that he noticed the ring.

"What's that ring? Where did you get that ring?"

I smiled. "Oh! Some ole silly friend of mine wants to think we're engaged." I laughed softly.

He stopped eating. "Engaged? What old friend?"

I kept smiling and passed him the bread. "You don't know him. He lives in my old hometown."

He didn't touch the bread. "You like him? Is that what kept you away so long?"

I stopped smiling. "Well—"

"You sleep with him while you were gone seven days instead of the two you said you'd be gone?"

I looked surprised. "Oh, I just stayed longer because things kept coming up for me to do. . . . And I knew you were alright."

He put his fork down. "No, I wasn't alright! Did you sleep with him?"

I laughed. "No! I don't just 'sleep' with people."

He picked up his fork. "Are you going back? Are you engaged?"

I smiled, looking at the ring fondly. "Well, I do have to start thinking of my future. And he is a good man."

He started eating again, slowly. "I'm getting sick of these men in these little hometowns shit."

I changed the subject.

Then the flowers started coming, signed only "Your Future." Beautiful red roses twice a week. If you don't know it, flowers are expensive! But I was investing in my future. Doctor would look at those flowers and pass on by, but soon he began to buy bigger bunches of flowers, and orchids too!

I had a friend write a letter to me from "Your Future," saying he was anxious for me to return and us to get on with our life. That he would be taking his exam for becoming a lawyer. That it had taken so long because of having to go to night school, but that his grades were the best in any class, so there was no doubt he would pass the bar. He loved me and wanted to set the date!

Oh, I know I sound terrible, but I don't believe so. I had my life to think of. I wasn't going back to that little ole shack in my hometown. Not if I could help it! And I believed I could help it!

I waited til the right moment when he came in the house, then I crumpled that letter and threw it in the garbage. Naturally he saw me. I went to set the table for dinner and I heard him going through the garbage. When I went back in the kitchen, trying to look guilty of something, he went upstairs. The letter was gone. Good!

Dinner was good that night. Special. But Doctor was quiet and ate very slowly. Sighing a lot. Like he was thinking. We made some of the best love we had ever made that night. We both sang light opera. I made him get up tho, and told him, "This is the last time we can make love . . . til I decide what I am going to do. I am so confused, Doctor. Loving you a little and longing to be with you and all . . . but also I have to think of respectibility. I don't like my lawyer friend like I love you, but if I decide to marry him, I can't go on cheating him like this."

Doctor looked like he smelled something bad. But I was really being honest at the same time I was lying, so I went on. "After all, we've been living here almost a year . . . alone. People talk. I have to think of my future." I was taking a chance, but I had come empty-handed and could leave that way if I had to. I had to take the chance tho.

About two weeks later, after several more crushed letters, flowers and such, Doctor came home with a beautiful diamond engagement ring. It was not as large as Miz Mavis' had been, but it's the thought that counts, and with this ring I thought I was going to get married! He took that pawnshop ring off of me and slipped that big one on. He looked worried but relieved. I grabbed him and hugged him for my dear life! We were soon married. I moved upstairs in MY house!

I quit full-time school but kept part-time because I had to take English so I could talk to my husband. You can tell I tried hard. Don't I sound better? To me, I had graduated a little, far as I was concerned.

In another year or so, I gave him a lovely baby daughter. Now, we both had everything. I thought.

You know what? I didn't REALLY love him . . . and he didn't really love me. I think we were comfortable and peaceful.

I entertained his friends when I HAD to, cause they were all college people. I couldn't get real comfortable with them. Some of them had such dumb philosophies. I also didn't want to have any extra affair. I didn't think my husband was a fool. I liked clothes but they weren't all I thought of. I didn't drink much. My husband and my child came first! And I didn't give a damm about nobody's business but mine!

So I was left out of a lot of their groups. I didn't really mind. We were happy. I really believe that. But life is still life.

Miz Mavis was still happy with her man down there in that little country town, but she was unhappy with her life. It was too poor. I would hear about her from her old friends. She was trying to think of something, somehow, so they could go into business and make more money to complete her life in the style she wanted. Her nights were fine. Daytime was the hard time.

She came to see me. Me! For some money! Doctor had refused her any. She rang the doorbell and just walked on in when I opened the door, saying, "Still answering doors, huh?!"

I answered, "It's MY door. Welcome to MY house."

She looked around the house, laughed a ugly little laugh. It wasn't from jealousy, it was from resentment. After all, I had been her maid.

She waved her hand at the house. "So nice and clean. You were always good at cleaning work. I need you down there at my other house!"

I waved my hand at the house. "I love taking care of my house. It shouldn't be hard taking care of your sister's house. It's such a small one."

She looked at me thoughtfully. "Well, I'm not here to play tag. I'm here because I need the money I told you about.

I asked, "Mavis, you have so many . . . friends, why do you come to me?"

She snapped, "Because I feel you owe it to me."

"Owe it to you?"

"Yes! You owe it to me! I'm the reason you are here!"

I laughed. "Don't be silly, girl. *I'm* the reason I am here!"

She was serious. "I brought you here. Innocently. Not knowing the kind of woman you were."

I was serious. "You let me come here. I paid my way. And if I hadn't been the kind of person I am, you wouldn't have kept me."

"Oh, you schemed all right! Innocently I—"

"You are getting silly," I interrupted. "You haven't been innocent in a long, long time. No one had to take anything from you. You gave everything away. The world ain't supposed to wait on you!"

"Nothing gave you the right to—"

I interrupted again. "Don't tell me about 'right.' If you had been 'right' you'd still be here! I was never the other woman til you had the other man!"

She was thoughtful. "You're lying."

I was thoughtful. "You're crazy. You come here to ask for money, then talk to me like I'm a fool."

She came to herself.

I didn't wish her any harm, so as it all turned out I got together two thousand dollars and gave it to her. She really did think I was a fool then.

She took the money, counted it and said, "This isn't any money!" Very properly.

I said, just as properly, "I isn't any bank!"

As she put the money in her purse I have to admit she did it with style. Didn't act like she was begging. Acted like it was naturally hers. Didn't even lie about paying it back. I was glad to see her still making it. In the end I was glad I had helped.

But that bitch!

As she was leaving she stopped and turned to me. "I know you think I did Doctor wrong." I just looked at her as she went on talking. "Well, I might have, but, it's what he asked for." She laughed a satisfied laugh and looked me up and down while she went on talking. "Doctor likes pretty things. Pretty women. He likes beautiful legs and long pretty hair. Pearly teeth and smooth skin. Style and . . . class."

I looked at her while I listened and thought. I did not have all of these things. I was not ugly, but I was not beautiful. Not like she was.

She spoke on. "He choose ME! He knew I went to college to find a husband with some money. Did not intend to marry a poor man and live like I grew up . . . poor." The way she said that word made you smell it. I listened because I could understand it. She went on. "Doctor knew just what he was getting! He wanted it! He loved me!" She looked around my new house—her old house—again and laughed. "Now . . . he's got a comfortable woman, a baby . . . a family. All warm and cozy." I almost smiled but she had a sneer on her face. "But now, bad as you think I treated him, he never played on me. Til you. And you were so convenient. And I was not here or he wouldn't have wanted you at all! He never had played around, so he liked what he was getting. Now, you!? He's supposed to have all the good things, with you. But the whole city knows he is one of the hardest afternoon-playing men in the city! He hits on practically every pretty woman he meets!" She threw her head back and laughed.

I could only stare at her as she turned to leave, but she wasn't through.

She looked over her shoulder at me, smiling. "I may have exchanged a wealthy man for a poor, good-lovin, foolish man, but he is MY poor man! You got yourself a wealthy man, but he belongs to anybody who will slip off with him, and you do know how many pretty girls will!"

Then she almost sang, "Well . . . good-byeee," as she went down the steps to that old Mercedes of hers and drove away.

With my two thousand dollars.

I slowly closed the door, went to the bar, poured myself a glass of champagne, sat down and thought . . . hard. You have got to decide about life while you are on your feet going through it. Is it going to be love . . . or money? If it's love you want, then you may only have to do without money. But that also means all the things money can buy. Ease. Comfort. Getting what you want (that money can buy) when you want it. That can mean a lot. If it's money, then you may have to do without love. Which, everybody knows, can also mean a whole lot. Did I want satin sheets, champagne and to sing the blues, or did I want to sing opera with sheets that may have holes in them? After I thought awhile, I decided. I can find a way to buy my own satin sheets, my champagne when I want it. Find a way where I could afford what I want whether the man I loved could or not.

I might not have believed her about Doctor, but I knew. I knew. Doctor had a new toy, a new skill. He was better, much better making love now. He had to show it off! One woman wasn't a big enough audience to appreciate his feats of pleasure (I read that somewhere).

I was sad, but I smiled as I poured another glass of our very best champagne. I looked around our home. I kept it so neat and beautiful. I did everything myself for my family. Then I got the telephone book, thumbed through it, found what I wanted, called and ordered a maid starting tomorrow. Called the best stores in the world, told them "I'm five seven, one hundred thirty pounds, tan-brown color. Send me two dozen of your finest for me to try on at home. Gloves to match each outfit. An assortment of purses. I'll come in for my shoes and hats when I have decided what I want." I also called the best caterer and ordered that evening's dinner catered. Then I took my bottle of champagne upstairs to my new room, showered and got in bed. Called Doctor and told him to arrange to have the baby picked up from nursery school. I put Billie Holiday, Nancy Wilson and Grover Washington on the record player, stretched out between my satin sheets and drank my champagne . . . and cried the blues. Just ordinary tears in $35.00 champagne in a $30.00 crystal glass. Oh shit, looky me.

I wasn't madly in love with Doctor, but I had been happy and thought he was too. Plain straight-out truth, I don't want NO man who has to have someone else's nothing! Rich or poor man, I don't care.

As time went by, I drank a bit more champagne, kept the maid, got a cook for weekends and all entertainment. Had Doctor eat out more, cooking for my daughter and me such things as we felt like. But I remembered Mama's advice about silly but not crazy. I was thinking, all the time, hard. I knew three things could happen. Number one: one day Doctor was going to run into somebody he was going to want to keep. It happens! And then I wouldn't be ready.

Number two: I could close my eyes and live with it and spend money like a fool, but in the long years I may have ahead, was that what I wanted? I'd almost have to become alcoholic or dope-addicted to do that, to keep my nerves from going to pieces, which they would then do anyway.

Number three: I could leave him. I could be ready.

I decided on number three. Now all I had to do was think of what I wanted to give me some security without Doctor.

I started back to school again; in case I had to take care of myself, I wanted to be able to afford me! In between times I watched older women to see what they did for security. I really didn't want to clean Doctor out. After all, he had given me my change in life and everything else, including my daughter. I never have understood women who make a man pay so much for falling in love with her. Myself, I just wanted to be kinda safe from this shitty world. It's okay if you got some money, but if you don't have any . . . Well, what do I need to say? At last, I remembered my mama thought a rooming house was a very fine thing to have and you would never have to worry again because there would always be roomers! That's what I wanted! Not just a ordinary house tho. I wanted a large Colonial-type house. Lots of rooms. Plush carpets, fine velvet drapes and shining white linen curtains, eyelet or lace, custom made. Chandeliers dripping crystal. Shower and basin with every room, wood paneling, gold and brass knobs, a small refrigerator. You know? Things like that. I started shopping around, I had much more time now.

Doctor was sweet. He was glad I had help now, but he didn't like the cook. Wanted me to do the cooking. He missed breakfast with us. I was usually stretched out in my satin sheets when he left for work now. He dropped the baby off at the nursery.

I smiled at him. "You want almost what you used to have . . . and you don't have that anymore."

He smiled back. "I want my private woman cooking for me in my kitchen!" He reached for me. I let him hug me; after all, we were standing up in the kitchen he paid for.

I kept smiling. "Well, I want what I almost used to have, but I don't have that anymore either."

He looked awful funny, like he was scared I might know something and he didn't want to talk about it. He said a few more words that hit the sink and the floor and the wall, he was turning so fast getting to the door. He went to work, I went shopping for my house.

Finally! I found one I liked! Lord in heaven! The price! But I only wanted the down payment from Doctor. The house was beautiful, with that special look old houses have. I didn't have a lot to do except customize it, put in the baths, wood paneling and things like that, because it had been well cared for. There was even a library downstairs with a fireplace that I could turn into my own little apartment. I'd keep it empty til the time came I needed it. It had everything! Even a fireplace in the dining room and living room!

I told Doctor I wanted to try my hand at investing and making money in real estate. He was glad not to hear no more about what used to be, so he gave me the go-ahead. Child, I went ahead!

My heart had been so heavy lately, but I was dancing a light step through life now, on my way to my homemade future I was making for myself. I was my own employee. And . . . I liked it!

I was still mindful of love in my life. But I had planned for that too. See, my rooming house was for bachelors. Doctors, laywers, businessmen who didn't want the responsibility of a house or apartment. Retired or otherwise. All potential bandleaders of the opera! No woman in my house after midnight! Cept me and the cook, and she was going to be old. I would be the only woman at the dining room table every morning, every evening. I would be looking good! Well! You have to start somewhere.

When the house was ready, I already had all the morning gowns and evening-at-home gowns and clothes I needed at that time. A little money saved for a light rainy day. I even had men on a waiting list. My cook received Social Security and would have worked for nothing but room and board, but I remember where I came from and I paid her. I knew she would always find something to do with money cause Social Security don't do much. Besides I knew room and board wouldn't be enough as soon as she got through being grateful for it and started counting my money. My old handyman came to chop and stack wood for the fireplaces and to keep the grounds pretty and clean. I charged a reasonable plenty. After all, they had lovely rooms and delicious meals with a homelike atmosphere!

I had seen my neighbors on each side of my house. One side was Black, the other, white. They didn't bother me and I didn't bother them. One of the young daughters on one side was often watching as the house became ready. When I would wave, she would go away. I didn't know why but didn't have time to worry about it.

Then, when the time came, I sat down and talked to Doctor, telling him I was leaving him so he could enjoy his life fully. He didn't want me to go, naturally. He was comfortable. I told him I wanted what he wanted . . . love. He went through two or three schemes to change my mind, but I knew he wouldn't be too sorry to see me go. He would miss his daughter, but he could see her and keep her whenever he wanted because I knew he loved her. I didn't try to clean him out or pay him back for not loving me the way I needed. I told him to just pay the taxes and the insurance on the house for two years, pay our baby's bills, set up a trust fund for her, put everything in her name, keep my medical insurance up for two years. I'd pay my own notes and in two years I'd take over all the house's expenses, he would have to pay no more, ever. He looked at me a long time, cause he knew with a little detective work, I could own him. I didn't want to own him . . . or hate him. It makes you tired and ugly. Letting him go was like letting myself go free. Soon I was gone. Now we both had new styles of life. I kept mine clear. I didn't want nothing nomore but what I really, really, REALLY wanted to keep.

Divorcing—I kissed Doctor good-bye . . . lovingly.

Finally, I was settled in. I loved my new home. It was MINE! And I was free. I had a little security and it was beautiful. The sunlight was suddenly freer. The wind through my windows blowing my curtains was free and good. I looked at everything I had . . . and it was good. I'm telling you the truth, I was happy! But I had no bandleader. Sang no opera.

I'd go to bed at night, drink my glass of brandy or champagne, slip between my satin sheets, lay my head on that satin pillow . . . and sing the blues.

I stayed in school part-time, cause I had money now. Had everything I needed and most all I wanted. Closet full of clothes, refrigerator full of food. Bed full of nothing but me and them rocks they always singing about. House full of men. Old, tired, young, greedy, ambitious, stingy or generous, truthful, sneaky, kind, cruel. All kinds. Not one of them appealed to me. Sometimes we would flirt for a little while, til I got to know their ways. Then I turned my eyes away. Nothing there.

If thoughts had sounds the whole city would have heard that house singing the blues in the middle of the night.

Finally in my normal run of taking care of my business I ran upon someone that I let make love to me. It turned out to be like singing swing or something like that. He was nobody I would really want in my homelife, so I just kept him as a stash. He lived way cross town and I left him there. I always went to see him.

Never let him come to see me. Well, when you are secure, you can do that! Anyway, he was a good stash. I didn't sing opera, but I didn't have to sing the blues either!

Five years or so passed. I never did regret my decision or bargain with Doctor. I was happier than I had ever been. I went to the theater, learned about the ballet, went with my class to hear another kind of opera sung, tried to learn to play tennis, took long walks, learned to swim. Oh, what life can be! I had my private apartment and my child. She was talking at her age like I had learned to talk at my age. I use to stare at that child and think about how I was raised. The kind of house I was raised in. I could almost cry I was so glad I could provide a different kind of life for my daughter. I was going to try to see that nobody killed her mama either!

I told you about my neighbors on each side of me. Black on one side, white on the other. Not going to tell you which was which cause I don't blive it makes no difference noway. During the five years I got to know them pretty well. I came to know the woman with the two daughters named Glad and Happy. It was really Gladys, but Gladys liked Glad better. Their parents musta really wanted them to be like their names. Wanted good things for them, you see?

Now, Happy was like she had just been to a funeral and wasn't back yet! Glad acted like she never would die. Happy was a very good baby-sitter. I was still taking classes, nothing special just whatever I liked. Interior decorating, painting, hat making, things like that. Didn't need nothing serious because I felt like I had already graduated. Happy was the youngest, in her first year of high school. Glad was going to graduate when I met them.

Their mother did a lot of civic duties and charity events, but was always promptly home at five. She then went on and got drunk. But I don't care what, she was always out there doing some duty the next day, sides Saturday and Sunday. She told me one day it was to be a example to her daughters. I thought about that, then decided, hell, she was human. It was really the daughters that interested me tho.

Now, Glad was very gay and happy most all the time. She was a pretty girl, had a way with clothes. Always smiling, laughing, playing. Always going out on dates. Had plenty beaus. Went to all the games and dances. Never had to look for a date. She was always in love or had a crush on some young man. And they crushed her right back! Older men with businesses liked her too! Her family was well respected, you see. I don't know bout whether she was a virgin or not, but I don't blive she fooled around. She changed beaus too fast. By her doing, not theirs! And the mother had told both girls, many times, they'd make better marriages if they were virgins! So Glad was just a very gay person. Never a worry a minute about getting married. She never had too many thoughts for anyone else but herself, I noticed. She loved herself enough for three people. Happy was the one who was full of love to give away.

Happy was the one who baby-sat for me mostly. She was the dead opposite from Glad. She was a good girl, but she was always gloomy. All the time! She suffered from acne real bad, not only on her face, but on her back, arms and wherever. She was always off by herself somewhere. Cry, at the drop of a hat! Close herself up in her room and read or sit and stare into space for hours—whole days even! Quiet, til she was over at my house, sometimes. She loved my baby. As I saw it, she loved a lot of things. She had a dog, cat, hamster, bird, goldfish . . . all them things!

Happy ran her mama crazy cause her mama didn't know what to do about her. How to help her. The girl had a terrible inferior complex feeling. She wanted love real bad and didn't blive she would ever have it! Knew she was ugly. But, truly, she was ugly cause she thought she was. Didn't do nothing to make herself better! Clean, that's all. Hair just hung on her head. Couldn't wear no makeup on accounta that acne. She said lipstick made her look and feel like a fool.

At her sister's parties she always stood around behind something like a silent lump on a log til she sidled on off to her room. Boys didn't ask her to dance or nothin; I guess that's why. But she was always pickin at her face and one of them pimples be bleeding or have a scab on it! She was always cryin, "I wish I could die!" Like no good, beautiful thing would ever be in her life.

I was talking to her mama once, about Happy and her sadness, and I told her I thought she was just going through a lonely stage. Needed more love, kinda. Her mama was pretty high that evening so she just spoke what was on her mind. She said, "I give her love. Her daddy gives her love. She has all those pets. She's just strange, that's all. There's plenty of love in this house!"

I didn't buy the part about plenty love—not in a house where Daddy was never hardly home except on some Sundays! But, I didn't say nothin.

She went on talkin . . . and drinkin. "This may not sound like it makes sense, but when Happy was a little girl, she put everything under her dress. We had to take her to the doctor when she was eleven and she complained about pain 'down there.'" She pointed. "The doctor got some things out of her . . . 'down there'!" She pointed again, hard! "A nickle, an eraser and a deflated balloon!!" It wasn't funny. Neither of us laughed. We thought a minute or two.

I said, "You know, the Bible says 'The womb is always crying to be filled.' Maybe hers just came down on her early and she didn't understand."

Mama just looked at me, took a drink and finally said, "The Bible says something for everything, doesn't it?" Dead like.

I just told her, "That's why it was written. It's sposed to tell us about everything in life so we can find our way through life!"

I took all that home with me to think about and came upon the fact that love has a whole lotta sides to it. I know God is love. But the devil makes some sad kinda loves too. He always tryin to do what God does! But he never can do it as good, if at all!

Anyway, that was the condition of the house on one side.

I had gotten acquainted with my neighbor on the other side of me, all at the same time. Slowly . . . but five years is a lotta time. My daughter was a friendly child, so she made friends first. The woman, Wendy, was the only part of that family I met for a long time. She liked to work in her yard. It was lovely! I learned a lot from her.

She was a awkward-looking woman. Like she was made a little crooked. Her face had a funny shape. Her bones were crooked even. Her legs, whenever you got to see them, were knobby, but nice. She liked to cook, and once we got to know each other, she was always handing cakes or pies over the fence for my daughter and me. I had to notice her husband was always gone a lot. Never saw them together. She never mentioned him and didn't seem to miss him, so why should I?

On the day I finally saw him, he was leaving out for work and I was coming back from dropping my daughter off at school. He looked so much like his wife, only better-looking in a way. I thought it must be true that when people live together a long time they begin to look alike!

He was pleasant and smiled, waving to me as he stepped into his Cadillac. I found out later he owned a men's clothing shop. That musta done pretty well, cause he never made his wife go to the store to work. They didn't have no kids and I thought they probly wouldn't now cause they was both above middle age. They never had ANY company the first three years I lived there. If company came, company came late cause I didn't see them. And I thought they was too old for midnight parties, when I was sleepin.

You know, you really ain't supposed to think too much bout other people's business! Cause if you don't KNOW, you ain't hardly gonna guess right!

Now, I never did see them together, but I never saw my other neighbor with her husband either. So, I didn't give it much thought. I had my own business to worry bout!

One day Wendy was helpin me dig a little space for asparagus plants. Got to plant em deep, you know. The shovel slipped and she cut her big toe in them sandals she had on. It bled somethin terrible! She went on home, naturally, to fix her foot. When she worked in her own garden that weekend, she wore house shoes. On that Monday morning I saw Walter—that's her husband's name—going to his car, limping. With a house shoe on the same foot she had hurt! He waved . . . or they waved. Walter was his own wife!! Or Wendy was her own husband! Whichever! That is one way to be sure the one you live with loves you!

I went in my house and slammed the door, sweating like a river!

I know life and love is strange sometimes. Every day, things may be goin on right in your face and you don't even know it . . . or understand.

Walter wasn't embarrassed bout himself. Just like he said, he wasn't hurtin nobody and it really wasn't nobody's business. So nobody just shouldn't have nothin to do with it! It was his life!

Walter was born Walter. Well, born a boy. Now, what Walter

told me came over a period of a year or so. And since I was usually speechless, I ain't goin to tell you a word-for-word description. I'll just tell you the whole story of after I learned it all. I like Walter a lot (and Wendy too) so I was sad for him. I cannot tell you about his pain. Life ain't always a bowl of cherries, honey, sometimes its a pit of shit! Life is sometimes cruel to children before they get a chance to understand what they are going through. Sometimes in the name of love. And mostly, they can't do nothin about what other people do to them.

Walter don't even know where he was born. Or his real mama and daddy. At least I do know bout mine, even tho it turned out bad! He was born in some hills, round a coal mine, he thinks. They was poor, naturally, and they had many children. He don't remember how many or even if they was all his mama's. He thinks they was all boy children. He remembers still nursing his mama's breast when he was bout six years old and there were three younger than him, still nursin too! That poor woman. He remembers the smell of trash, garbage and the taste of sour milk, stale bread. He still buys fresh bread and leaves it til it's stale. That's how he likes it. He remembers the smell of dirty diapers or rags that dragged on the floor, full of pee-pee or shit. Going naked in the summertime, never bathing. His mama was tired I guess. Hell, I don't have to guess! She never bathed either. Who cared? His daddy was always drinkin. Workin at something, but always drinkin. He never remembers his mama bein beat, only slapped. He remembers the sounds of their lovemaking, which was no love-makin . . . only a slap . . . a groan . . . a silent night-time matching of strength. To pry legs open, twist arms back, bite a arm or shoulder not in love but in force . . . a scream. Then his mama's sobs. Then, he thought it had been for the pain she felt.

Now he believes it was for the pain she felt for the new baby that had surely been made. Another child she could not nurse, feed, clean . . . or even love.

I grew to love Walter through his pain. Not as just a friend, it was more than that. Not as a lover, it was different from that. Here I had another kind of love.

Back to Walter's childhood tho. There was a bleakness, a emptyness, the deepness of poverty, want and need. There was no woman's warmth, no pride in a curtain . . . no curtain, no sewing scraps, no quilt of pride. No teapot even, to hide private money in . . . no money. No signs of a human woman cept children. No warmth, no warmth at all. No air of expectation, at any time, of anything . . . better. Even when it was quiet, everybody sleep, no activity ever except yesterday's same activity . . . nothin and always . . . sad. No happy memories.

Walter remembered his mother's bony hands and her hanging breast. Not her face. She looked like a old maid, tho she was married and had nine children. He remembered her, always vaguely, standing in the doorway nursing a baby, looking off toward the river where many woman like her had ended their lives.

I remember when he was talkin to me that I smelled boiling cabbage my mother was cooking the day she was shot. I know now that's why I can't stand to smell it anymore. I never cook it.

Walter does not know, naturally he couldn't at six, exactly what happened, but someone must have wanted a child. Someone who could afford one. They wanted a girl, probly, cause his mother dressed him in some borrowed girls' clothes. He does not know where she got them, and a girl's cap, left him barefoot and took him somewhere, telling him to shut up, not say a word. She sold him and told him he'd be glad someday. He was taken straight to a airplane where he forgot he was leaving his mama, his family, til the last minute when the plane was leaving . . . taking off. Forgot to cry until the last minute, then cried hisself to sleep. His mother had told him to hold his water til he landed in a new place. The poor child was in pain. He peed in his seat. The new woman-mother took him to her rest room. She screamed in shock. She had wanted a girl! She dragged him back out to the new husband-daddy, who had wanted a boy. She never touched him again unless he was wearing girls' clothes. Years later when the new daddy and new mama divorced, the man took him, raised him, sent him to school and college. That daddy seduced him. The man was not a homosexual as much as he was a child molester.

Walter grew up thinkin he was homosexual. Switching easily from men's clothes to women's clothes and even naming his female part. When he could no longer take the pain college life served him, the man bought him a clothing store and closed the door to him forever. Walter was too old for him. Walter was happy. However, they would not tell him where he came from, what his real name was or anything else about his life. Why are people like that?

When people ask, "What's love got to do with it?" I'll tell you! Plenty! There ain't much around . . . of the good kind.

Walter lived in one room while his shop got started. Over the years he prospered and finally he could buy that house next door. He's got money now. But he ain't happy. Well, you can say, "Who is?" Well, we know somebody is! Walter's unhappiness came from not having love in his life, and troubles when he tried to find it! Number one, he didn't know who to get loved! Walter or Wendy? That had given him plenty trouble from himself and other people too! He thought he was homosexual but he still liked being a man!

He had tried makin it with a new man but found a streak of cruelty and was hurt and beaten. He got away from that. He tried prostitutes, but his need for love was too great for that to satisfy him. He was lost. Said he couldn't court . . . too shy. Thought women laughed at him. He did look strange. But the strangeness came from the emptiness, the lonliness in his eyes, his face, his hesitant way of being hisself unless he knew you already liked him.

Out of his loneliness, he listened. Some visitors came to his door one day. They spoke of God. Walter had heard of God but didn't know nothin bout Him. He told me, "I know what the Bible means when it says, 'The truth shall set you free'!"

I said, "Of course!"

He gave me a strange look. "Do you really know? What did you have to be free from?"

While I was thinking he went on. "But people lay on homosexuals too heavy! The Bible says that fornicators—that's men or women, and almost everybody in the world does nowadays—NOR adulterers—that takes in quite a big piece of the world—NOR thieves—lotta people steal, legally and illegally—NOR the covetous—that includes almost everybody—NOR drunkards—need I say a word?—NOR liars!—shall be accepted by God."

He had my attention.

He went on, "Now He didn't say one was worse than the other! He put them all in the same group! Liars and thieves throw rocks and names at homosexuals, but they aren't any better in the sight of God! If everybody he named stepped off the world right now, do you know how much space there would be? We are all in this thing together! Ain't nobody better! Everybody hates a liar . . . but everybody lies! And I mean everybody!"

He still had my attention.

He kept it going. "So everybody who talks about homosexuals as a damnation better look in a mirror and try to heal their own selves. Who they call homosexuals do, at least, act out of their love. That's better than the hate a whole lot of people act out of."

I nodded.

He smiled. "Mankind ain't no accident. We are a miracle! Love is what makes us try to deal with what's wrong with us. Everybody needs it! Giving and taking! I removed myself from the world. I wasn't finding real love anyway. See? There is a symphony of love playing out there in the world. You got to listen and try to hear what song does love sing to you! Listen! We all have got to be saved! Save YOURSELF! Let the rest be between God and each one! That's the way God said He wanted it! Who are you, each person, good enough to judge another person, flesh and blood, like you? Who told you your way was the only way?! Whoever he was, he wasn't nothing but another man!"

I shouted "Amen!" before I even thought.

He was speaking almost to hisself. "But I needed love. I was so lonely, so lonely. Had everything. But no one to be glad about it with. So . . . I decided to love myself. I invented Wendy. She is my wife . . . my sister . . . whatever. I treat her well."

He did, too. He showed me her rooms, her clothes, her perfumes. She had everything!

He ended. "I am still lonely, but I am less lonely. I need someone beside myself to talk to." It pained me to see him so melancholy, so sad, with such a tired, patient face.

He finished, "I love myself. I talk to myself. I pray with myself. I buy things for myself. I please myself. I still need someone else."

It was not the life I am sure his mother thought she was giving him. So much better, maybe . . . so much worse, surely. I don't know. Who am I?

We had that talk sometime bout the time Glad was getting married. School over. She was marrying a big muckity-muck and was having a huge wedding. Beautiful gown, eight bridesmaids, chock full of flowers. Reception, long honeymoon, all of it! She was beautiful . . . how do they say? Ra-di-ant? I have dropped my English classes and sometimes I get it right and sometimes I don't! There was more important things I wanted to spend my time on! I had found the more better I spoke, the less people understood what I meant! Now, I can communicate when I speak like I feel. There are some words I liked because they saved you so much time, but they can mess you up sometime cause they can mean so many things to different people! If I can just say what I mean in a small way, most people get what I mean. Don't you?

Happy was struggling through her last year of school. She was eighteen now. Been held back a grade once cause she was going down to the lake setting there all day, spending her lunch money on food or books she wanted to read. Just sitting, looking over the water.

There had lately been a young man come to court her. Looked kinda like her. Same acne and stuff. But he also had braces. Couldn't afford them no earlier, she said. But he was through college and working his way up. She had met him sitting out lookin over that lake. He was quiet, read books a lot. Just lonely too.

He passed the mustard with her parents cause I guess they was glad! Probly they had been thinkin she was gonna be with them forever! That nobody would want her. She was shy with him, too, didn't talk much, but she did not run away and hide. Just got more pimples. I could tell she liked him, but she didn't talk bout him much . . . scared he may disappear one day. I saw a little happiness streak cross her face whenever we did talk about him. Then she would go back to her sadness, her confusion and pain.

Her private lonely grief and deep passion. I knew the passion was there!

Now, him being a simple, gentle, decent person, making it in his small way to his own small world, he honestly liked Happy's way! He must have seen the kind of love she had to give—that he had never had none of—while she still expected to be tricked by life, out of her desires or due, expected that this lover would leave her before loving her. She coveted love! Thank God, life got its own way!

My house was almost running itself. All my roomers were gentlemen. My cook came to cook dinner every day and break-fast on Sunday. Was a good cook, clean . . . and well paid. I had a waiting list, but nobody seemed to move except for when they got married again. I don't think any of them were too aware of our neighbors.

I had looked my roomers over carefully when they came in . . . checking them out, you know? For my bandleader. I never forgot opera! Nobody turned out to be HIM. I still had that ole stash I already told you about. I still wasn't singin opera . . . but almost! It was good enough to do til the real thing came along!

My neighbor, Walter, was stayin away from me. No cakes, no morning coffees, nothin! Shamed cause he had told me so much, I guess. But I liked him so much. He wasn't strange to me! Just human like everybody else! In time I worked it back around to our friendship cause I missed him and I wouldn't give up.

Then Happy was gettin out of school and getting married! She didn't get no big weddin like Glad. Just very close family and friends, a neat little dress, a little toast for the future . . . then off they went! Three days was all they could afford right then. She was radiating all over the place. Her eyes was so bright they lit up the room! She looked at the unhandsome man like he was the best of everything in the world! She looked like a child and a woman all at the same time! Ain't love somethin! She was eager to get started. Full of that love energy of life. Her face and soul seemed filled with magic! Then they was gone!

Then one day—all this happened so fast, I'm tellin it fast! I went to see Doctor . . . checking up on my teeth. He was doin fine! His hair was different, slicker. He had a mustache that made him look like John Juan or Don Juan, whichever one was the great lover! His nurse was younger, flashier. You could tell he made love (sex) to her cause she acted like it was her office. Too familiar with him too!

Doctor told me Mavis was back in town. Done left her band-leader man. Said she wanted my address. Didn't know why. I shrugged. Didn't make me no difference. Loans and gifts was over! We was created equal . . . we both had had a chance! I told him he could give it to her.

While I was in his waiting room I mentioned my garden yard and some trouble I was havin to a man who was sittin there sadly waiting his turn. He brightened right up and told me all kinds of things to do about it. I asked him if he did garden work. He answered, "When they let me."

I didn't know what he meant and brushed that aside, gave him my address and told him he could work for me. Doctor told me later he was mentally disabled and lived in a state home. I thought about all the intelligent things he had told me bout my garden. I shook my head in confusion. Now his sadness was mine but he had to live it, I only thought about it! I love people like that . . . quick.

To make a long story short, I got him to work for me. He loved workin the earth. He said he felt sorry for people who had no earth in their life, only stone and wood. Where he lived was all stone and you couldn't bother the earth. So cold like. You know what I did? After about eight months of knowin him I built him a garden shack in my huge back yard and moved him in. They, the state home, fought me. Guess they needed that money! But I got him. He lives there now . . . with a lady just like him. They both work. She loves to iron and clean, things like that. I pay them both a little and give them a home with food. That large bedroom, small kitchen and bath cost me eight thousand dollars to build. How come it cost the government bout a million dollars to build one?

I know you are tired of hearin bout all the people comin and going in my life, but I told you about them because I have grown to love them. Another kind of love. So they were important to tell!

Mavis did come see me. Did want, not a loan, but a place to stay without rent! I told her, "I already worked for you, Mavis. I'm not workin and gettin things together for you to use!"

She answered, smart as ever, "If it wasn't for me, you wouldn't have any of these things!"

I'm smart too! I answered, "Well, if you think you did so much for me . . . why didn't you do it for yourself? You didn't do this! I did this for me!"

She cut back, "I gave you the job!"

I cut too. "It wasn't the job you gave me that put me here! It was MY WAY with the job that put me here!" Then I asked her, "Where that man of yours? The one you was loving? You don't want him nomore?"

She leaned back, taking a breath. "You know, he taught me something."

I wondered out loud, "What could he teach you?"

She looked at her manicured fingernails and smiled at me. "He taught me that there is more to life than having an orgasm. Orgasms are not enough! He could make me laugh, but he couldn't talk to me." Her mouth turned down and her voice got hard. "From early morning when he left for work, I had to fix his breakfast, THEN go shopping for more food, clean the house myself if I wanted it cleaned, and it always seemed to be very dirty. Going to pieces. I couldn't keep it clean. You have to do it over and over, every day."

I said, "Every day."

She wasn't through. "Wash breakfast dishes before I cook dinner, then wash dinner dishes."

I started to say something but she kept on talkin.

"Clean up after him TOO! No help from him! If he couldn't afford a maid, you'd think he would help himself!"

I knew the kind of man she was talkin about!

She looked around my lovely room, saying, "At first, in the beginning, by the time I got to bed, good lovemaking was enough. Good enough to be enough! But . . . four years I took it. Just so I could feel good in his arms. By the end of that fourth year, all my nice things had been destroyed without any feeling by him at all. If I saved some money, SOMEHOW, and got a nice set of crystal to drink my own cheap wine from, his friends poured some cheap beer in them and usually broke them. Oh, not intentionally, just didn't know any better. Never had nothing! I missed my satin sheets, my caviar, my Mercedes. I let one of his friends fix my Mercedes when it needed a tune-up or something. We couldn't afford one. My car has never been the same. I cry when I drive it."

I thought of how proud I had been of her that first day she had jumped into her Mercedes and driven off!

She took a drink of sherry from the little crystal glass I had given her and looked at me, saying "I was raised in a poor house. I don't know how I forgot it. Busy having an orgasm, I guess. But . . . poverty is like a disease. The shabbiness." Her voice was disgusted. "The poor drabness of people daily living around people with dreary lives . . . except for their Saturday nights!"

I said, "Good grief!" Cause I know all she was talkin bout!

She lightened up. "Well, it just wasn't worth it to stay for a good feeling. I'm getting old . . . older. I need someone to take care of ME! In my style!"

I sat up. "Well, it ain't me! I ain't taking care of you!" I thought of that girl in Doctor's office who had been kinda snotty to me. "Why don't you go to work on—for Doctor at his office? It'll put you close to him. No tellin what will work out!"

She looked at me strangely. "You are cold."

I looked at her strangely too. "Life is cold. I am real!"

I started to give her a check but didn't want to start nothin I was not goin to keep up! I stuck some cash in her purse without her knowing it. Enough for a professional hairdo, manicure, pedicure and a good, practical new outfit. It was up to her! She left.

So much for that orgasm love! I wanted to sing opera, but I didn't want to sing it in the poorhouse!

When I called Doctor's office two weeks later, she answered the phone. Working there!

In time, he married her again! She was right! He liked that well-turned ankle! A face . . . a shape! Well . . . he had the money, he could afford it. I bet she don't say no when he wants to make love anymore. Not for a while anyway!

I looked up another day and Glad was back home with her one child. Separating and divorcing from her husband. That wealthy, fine husband. She had changed. She was quiet, sullen, silent and mean . . . gloomy. Marriage had changed her, too. Not for the better! Love sure can go any kind of way, can't it?

Cause bout that same time, Happy came by. She wore her name well now! She WAS happy and looked it! Skin all smooth. Body healthy, standing tall. And even pretty! Had two children and one on the way! This was what she wanted. Her husband was doin fine. Sometimes when he came by with her I noticed his acne was all cleared up too! They still together! Two more babies now!

Glad is still livin back at her mama's house. They both drink in the evenings now! She, Glad, goes out with gentlemens sometimes, then comes back and talks about them like they are dogs. I baby-sit for her now and then, cause sometimes she don't know where she is when it comes to dinnertime. Her son comes on over here. His granddaddy is gone even more often now! Love running amok!

You know, it's so much to tell I just can't keep up with everything! Walter, my neighbor, ended up adoptin two children. One disabled. He is gettin closer to the social welfare lady. She's a older, schoolteacher type. He said he blives she is smoldering, a passionate woman who wants to throw them books away! They are together a lot, goin places, doin things with them kids. He done even told her about Wendy! She wanted to see Wendy's clothes. I think he may have a sure nuff wife on the way! He may be askin for trouble, but he been havin trouble of a kind anyway and didn't ask for it! Least you ought to be able to ask for the trouble you get! I rather not have no trouble at all, but, if I have to have some, I rather it be some I ask for myself! He's bein loved. He can take it! And if he is lookin for his mama . . . and she wants to be one . . . So what!?

Now, me!

House full of men . . . old, tired, greedy or ambitious, stingy, generous, sneaky, gay, straight, kind or whichever . . . all kinds. Not one of them appealed to me, in no way. Sometimes one would for a little while . . . til I get to know their ways, then I turned my eyes away. Nothin there. Wasn't nothin in my bed but me and them rocks in the bed they always singin about! If thoughts had sounds . . . at night my whole house would have been heard singing the blues!

Now, I had paid attention and done learned a lot bout love ever which way I looked! It didn't look too good, but, truth? I knew it wasn't that bad either! So I STILL was on the lookout! I wanted my bandleader! I wanted to sing opera! I might be outta my mind, but it's my mind!

Then.

One day . . . early in the morning, they was pickin up the garbage, makin all kinds of racket! I raised the kitchen window to tell them to make less noise. Didn't they know where they were?! I looked out and looked into the warmest, biggest, beautiful set of eyes I ever want to see! Child! He was tall, big-shouldered, husky—well, fat really—and smiling up at me!

I was going to say, "Cut out all that noise! You ain't at the dumps!" Mad.

Instead, I said, with a smile, "You all are sure noisy."

He smiled back with laughing words. "If I'd a known I was wakin a angel up from her beauty sleep, I'd a tippy-toed back here like a mouse!" He had pretty teeth.

When he was gone I shut the window and said, "Oh, God! Not the garbageman! Please!"

I always woke up when the garbagemen came after that. Well, really you couldn't help it. But I didn't allow myself to look out there. Can you imagin . . . fallin in love when your eyes meet across a crowded garbage can?! I didn't want no poor garbage-man! No Lord!

One morning tho, they made so much noise I looked out the kitchen window again. He was just astanding there banging that can down on the ground! When he saw me he smiled. I opened the window some more, leaned out and said. "What's wrong with you? Makin all that noise! It's six-thirty in the mornin!"

He smiled on. "Girl? What's your day off? I want to see the rest of you hangin on the other side of that window!"

I smiled in spite of myself and my good sense. "Are you crazy?"

He laughed. "No! I just wanna take you to the best place in town for the best barbecue you ever ate! You ain't married is you? I don't take no married women out! But I might take you any-way! You married?"

I caught my brain. "No! I'm not married! But that don't mean I'm goin out with you!"

He said, sadly, "Baby, I know you can't tell nothin bout me in the garbage suit holdin a garbage can, BUT, if you don't have somebody to love you right, you betta take a chanct on me! You'll like me!"

Well . . . I'll just go on and tell you. We went to dinner. We talked and laughed and had so much fun. But I didn't tell him I wasn't the cook, workin at that big house. Tho I sure would think sometime, so what if you was a queen? If you don't have nobody to love you . . . right? So I took to even cookin for him sometime in my own house on cook's day off. But I still didn't tell him it was mine.

One of them days, I took him to my rooms, put him between them satin sheets. Honey . . . let me tell you. That man's feet and hands like to tore up my sheets, scratching them! I thought I had done a dumb silly thing and what was I doin with the garbageman! Then . . . we made love. I sang opera for the first time in a long, long, long, *long* time. He could have torn them silly satin sheets to pieces! I wouldn't care a damn! I had my bandleader, chile!!

Now, good lovemakin always make you want to tell the truth to your lover. I wanted to tell him the truth. I had to talk to myself quite a bit! I mean . . . I didn't think I had reached all this far, worked all this hard to get someplace, somewhere . . . and then find a man I would have to bring up to me! Oh, I knew he would still work! But I didn't want to live again like he could afford! I wanted what I could afford! Then, on the other hand, I could afford him . . . for me. And wasn't that what I had worked for? For me? I don't care how much money you got . . . you can be poor WITH money . . . if you ain't got no love. And I don't want money kinda poor. Rich don't make you ALL rich. Love make you rich too!

I told him the truth. He didn't blive me. Told me he wanted me without me havin to lie bout what I have!

I said, "Marriage?"

He said, "What?"

I said, "Marriage?"

He said, "What?"

I said, "Marriage!"

He said, "I don't know."

I said, "Then go to your own house and think about it! You a bandleader"—he didn't know what I meant—"but you ain't goin to beat my band til I know I'm goin to have a lifetime career of singin opera!" I meant that, too!

A week passed by. He didn't show. I cried in my satin gowns, on my satin sheets, into my crystal glass of champagne.

Let me tell you. I've had the blues both ways. Poor and with a little money. But it is best, by far, to have the blues, if you gonna have em, and cry into a satin pillow with the cook cookin downstairs and money comin in . . . than to have the blues and cry into a can of beer or a glass of cheap wine, layin down on raggedy sheets and a torn pillow with the feathers sneakin out with cold beans stuck to the cold pot sittin lopsided on the stove. If he didn't come back, I could make it on by . . . and by and by.

But . . . he came back.

He told me, "The moon even been blue, Bessy!"

I smiled and rubbed his arm.

He said, "I'm lovin you, Bessy."

I smiled and rubbed his arm and shoulder.

He said, "Spose you get tired of me . . . not havin much money as you and all that shit?"

I was serious. "You goin to work. We will work together, that's all."

He looked around. "I don't blive I can live here."

I said right back, "I'll fire the handyman. Cause you will be the man of the house."

He looked at me. "You think . . . and be sure . . . cause I don't want no divorce in my life nomore, Bessy. I done had one. That's enough for me. I want children . . . to go with your daughter."

I smiled even while I thought of Doctor's face. "I do too!"

He swallowed hard. "Welllll."

I said, "Well?"

He waved his hand in the air. "Well."

I said, "Well what?"

He laughed. "Well, hell!"

We had a opera duet that night.

We got married.

Now . . . the man had things wrong with him. He hung his

clothes over the tops of doors. I took to throwing away everything he hung like that. That broke that up. He puts them away now. I bought him $40.00 house slippers; he slid into them, walking on the heels . . . poverty type. I bought him house shoes with no backs to em. That worked better. He talked awful loud sometimes round my roomers, laughed too loud and talked that ole bad English, worser than mine! But . . . I had to remember, I married a man, not a book! When the roomers would be gone, he would still be mine! He soon learned to avoid them. Said they bored him! He don't care much for ballet. Says the only opera-singin he likes is mine! I haven't found anything about him bad enough to leave him for, or be sorry I married for love.

I been watching love ever since my daddy shot my mama cause he loved her. Everybody I know, I watch their love life. That's why I know love IS life . . . but life ain't always love. Some people don't love you for yourself . . . they love you for their self. I watched and I learned.

No . . . this man I have is sure not a perfect man, but I sure don't want to spend my life looking for something that ain't even there. And if he was perfect, he wouldn't want me, cause I'm not perfect. I'm glad I had sense enough to see my chance and take it! I reached for, took it . . . and I still got it!

I sing opera whenever I want to. And if we don't feel like no opera, it feels good just kissing his cheek before we go to sleep. We've got another house now, where we live away from my business. My husband (and me) is more relaxed this way. We have two other beautiful children now, too.

So . . . that's where my life is. And now, I better go take care of it.

(Pssssssst! But I'm glad I got some money, too!)

FEELING FOR LIFE

I was born in a strange little country town that may be like all other country towns, but I do not know. It was the world I was born to. The world is such a place *that* you need special things to understand it. I do not think I am a fool, but I do not understand life. It's like I am always standing in the dark somewhere. It could be on the edge of a cliff by a deep ravine . . . or on a flat piece of all the land in the world . . . and I would not know. I would not know whether to step or stand still. Either one could be a danger . . . when I'm alone. Some lives are like that. Depending on the kindness of everybody.

I was born blind. I have never seen my mother . . . my family. I have felt them. My first feelings of life. I have never felt my father. He has never been here.

My mother said some women cry because their man leaves them for another woman. She said it's worse when he don't want you so much he rather leave you for nothin. Just rather have nobody . . . than have you.

It's easier to *see* poverty than to feel it. I felt it. We were very poor. In the beginning of my life I was always the one who was fed first. When I got older, bout seventeen years old, and they were used to me, I had to provide for myself, with my mother's help.

My mother was sick. At night, when the others were asleep, she pulled and pushed herself to the dark and empty kitchen to gather whatever was left, bringing it to me to hide and eat when I was hungry . . . again.

That did not mean my family hated me. It means we were poorer since my mother could not work, our father was gone, and they must struggle harder to survive for themselves. They were, my brother and sister, old enough and strong enough to work, but they did not work.

I had seen nothin. My mother was my key to life. She gave me a life in this world after the one she gave me when I was first born into it. Mama was proud of the good little education she had had before she fell in love and got married, and now had nothin but us and a little ole falling-down house to show for her life and love. She was always teaching me words and things. It was really all she had to give me and I needed everything. There was no bus or nothin to pick blind children up and take them nowhere to learn nothin! Any word I know, right or wrong, she taught me. I picked up some new ones later, but she taught me the important words.

As I grew up and was always in the house, in the dark, except when we went to church on every Sunday til she got too sick, she began to find ways to help me live a little. As I think back now, I blive she was trying to get me used to getting outside that house, even if I was alone.

She began to take me out to the back yard, tie me to a lone tree with a long rope . . . and tell me to run. She pushed me, shoved me til I stumbled along. That's when I became aware of the feel of the sun . . . the feel of the wind, the breeze . . . the feel of space. I learned to go faster and faster, holding my arms up to the heavens I had heard so much about, where I might go to and not be blind anymore . . . someday.

Mama would say, "That's right, Christine child! Reach for God!"

I began to love it. I laughed and ran even when my brother said I was a crazy blind fool . . . running my ass off for nothin!

I thought my mama knew everything! She showed me other things, like how to be clean even if I was raggedy. How to listen so to know people by their footsteps. All new people had to shake my hand, so I could learn to judge them by the feel of their skin and touch. There are so many skins in the world: hot, cold, wet, dry, hard, soft, smooth, rough, wrinkled, young, weak, strong, all withered up, even. I learned to make judgments of people by their touch. My mama tested me and we made games out of what I thought a person was like and what she knew they were like. I learned.

My mama said I couldn't see what was coming at me so I better learn to listen and hear as hard as I could! I learned who was comin by their footsteps. I could even hear the barefoot ones. If I couldn't tell who was comin, I went in the house to be by my mama, or just shut the door if I was alone.

I still hadn't seen nothin cept through my mother's eyes and she was getting sicker all the time. It got to where she didn't care bout the world no more and nothin in it! She didn't teach me things nomore. Some kids, my friends who knew me, always usta bring dead things—birds, squirrels, snakes, butterflies, things like that—over to me so I could get to see what other things felt like. Then we would bury them in a decent grave. They always brought the little boxes, cause we didn't never have anything new that came in a box. So I learned that way, too. I'd show my mama how we was having a funeral and what we was buryin. She would pat my head with her weak hand and say, "Another funeral." My brother would laugh at me and tell me to "get that shit out the house." My sister just be layin down in that little closet room.

Everyone said my brother was almost good-lookin except he had a walleye. That means it floated round. Just one tho. He didn't like work and was always lookin for a easy way to make some money. Even my mama layin on her bed sick didn't make him go out and get no job. He just sat around waiting for my mama's check to come so he'd be sure to eat.

Everybody said my brother was a liar. So I did not know if all the wonderful and strange things he told me were true or not. But I listened anyway cause lies were better than just sittin round doing nothin cept staring at the dark inside my head.

My sister had a streak of madness from all the strains of life, and bein so poor, that took much away from her reality and gave nothin back. She had those epliptic fits sometimes—least, that's what they called them. She said that's why she didn't get no job even if there hada been one somewhere to get. I tried to give her of my poor spirit, but what did I have?

When my sister, Josephine, talked to me it was about love. Always love. So I knew of love. Her name was Josephine, but I called her Phine. She must have known bout love cause there were some men who came to see her. Specially after my mama was really sick and stayed to her bed. But they always came in the sleeping time of the night, through her window into our little closet room that was only big enough to hold a bed and a rod for clothes. When you stepped out of our bed you was almost in another room, the kitchen. I would get up and find my way to my mama's bed. I rather lay and rub my mama's back as she moaned than listen to my sister moan with them men. In the mornin they would always be gone. So . . . I knew of love.

I knew of death . . . my mother had told me. "Everybody got to go," she said, "I may have to leave you, my little blind child." She would cry when she told me that. I hated her to cry and I double-hated to think of her dyin. I feared both love and death.

I feared and wanted the love of a man. But, I thought, who will ever want me? I knew I would want death when my mother died. Yet! How could I know what I wanted? I had never SEEN anything! Never done anything! Never had anything.

I could touch and feel my mother and know the time for her dyin was close. She was dyin everyday. Oh! Jesus! She had been my whole and only life! What was I to do . . . in this house . . . when I'd be alone, with a liar . . . and a mad-woman . . . in the dark?

I remember that day . . . that day we had no food in the house at all. My brother was sittin on the porch studyin his feet, I guess, just sittin in the shade out that hot sun. My sister was layin in her bed, just layin. My mother was so sick, so sick. But she would not give them the money to go to the store cause they might not come back for a long time, a day or two even. Or when they did come back the money may be all gone, specially my brother, and we still not have any food nor money either. Then we have to call on the church people, and my mama was shamed when she had to do that. She got a check for $65.00 from somewhere once a month. The grocery store, way up the road, cash it and sell her food. Their food was high, she say, but they would cash the check if she bought there.

My mama got out of bed, slowly, and tried to dress. I had to help her. Told me to get a wet rag so she could wash her face and under her arms. I did. She was hot to my touch. Her skin was damp, yet dry and withery.

She took my hand and we went walkin to the store. She leaned on me. The blind and the sick. Store bout a mile and a half away. Sun hot. Insects, bugs batting round us. I didn't know what they were and when I ask, Mama didn't say nothin. Saving her strength for walkin, I guess. She had to stop and rest by a tree lots of times. I circle her body with my arms, huggin her to give her my strength, til she push me away, saying, "It's too hot." Then we go on. We both tired and hot and sweaty. But we hungry.

We finally got to the store, finally. I was a little excited cause I knew I was gonna get a candy stick, but Mama wasn't excited, she just kept countin that money, over and over. She did get me my candy stick tho.

Well, we got everything and was bout halfway home when the rain came down from nowhere all of a sudden. Mama began to drop things out of her bags, then the bags was so wet, everything dropped. Mama started cryin. I felt her cryin. It made me scared and I cried too. I made her lay down even on the wet ground under a big ole tree she led me to. Then I groped around for the groceries in that wet clay and dust, with her telling me which way to reach. Since I was a child to me, I could take off my dress without no outside trouble, cause I had a slip on. I wrapped the groceries in that dress.

When the rain stopped, as suddenly as it started, we started out again. When we finally got where Mama said the house was in sight, Mama seem to almost give up. She got to hold that big dress full of food and she got to hold on to me, or I got to hold on her dress, but she say that pulls her down. We both barefoot cause she had done lost those sliding shoes she wore and I couldn't help her find neither one. She was sweating even tho the sun wasn't so hot now and it seem like I could hear her crying again. Then her step became stronger and we made some more road go by. Do you know . . . we was almost to the gate, then my brother, who I know had watched us comin, came down to help us get in the house. His hand already reaching into the food.

I put Mama to bed, tho she kept pushin at me to go get something to eat. My brother and sister were arguin. Phine came in to look at Mama and ask her what she want to eat. Mama say, "Anything, nothing. Feed this child, please, first." My sister grunted and went on in to cook something. I lay down side my mama.

Then my mama raised up suddenly, like she just remembered somethin. Put her hand in her bosom, I know cause I had my hand on her arm. I heard paper money, a wrinkled, crinkly sound, then she was pressin it in my hand. Said, "Hide this where only you know where it is!"

I ask, "Why?"

She say, "Just do what I tell you!" She lay down again with a deep, ugly, painful sigh.

Well, I had a place. I went out to my graveyard where all my little dead friends are buried, my animals, my pets. I buried that money in a box by the post of the house so I wouldn't lose it. Only had to find that post and I would know where the money was. I could hear my brother fussin with my mother bout money, and my sister in the kitchen, so I knew they wasn't watchin me. I went back in and lay down by Mama again.

Mama couldn't eat that evenin, but I did. I felt starved. Everybody else ate too. I could hear them.

That's the night my mama died.

Nobody was in the room but me. I could hear my brother and Phine arguing playfully. Full now. Then they would get serious in arguing every once in a while. They was in the kitchen, bellies too heavy to carry away.

My mother sat up and was looking at me. I know that; tho I am blind I knew it. Then she said, "Oh, my child. I am lovin you. I am lookin at you and cannot stop. Because . . . I am leaving you . . . undone and alone. Oh, my blind child left in this here world in this room."

She fell back. I reached for her, holding her tight! I cried, "Where you goin? Mama, you dyin! Mama, don't leave me! Don't leave me . . ."

She say, "Death ain't so hard, chile, not for me. Not for the dyin. Only for the ones left behind." She held me tighter. "My blind baby."

I cried, "God! Don't make my mama die! Please, God!"

Mama say, "God don't call everybody to death. Don't cause all dyin. People do it too. Don't pray for me, pray for yourself. Cause you left here . . . with people." She was breathing heavy, gaspin even. I felt the effort she made to roll over on me, holding me while I held her. Her poor little small, wet, sick, sweet body next my blind one.

That's when she gasped her last breath . . . and died.

I pushed her over, clawing, grabbing at her body, rubbing her face. I even tried to breathe life-breath through her lips. But I could not hold her life. She was gone! Still in my arms . . . but gone. Forever.

I didn't tell my brother and Phine that our mama was dead.

I lay and sat with her all by myself that night. The last person I could truly trust was beside me, unseen, only felt. Dead. Gone. I wanted to hold her to myself, by myself, as long as I could. I did. I fell asleep and woke in the morning, scared, empty and friendless.

My brother knocked on the door asking Mama if he could borrow a dollar. My sister, Phine, hollered at him, "If you take your lazy ass to work somewhere you would have you a dollar!"

He hollered back, "If you was to charge some money for all that whiff you give away, we'd all have some money!" He knocked again. "Mama!"

I opened the door and screamed in his face, "Mama's DEAD!" The house got very quiet. Nothin but the faucet drippin in the sink. But I could feel it was not the silence of grief. It was the silence of confusion and fear. I know in my heart that Phine checked over the food in her mind. My brother thought of what money might be left . . . then my sister did too. She read his mind.

Phine said, "We need that money for to bury her."

My brother didn't say nothin.

Phine said, "Brother, go tell the minister Mama is dead. We need a funeral."

Brother said, "I know why you want me to go! You want me out of this house so you can find the money!"

Phine slapped the table, or something. "Oh shit! That's our mother! If she got any money, we got to use it to bury her with! Go on now! I'll clean her up. Tell somebody to come help me! Go on now!"

Talkin over his shoulder, he said, "She won't need all the money to go into the ground. Sides, if they don't think we got no money, they'll take a collection and bury her anyway!"

Phine laughed, said, "What you know bout what they do at church? You don't never go! And just how much money you think Mama got? You done ate up most of it last night, fool! Go on! Go tell em what we need!"

He left, mumbling.

When he was good and gone, Phine looked through Mama's things. I could hear her. She asked me, "Where she put her money?"

I didn't know what to say. Keep the money like my mama say or give it up to bury her with? I decided to wait on the minister, or somebody.

They came, but before I could tell him anything, they had done decided how to bury her in the churchyard cemetery without no cost. So I kept quiet.

My brother and Phine, together now, looked for that money all that night. They only knew the rent was paid for two more weeks only . . . til the next check came. Each one thought the other one had found it and was holding it back, pretending. They argued and said a lot of mean, mean things to each other. They told me to sit down and shut up, cause I couldn't see it if it was in front of my face. I sat down and shut up, cause my mama had taught me bout some things.

Now, I have seen or been round some of all kind of things in my life, but it's one thing I do know. People say I am disabled because I am blind. But the most disabled people I know are the one's without love or kindness in em. You set your life by what you don't have as much as by what you do have. I have found that out, over and over.

When they buried my mama I remember everything I smelled that day: the trees, some flowers, heat smells too: sweat, dirt and my rough-dried, damp, almost not ironed dress. I still taste my tears. They had to hold me! Carry me and everything. I held Mama when they let me near her. Then I held the box she was in. They picked me up cause they couldn't drag me away and I tried to walk the walls of that little church, screaming. I didn't care bout my raggedy underwear showin or nothing. Then we was at that big hole in the ground was gonna keep my mama forever in it and I heard the men groaning as they let the coffin down on ropes. I heard that box hit the sides of the grave as it traveled down. My mind died, my heart died, my life died. I don't know who said it bout death not havin a sting, but I do know it does have more than a sting.

Back at the house, people brought lots of food. They must have liked my mama. They talked bout her and old times, so I listened, hard, to get everything I could bout my mama. Then Brother and Phine argued bout nothin and everybody was goin. Only us three was left.

I moved in Mama's room. Nobody argued with me cause they thought death lived in there. Phine still kept company coming in thru the window, only now I could hear them arguing bout money. My brother was in and out all the time, looking in things, over and over the same things.

Finally, the month was over. Rent was up. Brother and Phine lived on the front porch practically, waiting for the mailman to bring that envelope with the check. Didn't nothin seem to bother them but that money.

To me, it seemed like the house and the world had turned on its side. Was crooked. The heat, the flys, mesquitoes pressed in on me. The souring food filled my nose and throat. My pain in that empty place in my chest. My tears that wouldn't stop, so much that Brother kept callin me bitches, snot-nose bitches.

I wanted to die and go find my mama in heaven and hold her tight, never let her get away again. I wanted to die.

When the check came Brother was in the toilet so Phine got it. She gave it to me, saying, "If I cash this check it's gainst the law. If you cash it, it'll be alright. Don't tell we got it to Brother! We'll cash it tomorrow. You hear me?! Now do like I tell you! and wipe your nose and shut up. I'll buy you somethin sweet."

I didn't say nothin. I wanted to tell my sister bout that money I had. I tried . . . but my lips just wouldn't open. My brother came back out and sat on the porch looking at the mailbox or the road all day. Frownin.

My sister finally jumped up like she was tired of waitin, took my hand and said, "We goin for a walk."

Brother said, "Where? You ain't been takin Christine for no walkin!"

Phine answered from the steps. "Mama gone. Somebody got to! You ain't!"

Brother leaned forward. I heard that old chair creak. He said, "Tine! You tell me if Phine take you to the store and cash a check! You hear me!?"

I nodded. But I was thinkin, Do they think bein blind makes me dumb?!

We walked that long road to the store, the road I had last walked with my mama. Phine had signed Mama's name already when she gave me the check to cash. She took the money, put it in a little ole purse of hers and pinned it to the inside of my thin dress. We went home with a box of oatmeal, a quart of milk and a small box of sugar. She bought me a banana and told me it was the same color as a lemon and the sun. I thought I was tasting the sun. She let me taste her lemon and it confused me bout the taste of the sun cause it wasn't like my banana at all. Phine like to suck lemons. I didn't like it. And, truly, I didn't like yellow for a long time and told everybody when they was goin to buy me somethin to wear, "Don't get yellow, please."

When we got home, Phine locked me in Mama's room. When Brother got back, he looked at those few groceries and knew somethin was up. Brother and Phine fought that night. Actually fought with fists! I know he hurt her, but she musta hurt him too! For some reason he didn't kick my door down to see if I had the money. He musta thought she didn't trust me either. If I hadn't had all this darkness in my head that kept me from knowin what way to step next, I would have split with her, but I would have surely been gone!

As it was tho, I left the money pinned to where she put it. I wasn't goin to get beat bout no money! I slept in that dress that night!

Brother shouted, "That money don't just blong to you! What you gonna do with it?"

Phine screamed back, "I'm gonna pay the rent! For everybody! So we have a roof over our heads! That's more'n you would do!"

Brother shouted again, "Where the food then?! You ain't spent but a dollar on no food!"

Phine screamed again, "We got to plan it!! So it will last all month!!"

Brother thought a minute. "What's gonna happen then? You ain't plannin for nobody! I ought to report you for cashin that check! You a lousy, crooked, cheatin bitch!"

Phine answered right back. "Then we won't have no roof and no food neither!"

Brother's voice changed. "You ain't thinkin of that poor blind chile in there either," he whined. "You just thinkin of yourself. What me and that chile gonna do?"

Phine just said, "Oh shit! Now just what are you plannin to do for your 'poor blind' sister? Jesus sake! I'm tryin to help ALL of us!"

Brother said as he slammed out the door, "ALL of us, some shit!" Then he came right back in to argue again.

It went on like that all night. With quiet in between til Brother thought of a new argument. I went to sleep, finally.

The next mornin, early, cause Brother musta gone off sometime durin the night, Phine knocked, got me up and dressed and snatched me down that road. I could hear her feet was bare. She would step on them stones in the road with bare feet and never make a whimper. They hurt my feet and she was half draggin me. Wasn't but bout thirty minutes and we was at the church. She walked me right up to the steps.

I stood still as she unpinned the purse with the money. I can count in my head. I knew there was bout $63.00 left. Unless she had paid the rent and I knew in my heart she hadn't! She gave me $5.00, she said so. She took what I think was the remainin $58.00.

She pat me on my cheek and said, "You at the church. God gonna take care of you! Me, I got to look out for myself! Now, you wait here or go in, whatever you want to. But, me . . . I gotta run now."

I grabbed her arm. "Why you leavin me? Where you goin?"

She loosed my fingers. "Mama finally gave me a way outta here, and I'm goin!" Another pat on my cheek. "I got to run now! Bye!" She was moving away, but she turned back once, said, "You know, you blind . . . but you kinda pretty, and your bust is nice.

Long braids, nice teeth. You can make it. You gonna make it. Well . . . I got to run now, for sure!"

I stood there in the early mornin sun listenin to the sound of my sister's bare feet hittin that gravel til I couldn't hear it no more. The sound of somebody I thought was my last friend, was leavin me. I wanted to cry . . . but I didn't have time. I had to think. Was Brother who I was gonna have to depend on? What must I tell him?

I felt like I was in what my brother called prison, only the bars was the darkness inside my eyes. I was a prisoner inside my head. Nothin! Nothin! I was standin in the dark without knowin which step to take. Which way? I had to wait for somebody to find me, oh dear God! Phine's words echoed in my head for a long time, *I got to run—I got to run—I got to run—I got to run!*

There I stood. Couldn't even take a step.

I had just started smelling the trees, hearin the birds, feelin the sun, when Mrs. Minister found me. Came round the church, saw me and said in a very nice holy voice, "Well, good mornin, Christine! You up an out awful early. Where your family? Who's with you, dear?"

I started cryin. "Nobody."

She asked, "Nobody? How'd you get here, dear?"

I cried, "Phine left me."

She asked, "Well, where you goin, uh . . . dear?"

I was really cryin then. "Phine gone off. She not comin back for me. Ain't no rent paid and ain't no food." I forgot the oatmeal; I guess I wanted to.

Mrs. Minister said, with a change in her voice, "Oh, for God's sake! Damn it!"

I said, "Yes'm."

She snapped, "Well, why they leave you here? This ain't no charity hospital! Damn it!" Then she hollered, "Ray! Mr. Minister! Come here!" He came and they stood looking at me. He finally told her they would talk about it later. Said, "This child is scared and probly hungry. Let's bring her in and think about what to do."

Now.

Well, it turned out I would stay and sleep in a church room, cause they had two kids and no room in their house. I would do light work in exchange for room and board til they either got my mother's check changed to me or got me one of my own, or find a place in the bigger town not too far away where I could stay as a ward of the state.

They ate good. Some different things than I had ever had or things we had only had on special days, the best Mama could do. And it was hot and fresh. I could drink all the milk I wanted, at first; then Mrs. Minister limited me to two glasses a day. Told me God was providin for all of us, not just me.

Now, you may fault God for this woman who said she was a Christian, but you can't fault God for what people do. They got freedom of choice. That's a gift from God. And if God give it to them, how come you goin to take it away? People just need to know what to do with that gift, that's all.

Anyway, I had been there for bout a month when they found out they couldn't get my mother's check turned over to me. I had to eat my meals in my room and they wasn't always hot no more. The minister tried, but I know they was poor too. Dependin mostly on the flock. Mrs. Minister started havin people in the flock take me home with them for Sunday dinner, every Sunday and sometimes Saturday.

All the only work I could do was dust the benches and things in the church. I could wash when she fixed the water and sat it where I could use the washboard good. I overwashed all those things good as I could. Well . . . I was workin for a home! And on church meetin days and nights I loved listenin to those rich low and high voices singing those rich words of love and trials, tears and smiles of joy, God and heaven. Heaven and my mama was on my mind.

One night, after I was gone to bed in that empty church that had just been swollen with the sounds of tribulations and joys, I was just layin there driftin off to sleep thinkin of my mama and my now life. I heard footsteps. I thought it was someone I knew, but these feet were bare and I hadn't heard bare feet, nor these bare feet at all, in a long time. They stopped just at my door. I called out, "Who's there, please?"

No answer.

They moved closer and put a hand on my head. Don't ask me how I knew it was a man. I jumped because nobody touched me much and I hadn't expected it. It was a man's hand. There was more weight to it and it was gentle but not gentle.

The hand smoothed my hair over my head, over and over. I said again, "Who are you, please?"

No answer.

He was not hurting me, so I said nothing else. Just fear came from somewhere to somewhere.

Then, the hand was joined by another hand. They slid down my cheeks, over my neck, down my arms. Up and down, up and down, my arms. My mind tried to feel safe—I was in the church! For God's sake!

The hands moved over my back for a moment before they slowly moved to my breast. I knew this was going too far. I put my arms across my breast. I turned in the direction of the breath

I heard, saying, "Don't do that to me, please." I begged. "Please don't."

The hands stopped a moment. Then the one on my back started again, gently, gently. The other hand, then placed itself on my thigh . . . and rubbed toward my knee. Fear moved up my body, bringing tears to my eyes. I began to have chills. I was scared, scared. It was hard to take a breath because my breath seemed to choke me.

Then . . . he spoke, in a whisper. "I want to hold you like your mother held you. With love. Aren't you lonely? Don't you need someone to hold you? Don't you need someone to hold? Someone to tell you not to worry bout anything?"

I was listening without realizing he was lowering me back to the bed. I was still scared but he had set my mind to dreaming and wishing to be held by my mama. I was layin down and he was next to me, laying down, fore I realized it.

I had my thin little nightgown on. My skin was prickly. I took a deep breath to scream. Somehow he knew that. He covered my mouth with a hand and rolled on top of me. He changed. He was no longer gentle. He forced my legs open with his knees. He lay there touching my private body with his. He lay still. Then in a few minutes he took his other hand, not the one over my mouth, and began stroking my head again. Telling me I needed to be held. Reminding me of the love my mother had for me . . . that he would have for me. That I was grown, that I needed him.

My mind was so busy . . . because I could not move my body to throw him off. He was entering my body before . . . before . . . Before what? I tried screaming again, but his whole hand covered my nose, my mouth, hard. I could not even move my head. The other hand kept stroking, gently, gently. Then he was through my virginity. I felt the pain. Then, God forgive me, I felt my body grow warm with feelings hitting me in places not even known to be alive. God forgive me, I did not make this body and it was betrayin me! I cried from shame. Spit, mucus and tears soaked the hand over my face. My body opened and reached up for him. I cried for shame through his fingers that were releasing my face. The other hand still stroked me, gently, gently. I felt no more pain. I only felt a wave of somethin that moved my arms up to hold him, to stroke him, to sob . . . even as I hated him. I came to him.

He lay there til his private body dropped from mine. Holding me, quieting my sobs. Then he was up. Then he was gone.

I didn't scream. I just lay there hating myself and, tho I knew not who he was, him . . . and life. Til my body pulled me to sleep.

The next day I washed my own sheets and my towel. I was ashamed so I did not tell. I kept goin on, doing as I had always done, cleanin things up.

I had already found a place to hide, so when the footsteps came again, I hid. Do you know, my body tried to make me go out there where he was?! My mind refused. I did not go!

In the next two months Mrs. Minister was lookin everywhere and trying everything to find me some money so I could get out of there. I have her to thank for finding out that my mama was not rentin that little house, but was buyin it by paying on a little loan. The house was in my name. Only mine. Two months behind in payment.

My brother had moved, somewhere. Mrs. Minister and I went over there, cleaned it up. While we was cleanin, Mrs. Minister found some pictures. Said one was of my mama and daddy. I asked her to get em all and give em to me. I left everything else.

We rented it out cause Mrs. Minister said I had no money and no way to work to pay the little note. I got my money from that box by the post and gave it up to pay one back note. I felt good! I had a piece of property back of me, even if I couldn't afford to live in it. Poverty is somethin! I was too poor to live in my own house!

The footsteps kept coming. I kept hiding.

Mrs. Minister was getting tired of me. She said this was no future for a young woman, blind or not. Said I needed schoolin. When I started throwing up she said I needed a doctor. The doctor said I needed a husband cause I was goin to have a baby.

Mrs. Minister screamed and asked me whose it was.

I told the truth. I did not know.

Mr. Minister quieted everyone down by sayin he would make a few calls to the city to see bout a home for unwed mothers, or a abortion. He did. But I did not want a abortion. This was my baby, not his, whoever HE was. I had no mama, no sister nomore. And my brother didn't even come check on me. I needed someone of my own even if I had to give birth to it. I needed a friend who cared about me and I knew my child would cause I would be a good mother.

I qualified for the home and the abortion. When I said, "No abortion," Mrs. Minister said, "You want that baby just cause it was made in a church? Honey, that don't make it no immaculate conception! That baby ain't gonna be no Jesus Christ!"

I stayed on my ground, said "Just bein my baby is enough for me."

She stayed on her's, said, "How you gonna take care a child? You can't see how to do nothin! That baby don't need no blind mama!"

I didn't say nothin cause I knew she wouldn't understand me. Sides, I didn't have to explain. The baby was in MY body.

Soon, one mornin early, we left. Mr. Minister was driving me to the city, a few hours drive. Mrs. Minister hugged me good-bye and said in a low voice, "If that baby is born with six fingers, let me know! I mean it!" She gave me a dollar in a envelope for the call and said good-bye again. I think I heard a smile in her voice when she said, kindly, "You can also call me if you need anything reallllll bad, cause I need everything I got real bad, too. But, I'll do what I can, child. Take care yourself."

I was really nervous and scared. I was goin to God knows where and Lord knows who! But what other road in life did I have? So I said, "Good-bye. I got to run now." Just what Phine had said.

Then we were gone.

Me and Mr. Minister didn't talk much on that ride. But I did somethin I had been wanting to do. I asked him for his hand. I wanted to feel it, see if I recognized it. He gave it to me with a friendly little laugh. I felt it, but I was concentratin so much, he snatched it away. Without that friendly little laugh.

Neither one of us said nothin for a little while. Then I asked, "Was you born with six fingers?"

He asked, "How could you tell that?" Surprised.

It was my turn to laugh that funny little laugh.

We didn't talk the rest of the way. Then the car was slowin down and parkin as Mr. Minister said, "The house is all bright and shining on the outside! Welcomin you!" I got out tryin to smell it and what was round it.

Through the doors, after he introduced himself and me, a woman's bright, cheerful voice said, "Well, hello! We are so happy to have you here with us. I am Mrs. Doll! You can call me Doll, Christine!"

I didn't say anything. I was tryin to feel the house, the people, the feeling.

I heard a new voice say, "Girls! This is Christine. Several voices said hello, hi, whatever, and Mrs. Doll named them all. I forgot them, all except for the girl I was to room with, Dancer, a girl in a wheelchair who it turned out had been there several years. She said later that nothin ever changed for her except the size of her wheelchair, which I learned to push with Dancer directing me.

Now, my biggest dream was to find a way to make a livin so I could take my baby and go to my own house and live. Dancer's biggest dream was to dance. Her only dream. I decided then I would take Dancer to my home with me. Then I could tie that wheelchair to that tree my mama use to tie me to and push her fast, fast, fast through the wind over the ground. That would be a way of dancing she could do. Cause she told me she would never get out that wheelchair.

All over Dancer's side of our small room, she told me, were pictures of the world's greatest dancers. Ballet (I had never heard of), modern, jazz, whatever kind there was. She even had a pair of ballet shoes she had saved for and bought herself, that she wore on her shriveled, useless little feet. She put them on and they just hung in my hands when she had me feel them. She talked a mile a minute for a few minutes, then she was quiet. I heard her roll from her wheelchair into her bed. I heard her crying softly. I lay and stared at the ceilin with my shriveled, useless eyes. Sooo alone. Cryin softly, for her and me . . . and even my baby.

After a while Dancer said, "I'm not always like this. I'm usually very happy. I just saw your fine, strong legs and I got unhappy. You are so lucky!"

I could only smile, to keep from cryin out loud bout my luck . . . and this thing called life.

It started raining. I could hear Dancer's strugglin movements as she got up to roll to the window to look out at it. She said she loved the rain, cause it was so sad, so pretty.

I asked her to tell me about the rain. I mean, isn't it strange that water could fall from above us without drownin us? She laughed. She had a nice little tinkling laugh, gentle but full, sweet. She said, "Put your hand out! You've felt rain. It's soft, wet and smooth. The color is silver-white. You can see through it. It's always moving whether it hits your hand or the ground or the house. It drips, runs. See how it feels to your hand? Like little kisses." We laughed. How we must have looked standin at that window laughin like fools. Happy fools. Over rain.

I asked her to tell me bout this house that would be my home, til my baby was born anyway. She changed and her voice got kinda mean, disgusted like.

She said, after a moment, "It was a abandoned house. It is ugly and dirty and decaying and sits off by itself. It is mostly always silent until somebody has a argument or fight. It has long, narrow, dark halls that sometimes echo in the night with sounds nobody can tell where they come from. The rooms are mostly tall . . . and half empty. Almost all the doors are cracked and warped and hard for a cripple person to move. The bathrooms don't always work. The ceilin's old and covered over with so many coats of paint that the yellow comes through and it's always peelin. They put the wallpaper on crooked, mostly. It keeps hangin down no matter how much you glue it. Some girls cover it with pretty posters. Like me and my dancers. They ain't never gonna get these rugs clean. Always try to wear shoes or your feet will get dirty!" She laughed that different laugh. Kind of a dancin crippled laugh. "It's filled with dreams and a lotta bad memories." She closed the window, directed me to my bed and rolled to hers. I heard her voice turn to me. "The only friends you're gonna have in this house are your dreams."

I said, just to make things better, "It's better than bein in the street." Which was true.

She said, "Yeah . . . it's home."

I forgot to say anything cause I was thinkin.

Then, her voice brightened up. "We have a tree tho! It's a sad, lonely, ole tree, but it's holdin on. Ever once in a while a bird comes and sits on the limbs and talks to me. I leave food for it!" Then she laughed that nice laugh of hers. "I also have a mouse for a friend! He comes in here and I feed him bread or whatever I have! Be sure and give me all the food you leave on your plate!"

I raised up to smile.

She went on. "I sit in my bed and watch him. He only comes early in the mornin or late at night. I watch him when he eats and watches me!" She got sad again. "I had a spider for a friend once. I was afraid of her at first, but, she alway's came back and sat, lookin at me, I think. Until I began to know her, talk to her and push crumbs in the crack she came from. Then, after bout two weeks . . . she didn't come back anymore. I think she was killed by somebody who came to clean. They left the dirt, but killed my friend, Miz Spider, when she came out thinkin it was me out here. Or . . . Miz Spider just danced away, sayin, 'I have to run now!' Anyway, she was gone."

I felt her look at me.

Her voice sounded strained or somethin, she said, "Don't ever kill a spider. I don't kill spiders anymore. I just leave them alone to live their short lives out." Her voice changed again. "Do I sound crazy?"

I laughed. "No. You sound lonely." Then it was time to go eat.

I could tell by the conversation of the girls I heard who lived in this house that certain ones stuck close together. I heard snubs and coldness in their words for each other. I heard little cruel ways, mean gossip, backbitin! All but a few seemed to hate Mrs. Doll. I heard bracelets clink, teeth bein sucked, food bein spit out, slaps, threats and dirty words. They did not bother me except for a few jokes like hiding my food or messin with it. I heard things like, "Don't give her that, Girl!" Another voice; "Let her have this!" Then laughter. Only Dancer said, "Bitches!" and fixed my plate. I thanked God for her. She treated my plate like it was a clock and told me where each food was by the time it would be on a clock. The top of my plate was twelve o'clock and the bottom was six o'clock. She didn't put things IN my hand like I was a baby, she just put my hand ON things and I could work it out for myself. She took thought for me.

Later, back in my room, I would lay in my bed in this strange new home of mine and think. Who were they to talk about my blindness. I would rather be blind then evil and mean. They were more of a threat to the happiness in this world than I was. And isn't happiness more important than anything? Isn't it what we all want? They thought my blindness was a great trouble, a weakness. But I thought their meanness was a greater weakness. Blindness was forced on me before I was born. They had accepted and helped to make grow their small, mean, hurtin ways and blamed it on bein poor and the lies that were told to em. My mother taught me from the Bible that we have free will. We don't have to be liars that fool people or thieves that steal hearts, souls and things, and time, or people who give pain to other people cause they were given pain from somebody else!

Deep, deep loneliness moved over me in my borrowed bed

and covered my soul like dirt in a grave. Lay down on my face and grabbed my heart, curlin up in my stomach.

But my womb was full. I held my belly and thought of my child. I would not be alone. Loneliness was not here to stay. I pushed it out of my lap. I wiped my tears away and thanked God for my child and slept.

The next day was a visiting day. Well, all days were. Your family could come anytime, but the girls seemed to look for them on Saturday or Sunday. Not workdays, you see. Few came to see anyone living there, so the misery stretched out and filled that sad house with some kind of quiet pain that changed by the end of the day to mean anger until arguments and fights were heard all over the house. And the hate . . . for those who did not come to see them. Now I know it was the pain of that same loneliness I had, untied and let out.

Dancer and me stayed in our room between meals. She told me what was outside the window. And about the bird. I heard him speak. Dancer talked to him as like a friend. He chirped back. She told me when he cleaned hisself and smoothed his feathers and ate the bread crumbs she gave him. I was so glad to have Dancer as my friend. And I wanted to hold and kiss the bird. She called him Nijinsky and he sang in answer cause he was not afraid of her. Nor me either.

Dancer said her sister would not come to see her until the first of the month, when Dancer had a check, therefore some money.

That's what happened. Dancer's sister came whirlin in, dancin in. Talkin, talkin, talkin. I could feel breezes as she flung her coat and moved around the little room. She threw "Hi!" to me, then turned to her job on Dancer. Sure enough, Dancer gave her $10.00 that the sister fussed about, but took. I never did hear her say thank you. I never heard her kiss or hug Dancer. I heard her leave, saying, "Well, I've got to run now! Bye!" She was gone.

I didn't say anything, just sat blindly smiling like a idiot. Dancer gave a crippled little laugh with just a little meanness in it. Said, "I only gave her $10.00, that way she'll come back next week! Then I'll give her $10.00 more. Then I'll do it one more week and that way I'll have three visits steada one!" And she did. The sister always comin for the ten dollars and always leavin saying, "Well, I've got to run now! Bye!"

It seemed everytime there should be somethin to be happy about, it seemed the part of it that should be human, wasn't. Or was it?

Then I had my problems. New ones. I got a worker to talk to me bout my life and what I should do with it. In all the talk I heard round the girls bout workers, it was all mostly sad and bad. Girls usually came from the talks cryin or mad and hopeless. Some of the girls, far as I could see, were nice, and a few, smart. But, some were mean and dumb, didn't want to go to school or nothin! They thought they knew it all!

Now, I had learned my ABCs and spellin from my mama. Since I could remember, when she was well, my mama had me spellin words, drawin the letters in my hands. I could count, too. Just had never seen the numbers and letters. I wanted to go to school to learn braille. I wanted to READ. I knew I had to learn somethin to take care me and my child with. I looked forward to my worker. Dancer told me all kinda things to look out for. I went.

Miz Somebody, I never remembered her name, started right off tellin me why I must not have a baby. I must have a abortion. I understood what she was sayin, but I couldn't understand why she said it. She didn't know me nor nothin I could do. Also, I didn't like how she said it. She really got mad when I stuck to havin my baby. Now, just listen:

Miz Somebody: You know, you belong to the three Bs.

Me (I wish I coulda seen her): What do you mean?

Miz Somebody: You are blind, Black and broke!

Me (I wished I could hit her): I got a brain!

Miz Somebody: And . . . you're going to have a bastard.

I didn't say anything, just wondered was she paid to talk to me like that.

Mis Somebody: Who is the father? Do you know which one it was? Maybe we can make him pay.

Me: I was raped. I can't see. I don't know who he was. (I didn't want no father for my baby. It was mine. I needed it all by myself.)

Miz Somebody (she gave a cheap, ugly little laugh): Everybody is always raped.

Me: Even you?

Miz Somebody: You don't have any way to take care of a child. You can't raise a child if you can't see. Your child would develop special problems.

Me: Seem to me everybody in the world got special problems, and they mama wasn't blind!

Miz Somebody: You don't have anything to give it.

Me: I'll give it love. I'll find some kind of work. I'm goin to school now.

Miz Somebody: Learning braille. That won't help you. You're not being bright.

Me (almost cryin): How you know what I can do? And don't you call my baby a bastard nomore! There ain't no bastards! Everybody got a daddy!

Miz Somebody: But yours won't know its father.

Me (mad now): You ever think you might not blong to the man your mama told you was your daddy? You might not know your daddy!

Miz Somebody (she got mad too): I'm not in trouble here, you are! And the state is not going to keep sending you to school after that baby comes! The state will have to give you some money to live on as it is! You need to have an abortion and get fixed so that if you are going to go around screwing everybody you will not get pregnant again! Then you need to go back home where you came from! Where is your family?!

Me: In my stomach!

Miz Somebody (she sounded like I was dumb dirt): Oh God help me! You girls are the dumbest bunch of people . . .

Me: You better call on somebody who knows you, cause I don't blive God do! And did you went to college to learn how to call people dumb and tell them to get a abortion?!

I got up, waving my arms tryin to find her. I never been so mad! No wonder all them girls come out cryin and mad! I decided to leave.

I screamed, "Where's the door? Where's the door?!" Just awavin my arms, bumpin into furniture and things. Somethin fell off of somethin. I kept movin. She was talkin, but I didn't hear her. I got to the wall and followed it to a corner, then went the other way. I was talkin too! And cryin. "I'll find a way! I CAN do it! There's somethin I can do! You went to college and the alphabet got twenty-six letters in it, and high as you can go is to the Bs." I finally got to the door and flung it open. I turned to her direction and she was tellin me I better sit down, control myself, stuff like that. Said my behavior was against me. Them "Bs" again.

As I left I said to her, "You like them Bs so much, I'll give you some! *B:* Bye, bitch! I got to run!" Somethin I learned from my brother was finally useful! I never before in my life talked to anybody like that! I don't like to feel that way and talk like that! I stumbled down that hall holdin the walls. I got somewhere where Dancer was waitin and went to my room, breathin heavy, hurt and mad. These must be the kinda people my mama was talkin bout!

I did learn somethin from her tho. They was goin to keep sendin me to school til I had my baby, and I would get a little money to live on while I found a way to take care my own baby.

I studied harder. If we got one chapter to read for homework, I did five of em! Til I fall off to sleep. I loved learnin. I wanted to know more and more and more. I might be blind and Black, but I wasn't goin to stay broke. And . . . my baby wasn't no bastard either! Damn them Bs! But . . . honest to God, I was scared. Of life.

Dancer and me got closer. She helped me do everything she could. She even read to me from her books. She said Shakespeare went with the ballet. He was a alright writer. I didn't always understand him, but some things he said were beautiful and made some things so clear the way he explained people. But one thing he was wrong about. That "To be or not to be?" is not the first question. "What is the truth?"—that is the question! Then "To be or not to be?" is the second question. Oh, well, I don't know nothin noway. I loved to hear her read him tho.

Anyway, time passed. Months. My time was drawin closer.

Dancer was growin happier for me, but sadder for herself. Now she not only wanted to dance, she wanted a baby. Mostly I think she wanted somebody who would make a baby so she could give them all that love she wheeled round in that chair in that small shriveled-up body of hers. I always heard her cryin herself to sleep now. Oh God, it hurt me way, way down deep in my soul's soul.

I tried to get angry with God for these things that happened to us, the sad ones. But I couldn't, because God was not doin this to us. Mothers, fathers, relatives and friends, just plain people were doin this to us. Not God.

Dancer knew I was goin to be movin. They were tryin to talk me into lettin my child go for adoption. Said all the same ole things bout bein blind. I said all the same ole things bout makin it. Dancer stood behind me.

I was so wrapped up in my struggle for survival, I did not talk to Dancer bout some of my plans. My life was so strange I wasn't sure what my plans were. I wanted Dancer to come live with me if it was possible. She had eyes and I had legs. Between us we could take care babies or find SOMETHING to do! I loved Dancer. Her sweetness, her goodness and kindness. Her pain and loneliness was mine.

Near the end of my time, when I was so heavy and tired, I pushed Dancer's chair and we went all over, far as we could go, with her showin me the way. Lookin for a place to rent. I got a temporary room and kitchenette with a little—very little—monthly check I was gettin that they give disabled people. It seems somebody rather spend it on war and gettin more people disabled.

I hadn't told Dancer yet, but I was gonna find a bigger place later if she was gonna move with me and my son. I knew it was a son. I needed a son, a man in my life. Before I got round to tellin her, my labor pains came on me. I planned to tell her when I got back.

Labor pains. As I look back, there was more labor in how I got him, how I kept him, how I lived for the nine months I waited for him, than during the time I gave birth to this little heart of mine wrapped in the body of my child. I felt him. Oh, I felt him! I could not get enough of feeling him. My son.

I would beg the Lord to make him hungry so I could nurse him again, soon. I loved, loved, had loved, do love, will always love, my child. I named him Maman. *M-A-M-A* for my mama. *M-A-N* for my man child. Maman. I gave him my own last name. Even tho when they told me bout his sixth finger, now cut off, I knew who his father was. I wanted him all to myself . . . and Dancer . . . a little.

I went back to the house to move the last of my things. To tell Dancer my new plans for us. You see, they hadn't told me. Dancer had taken her own life while I was away bringing my son to life. With her little ballet shoes on. She just wheeled through that house when most people were gone and those left, paid her no attention. Collected all the pills she could find . . . and took them. She left a note . . . for me.

My dear sister friend,
    You are going on to your new life—Be happy. Take whatever you want of mine—People always do. I love you. And your son. Anyway, I've got to run now!
Bye.
p.s. That's a laugh.

Ahhhh, I cried. I cried. I should have told her my plans for us! I should have, I should have. I should have had some kinda faith in myself and her that we could make it on our own, helpin each other. She should have waited! One more day! Waited to see what tomorrow would bring! Because I didn't want to lie to her and say somethin that wouldn't come true, I didn't tell her nothin. I should have lied anyway. Given her my dream for her to have a dream. I rather lie and have her live than say nothin and let her die. Ahhh, I cried.

I went to my new little home and felt the lack of Dancer, who had never lived there. Then my son became so many problems for me to learn and do that he took over my life. Gave me a life, not just me givin him one. And . . . he could see! It was hard, hard carin for a little baby I could not see, but I learned, I learned. I did it!

My new home smelled of sweat, beer and dust and grime. It was another old beat-up building. The tenants were a lot like me, disabled in some way.

The landlady, she let me feel her face as she laughed a hard little gruntin laugh under her breath. Her face felt like hard, dry bone and skin. She had big, bulgin eyes that my fingers told me stared at me, at everything. Her hard skin was wrinkled and her chin jutted toward me. I moved my hands fast, from the cold. She smelled like perfumed liquor.

She told me they did not allow children, but since mine was a baby and could not move round, if I kept him quiet, I could stay until I found another place to move to. I was grateful. Cause who could I turn to to help me find another new place? I was weak from havin my son and hurt from losin Dancer and did not know anybody cept those from my old home for girls, and they had forgotten me even when I was there! My worker was tired of my life and hers. So . . . I was grateful, I mean!

I started not to call Mrs. Minister bout her evil thoughts, but decided, what the hell? I called. Told her the baby was born with five fingers. She said, "Well, of course he was! That's good. Now, take care yourself." That was that. But bout two weeks later, Mr. Minister found me, came to see was I doin alright and to see the baby. Put some money in my hands, paper money. Told me my house was doin alright and he would see to the taxes bein paid. Didn't know when he would see me again but . . . I wanted to ask him why? bout this money and taxes stuff, but I just kept my mouth shut. He didn't touch me or nothin, cause if he had, I'd a tried to kill him. I was glad bout my baby, but there was some madness deep in me somewhere bout what he done. Then he left.

I kinda felt alright! Life is somethin to watch! I couldn't see the pieces of the puzzle, but . . . I could feel them!

I didn't have no time to live in a dreamworld no more. Life was hard, not gonna tell you no lie. Life was hard! You hear me?! I had to find my way to stores and musta asked a hundred people a thousand questions. Then I had to find my way back home. I didn't have no seein dog, just a stick. The sounds of the cars and people scared me to pieces! I felt like cryin right out there in that street sometimes. Sometimes I did cry. I felt lost! But my baby was at home. I learned. After bout two weeks, I had the grocery store and the drugstore down pretty good! Then I was proud.

I had to learn that stove in my kitchenette. I have burns and scars to show for my trials. But I learned it. I had to. I washed diapers in my sink. Couldn't afford and didn't want them paper things. I hung wet clothes to dry all over my room on everything. That was okay til winters, then the dampness in the air made the room colder. Money don't stretch. Stomachs get smaller, that's all. I chewed my baby's food for him and got my nourishment from that sometimes. But Maman never did without what he really needed. He didn't have all I wanted for him, but he had what he needed. I had to steal his rattles and little toys. I know somebody musta seen me, but they musta not told. I had to give my baby somethin to look at . . . to see.

I lived. I cared for my baby and we lived. I hate to keep sayin how I love him, but I loooooved him. I built a world in that room. A world of hard, real life and a world of dreams. What WE would be when he grew up! Because he could SEE!

God was good, again. My cross-the-hall neighbor, Jane, was a kind woman. She was what they called slightly mental retarded. She was always talkin bout love. All the time. It was her answer to everything!

I felt her face. She wanted me to. It was soft and had small features placed crooked on it. Her eyes blinked real fast. I know her body was full and soft cause she put my hands on her self. She was short. Moved slow, sometimes clumsy. Her feet were wide and bare, with bunions. She was warm. I felt her smiles. Then she said she closed her eyes, and I let her feel my face. I felt her smiles again. She sees love in everything. Sees no ugliness cept in meanness. She hates our landlady. She sometimes cried easy.

When I went into her room for the first time, she had me feel her "children." She had rows and rows of dolls, all sizes. She said all colors. Some with hair, some didn't have none. I felt the neat clothes they had on. Most knitted and crocheted. See, she could knit and crochet, fast and good. (That is the most confused and mixed up piece of material I have ever felt and to think they do that with long, pointed, straight needles! I will never understand it!) After that she started knittin for Maman. All kinds of things. Even diaper covers! When he got bigger, she knit him suits! Everything! I could feel the warmth and beauty in em. Or maybe it was the love she put into everything. She loved Maman.

He was her real doll! She watched him when I went to the store or anywhere. I never worried.

Jane couldn't go to anywhere less she had somebody with her. The landlady had a contract, or somethin, to watch her. See, if Jane went out alone, she always picked up a man and went off with him, then people have to get out and go find her. She was always tryin to sneak out that front door or even go with me. That landlady had eyes like they say a hawk do! She most always caught her, and she didn't let her go with me cause I couldn't see her when she got away. Jane didn't do that all the time tho, just certain times of the month. The moon, she say, makes her love come down. I use to wonder how love "came down," watched for it, but didn't never feel it. Less it happen when I was sleep.

In findin my way in the world, hands were very important to me. They have a certain sound-feelin. And I always listen carefully to the sound of people's voices because that's all I have to go on when I make judgment of strangers. The sound of what they say and the way they say it. I could almost tell a person's age by their voice, almost tell their size, if they was kind and good or mean and evil.

It was in my classes, cause I still went to every one I could get to, that I started payin attention to the sounds of words for real. Each word started to have its own special look or somethin. Some words did not mean what they sounded and other words got on my nerves. Some seemed like wicked, mean words tho they could mean somethin nice. I began to take the only tool I had, speech, and roll the words round in my mouth. You can taste some words. They feel good to your mouth. Sounds just got so important to me! Then I graduated to higher classes in braille. Can you blive I cried with joy?! Books! I had worlds . . . worlds! Open to me! Oh God, you are good!

But there was not enough books. Not enough. I read what I could get, twice, three times. To me, it was my life, almost like my son. I, a mother, could READ to my child as he grew older. I read to Jane. I. I had somethin to give those I loved.

Jane could count money, so she helped me when I shopped. We put straight pins in paper money. One pin, one-dollar bill. Two pins for $5.00, two pins crossed; $10.00. If the bills was larger we put them in a special envelope, knitted, and I asked for change and put it back in that special envelope for Jane to check. My store man was usually honest with me, but not always his kids.

No matter how many times I started out for that store I was always scared and a nervous wreck. I knew where that store was exactly, that was no problem. The problem was that outside things changed every day. The people, the cars, the dogs, little runnin children, a box left out, a garbage can, somethin slippery like fruit on the sidewalk. There were so many things! Just walkin to the store, I might never get back home again! But it had to be done. I made it. Alone.

I got tired of gettin burnt all the time. I got some credit; it was the hardest thing to get that store to trust me. I was blind, Black and broke. But finally I got a small stove that clicked or rang to tell me what was going on. What was lit and what was out. I learned to cook more things with the timers. I made a few mistakes, but my son and me ate em. And my son was growing.

Maman was such a good child, quiet. I waited, every day, for the landlady to tell me to move. I was scared to death cause I didn't know where I could go on my little money or even how I could find somethin else that would take a blind woman and a child. But Maman had gotten to her heart through some long, cold tunnel in some way. He could do useful things round the house by time he was five years old. Some cookin, some cleanin. Ah, my son was growin.

He started to school. I missed him. He started a paper route. I missed him. At nine years old he started deliverin groceries and shinin shoes. I missed him, but . . . he was a man. Growin. I felt sorry for him havin blind me for a mama. See, I loved him.

He changed my life every day. He described everything to me! He had a piece of some broken crystal glass he had found somewhere on his little travels. He told me the things the sun did to it so splendid! Told me it was like the sky that was so huge like the ocean that was so deep like the sky that was so blue like the ocean. He told me about people and, oh, all kinds of things I never even knew was out there in the world. He said HE was lucky to have me because *I* made him see more!

Ahhh, now. My child was such a big somethin to me. There was no end of it. He took the place of life. Gave me joy and warmth in his little arms. So tender, such strength. I had no terror nomore when he was in my life, cept from the outside world that needed money. I had . . . peace, as much as possible. When he was away, I sometimes cried with happiness. And forgot I was blind. And he was still growin.

Don't think we didn't have some hard times! We had more than our share and more. I knew my son's clothes wasn't right. Knew sometimes he wasn't warm out there in that street in the winters. Knew he didn't eat lunch at school all the time. Knew he was hungry when he brought somethin home to share with me. If he complained, you did. And I don't know you. My son was a man.

We give each other nuts and fruit for big holidays. That's all we could get. But I found out my son loved music. Them records and things. I went right on back down there where I got my stove and got my son a record player on credit. They trusted me now, if I didn't get too much. My son bought two secondhand records. You know what they was? Stevie Wonder and Ray Charles! Blind men! But I had made him happy. He cried! Happy!

I was just gettin so good at things. Walkin to the store or wherever I had to go! You know I had started out in this city by hittin posts and people, steppin off the sidewalk into sewers filled with water sometime. I even ran into parked cars. I had to listen hard for everything! At street corners for cars when I just had to get cross em. Listened for footsteps in front or behind me so I could stay lined up with them, stay out the sewer. I could almost tell if it was a man or woman. How much they weighed. I started out keepin my hands on the buildings, fearin the space of the whole world on the other side of me. I made mistakes, many mistakes. But I had many quiet miracles. I made it on my own. I am here, ain't I?

One day a dog "followed" my son home. He got that hard ole landlady to let us bring the dog in and feed her if she slept out at night. We soon worked that into keepin her in from the cold. Darlin was a female. She was so feelin, so sweet. I loved to bury my hands in her warm fur. Maman got a rope and soon she was leadin me where I use to go more slowly. She seem to know I was blind. Maman walked with us at first, showin her. Then just her and me went, alone. She was untrained! She was just full of love and wanted a home. Well, she had one. And ate when we did!

I can't even begin to tell you the freedom such a dog-friend gives you. You feel safer. You feel good. You feel almost normal. And you can GO places. My world got a little wider. You see, we had no phone, no doorbell, nothin like that. We really didn't need em. I did not miss the hard, blastin sounds nor the people that might be behind em.

We had Darlin to love bout two years til, one day, some boys was chasin her, throwin rocks at her, and she ran into the street . . . and got hit . . . and died. They said we coulda saved her if we had some money. Ohhhh, God, we had NO money. NO money to save our best friend! NO money to keep our little love alive. Money, money, money. The only doctor we could get to, said it would cost too much and she wasn't nothin but a old dog anyway and we just as well go on and let her die. We didn't let her, but she died with my son holdin her and me holdin both of em. Just tell me, what's money got to do with love?

We wouldn't let the vet man keep her cause he was just gonna put her in some oven like she wasn't nothin! And wanted to be paid to do that, too! No, we took her home and that landlady, she was nice after all, let Maman bury her in the little back yard and we prayed over her. Later we got a tiny little evergreen plant, cause she would like that, Darlin would. Then we went upstairs and I got my son to put on one of them records, says, "The song has ended, but the melody lingers on," and cried and cried and cried. Then a terrible loneliness came over me. I still had my son . . . but it was a new loneliness born in me somewhere. It seemed I wanted to run somewhere, to somewhere, for somethin! But not only did I have nowhere to run to, I couldn't even run.

I was already makin little art things, like gluin pretty pieces of wood and rocks to base blocks my son cut for me at school. Sometimes I sold em. Little extra money, you know. I started doin more volunteer work at the center to help fill up that lonely place in me. Then I started taken out them pictures of my family and just sit, holdin em. They were only flat pieces of cardboard to me. I couldn't see em and I couldn't feel nothin. My son caught me cryin over em one time when he came in one evenin. And you know what he did? He took em to school, brushed em with several coats of a thin waxlike somethin and when it was almost hard (he told me this), he took a instrument and rubbed the parts outward so I could feel em! The nose, cheeks and things! Pushed in the eyes, made the hair feel like lines! I could feel the faces!

Maman's teacher saw what he was tryin to do, so he taught him how to do it, put the likeness on metal. A bigger piece that would never break! That's what my son did for me! I told everybody at the blind center and most all of em had pictures they wanted to "see," so my son got a little business of his own started, tho he didn't charge them much. And now I can feel my mama whenever I want to! My son was growin.

Jane knew bout my loneliness, she said I needed a man, needed some lovin. That was so funny I laughed til it wasn't funny, then I cried. Who would want me? Feelin my way to the bed? But . . . for once in my life . . .

Now . . . through these years some men had spoke to me as I did my chores in the street. But they only wanted to see what it was like to have sex with a blind woman. One certain man came in handy one time tho.

I wasn't goin to tell this, but I have told everything else, so why not? There was this man had a shop down the same street I lived on. He was always speakin to me, grabbin my arm, givin me somethin like candy, gum, little things like that. But what he asked me is didn't I need some money, sayin, "You know if you ever need some money, I got some for you! It's got your name on it. I got it right here!" Then he take my hand and pat his pocket with it. I snatch my hand away cause I know what he's doin and I don't like it!

I say back, "If it got my name on it, give it here now."

He say, "You got to come back after I close, you know what I mean! Make me know you preciate it!"

Well, I hear a heap in my life, so I know he mean a sex trick. I call him a nice bad name, snatch myself on away from him and go on my way. Him just laughin behind me, sayin, "Don't forget! Just let me know!"

Over the years he told me how much. It went from $10, to $20, to $25, to $30, to $50.00. He wouldn't go no higher than that. But he say if I do him realll good, I'll get a hundred-dollar bill. Just lyin. He kept this little game up all the time. He talk so much all the time that when he told me a man was followin me everywhere I go in the evenings and on weekends, I didn't blive him! Why should I? I thought he was foolin, or talkin bout hisself.

Then somethin happened sometime soon after that. Maman came down real sick. Now we needed money. I didn't ever ask nothin from welfare for Maman cause I didn't want them to see that little room in that dirty house and me blind. I thought they would take my only love, Maman, away from me. I didn't get much for my own disability and now we didn't have the money he brought in either. We needed some money for medicine! My heart was breakin when I listened to my son and my brain was just goin wild! Tryin to figure a way! I didn't know what to do!

I thought of that man and his fifty dollars. I went right out to walk by his place, wait for him to grab my arm and ask me again, so I could tell him yes. I slowed when I got near his shop so he would have the time to see me and come out as he usually did. I also slowed because my heart was so heavy from havin to do this I could hardly carry it. Just think on me! The first time, my body was used for rape. Now the second time I was ever gonna be with a man is a sex trick. God, I needed love, love. For once. Just once.

Anyway, I made a mistake when I lingered, waitin for him. He musta seen me! I had to walk by that store bout four times . . . then he came out. His voice was different. When he found out what I wanted, he made me stand round there a long time waitin for him to tell me what time to come back or whatever I need to know. Right away, he came down to $25., then to $20. That man saw all my desperation. Every piece-a brain in my body, every nerve, screamed inside my head at this man. But . . . I said alright . . . anyway.

I went back when he told me too. I was grateful to him for the money I needed, but I hated that man. He was rough . . . and sweaty. He was nasty. He kept wantin to "look" at things and poke his fingers at em. He wanted me to keep my eyes open, even tho I was blind. I wanted to squeeze em tight shut to put him further away. My body was dead, it didn't do nothin. Somehow we got through. I went home holdin tight to my money.

When I got home I ask Jane bout the bills in my hand. Was sposed to be two $10. bills and one $5. bill. She said it was one $5. bill and two $1. bills. My body was so hurt and I was so mad my eyes almost could see!

I got a brick from my own room, cause outside I never would find one on the street. I went back down there to that man's shop. It wasn't too late and he had opened up again. I felt where his plate glass window was and stepped back . . . and shouted! "Mr. So-and-So! You better give me my $50.00"—I went up—"or you gonna spend it on this window!" People started crowdin round, askin questions. I told em, "He took my fifty dollars!" Well, he had, you know! That was at *least* fifty dollars worth! Cause it hadn't been touched in thirteen years and was brand new anyway!

The people started hollerin at him. He was standin there lyin, but he couldn't grab me and take that brick on account of those people! And he must didn't want to tell them the truth cause his own friends in his shop would know his business! He finally said he musta made a mistake (he sure did!). He gave me the whole fifty dollars. I knew, cause the people counted it for me! Then I went home. He never, never bothered me again! I wasn't ever gonna do that again anyway, if I could help it, with anybody. But my son got his medicine and we had a little party of good things to eat for him, me and Jane. He got well and kept on growin. Forgive me, but thank you God.

Now, you know, I didn't want to do that. That ain't no kind of lovin at all! What I wanted was a real kind of love. Married love. But I knew in my deepest mind nobody would really want me, a blind woman. Some blind men at the center had talked to me bout love and things, but I didn't feel any sparks or whatever it is they say love makes you feel. Not cause they were blind, that's normal to me. Just cause. So that lonely place in me just grew and got bigger and heavier.

Now sometimes, I've noticed, everything happens all at once! Two or three weeks after my brick day with Mr. So-and-so, this happened: a man came up close to me as I was walkin home with some groceries. I felt the closeness for too long and I got nervous. It was too close, too steady.

After a while I asked, "Who's there, please?"

In a slow, sorta singin low sound he said, "Me."

I say, "Who are you? Do I know you?"

He say, "Not yet. But you can if you want to."

I slowed down, said, "What's your name?"

He said, "Skip. I already know your name is Christine and they call you Tine for short."

I ask, "How come you to know so much bout me and I don't know bout you?"

He laughed a little. "Well, I been watchin you, Miz Christine, for a long time. I know your son, too."

Well! I asked, laughin a little, "You know my son? He know you?"

He say, "Yes. . . . We talk . . . sometimes. He shine my shoes sometime. I buy his papers sometimes. When he have a big loada groceries to deliver, I help him carry em, sometimes. He a nice kid, a real nice kid."

I laughed easily now. "That's my son!"

He touched my shoulder. I jumped. What now?

He asked, "Can I carry that bag for you, Miz Christine?"

I didn't know. Jesus, I couldn't see him! And there are so many things in this world to watch out for!

I tried to smell him. Sometime you can smell things that tell you somethin. He only smelled like some shavin cream or some-thin.

I stopped smilin. "I don't know, Mr. Skip. I don't blive I need any . . ."

He took the bag. Said, "Just call me Skip. I'll take the bag and I'll walk you home. You miss your dog, Darlin, don't ya?"

I had to laugh with surprise. "You knew my dog, too?"

He walked beside me. You know I began to feel safe with this man I didn't even know.

He said, "Miz Christine . . ."

I said, "Call me Tine."

He said, "Tine, I know most everything bout you a man can tell with lookin! I'm the one planted that big flower bush by Darlin's grave, too."

I smiled. "My son told me bout that flower-bush plant! He said it's very pretty. Why did you do that?"

His voice got realll low. "I love everything that loves you."

I stopped smiling, frowned. I don't like to play with grown men. I said, "What do you mean, Mr. Skip?" Now, inside of me is all this darkness. This big, empty space of loneliness is dark too. Do you know, a little light, just a little light peeped inside of me when he answered me.

He said, "I love you, Miz Christine."

Now, ain't that somethin! To happen to me!? I didn't blive him. But, I wanted to blive him. To blive anybody who said they loved me.

What I did was say, "What?"

He went on talkin. "I been followin you, watchin you, for a long, long time. I seen how you are. I seen you with your son. I watched your face when I could get that close to you without you knowin it. I like the way your face show most everything you think. I seen you thinkin bout your steps fore you make em. I seen you think bout sounds you hear . . . and smells you smell . . . and things you run into sometime. I heard you cuss a coupla times. I seen you always lookin nice. You ain't mean!!"

Now, I was bout to call this Skip man a fool and tell him don't be followin me around like no crazy man!

Then he said, "You a pretty woman, Miz Tine. And over all this time I been watchin you . . . strugglin along, I done fell in love witcha!"

I didn't say anything. And I know I was a fool. But my heart turned over a little in my breast. Little sparks, just a few, flew round in my body. I didn't know what to do. By that time I was at the house, sorry to get there.

He say, "I mean what I say! I love you. And you don't need to love me back, if you don't want to. Just let me be with you sometime. Let me help you with your packages and your chores."

I was outdone! Here is all this out the clear blue sky, whatever that is! Now I know what flabbergassed is all about! But he went on talkin.

"I know what happened down there at the shop coupla weeks ago. I seen you go in and I seen the lights go out. I knew then what you was doin, cause I knew him too. That hurt me. That hurt me bad. Cause I knew you never did that before and you musta needed somethin and you didn't know you could ask me for it without worryin bout nothin. That's when I made up my mind for you to meet me. Now . . . you don't have to do that again. I'll help you when you need it. Cause . . . I love you, Miz Tine."

Every word the man said was rock-bottom, sure nuff what any woman wants to hear. I ain't never been on no island listenin to no violins, but I sure nuff felt the breezes on a island, heard the trees wavin in them breezes and heard the violins! Music in my soul.

But I brought myself back to where I was. I couldn't blive this man! Was he lyin? Was I a fool to be listenin to him? Sweet, sweet Jesus, have mercy. You probly think I was a fool, but that dark, lonely place was awful, awful dark and the loneliness was pullin me down a little more every day. I listened. He kept talkin.

"When your son got well and told me he been sick, I knew why you did it. Don't do that nomore, Miz Tine. I work two jobs. I'm a welder and I fix cars and know how to do some carpenterin too. I ain't got nobody. I left home at age of twelve cause my mama married a man that didn't want me around. So I left and I been on my own ever since. That's how come I notice your son, Maman. He a little man! Anyway, all I do is save my money cause I ain't got nothin to do with it but pay rent and buy food. I cooks! My car paid for. I don't care bout no clothes. And . . . I ain't got nobody."

My whole body screamed inside my head, *This man is lyin!*

Couldn't nobody make him but a fairy godmother and I don't blive in Cinderella! I didn't say anything tho. I musta looked stupid tho, with my mouth hangin open and my eyes starin without seein a thing.

The man wouldn't quit! And he had a whole symphony playin in my heart! He said, "Lady, Miz Tine, I'm tryin to tell you I love you. I done decided I better speak up now!"

I found my voice. "Man, you don't know me! How can you love somebody you don't know? Don't you know I am blind?"

He said, "I told you I been watchin you for most two years and more. I know what I love. And you bein blind don't mean nothin to me. I don't love your eyes, I love you. I mean, I do love your eyes cause they part of you. But . . . eyes ain't what I'm after! I got some eyes of my own!"

I thought I had him! I asked, "What are you after?"

He said, right off, "You!"

Since he talked so strong I decided I would too. I felt just like a fool anybody could walk up to and say "I love you" and I would stop and listen! But I'll tell you somethin, them words are powerful! They will stop you if the right person say em right!

I ask, "You want me? What for?"

He said, "First, I want to see will you like me . . . maybe love me, someday."

I ask, smart now, "How you goin to find out?"

He laughed, said, "We can start today. Will you go to the picture show with me?"

I said to myself, I knew this man was crazy! Why he have to be crazy?! I said to him, "Mr. Skip, since you been watchin me you must know I cannot see no picture show. I cannot see!"

He said, just as smooth as could be, "You can hear! Picture shows talk now!" So I was the foolish one.

We both laughed. I nodded yes and said "Yes, what time?" He told me. I took my bags and started up my stairs.

He hollered good-bye, said "Til later."

I hollered good-bye, said, "Til later then."

I started floating right after I shut the front door. I floated on up the stairs, up the hall, all the way to my kitchenette-room. I floated to my bed, lay down and laughed til I cried, then cried til I laughed again.

I had a date! And allll kinds of sparks was flyin round in that empty, lonely place in me.

We went; I listened. But mostly I was feeling him beside me. He bought me all kinds of things. I had chips, popcorn, candy, ice cream and a hot dog! I had the best time I ever had in my life since I been away from my mama . . . cept for my son.

We left the show, stopped to eat. He wasn't shamed of me. He talked and talked and talked about us. I listened and listened and listened. I began to be-lieve by the time that man took me home . . . and kissed me. (Yes, I let him kiss me. I didn't care if it was my first date! It could be my last date!) We kissed. And that kiss gave me joy in him and in myself.

You know, eyes are the way most people make friends. Ex-changin looks. Flirtin. I couldn't do that with my eyes. Lip is how I was able to feel his heart out. He felt like he had a good heart.

I just must tell you bout my kiss. First, the world started turnin real fast. I heard water in my ears. I felt his shoulders, hard and strong under my arms. My head got shaky . . . I wanted to hold it with my hands to keep it still, but I didn't want to let go of him. Then I felt the rest of my body. I felt my legs all the way down to my feet. I felt every hair on my head. My little heart turned round inside my little soul and I almost couldn't bear it. Somethin inside me whispered to me, *Tine, Tine . . . Is this love? This is love. Oh! let's trust him. Lets keep love.* I whispered back to that voice, "Oh, yes. Oh yes."

When he let me go, shame of all shames, I fell! In front of that man! Oh, God, I hated my eyes! My no-eyes! I fell . . . and he picked me up so gently I was almost glad I had fallen. But I was so mad at myself I got mad at him. Til he kissed my arms and hands, where he thought I hurt myself.

Will I seem like a fool to you if I say my heart opened wide open and somethin warm, my love, just poured out for him.

I don't know how I did it, but I finally got in the house. I floated up those stairs and up the hall again. I was still embarrassed bout fallin; then at last, I knew he didn't care. So I didn't either nomore. I hugged myself. I floated to sleep huggin myself and kissing those spots where he had kissed my hands. I tried to fold my lips in where he had kissed them. But I realized, I can't kiss myself and get all those feelins back. I need him to kiss me. Again . . . and again and again.

That man Skip brought me flowers and we smelled them together. He brought me perfume and we smelled that together when I wore it for him. He took me everywhere. Things I had never done. We went on a picnic even. He made the lunch. I wanted to show him I could do things so I made a potato pie. Jane sat with me. She was almost excited as I was. He took me to the beach. We played. We laughed. We kissed, kissed, kissed. I couldn't get enough of his kiss.

I ate my first avocado. He said that was the color green. I like green. He bought me a sweater that was green. I still wear it. An orange was the color orange and shaped like the earth, pits and all. I like the color orange. I knew bout yellow. He said his skin was the color of the inside of my eyes, Black. I liked it, it was smooth. I ask him my color and he bought me pecans. I like my color. It taste good. He told me I would look good in red. I ask what that color was. Watermelon told me it was a sweet color, but he said it was more. So he put my hand in a bowl of ice water then held it over the hot stove and that, he said, was the color red. It excited me. He bought me a red dress. Oh, all kinds of things like that did Skip do. He made my world bigger, better. I wrapped it around him.

Once, at twelve o'clock midnight, when the streets were most empty and we could hear our footsteps, he said that was like the color dark blue, midnight blue. Twelve o'clock in the afternoon was light blue like the sky. The feel of his tongue in my mouth was pink. I loved pink. He bought me a pink blouse. It was soft and smooth, too. And, oh, all the perfumes to smell, to bury my face in, to wear for him, to bury his face in. To learn. To know. All kinds of things came from him. All kinds of things. But still, he never touched me funny or talked bout sex. Never mentioned the bed.

I had planned on what to tell him bout why I couldn't go to bed with him on accounta I wasn't that type of woman. But when he didn't ask me, never, I got worried. Didn't he want me that way? Did my being blind turn him away from sex with me? Then I began to want to ask him! I wanted to make love with him! So, I asked him! Well, I had to. I had stopped floatin to sleep at night and instead, was having a hard time sleepin on them rocks in my bed!

Can you blive! He said he wasn't goin to do that til he got married. Til HE got married! I didn't say nothin for a while, then I asked, "Well when YOU plan to marry? Who you goin to pick?"

He answered, seriously, "I would ask you, but I don't want you to turn me down."

I laughed, seriously. "What makes you think I would turn you down?" I knew marriage was too much for me to pray for.

He said, very seriously, "Well . . . I . . . don't know. See, you ain't never seen me cept with your hands."

I said, quietly mad, but scared, "Well, if you wait til I see you, you ain't never gonna ask, cause I ain't never gonna see!"

He moved away from me. Said, "Well . . . I . . . don't know." Then he said he had to go and he left. He didn't come back the next evenin like he usually did.

I didn't smell no perfume, either. I smelled shit. And it hurt. It hurt. It hurt. You know what I mean?

I had the blues. I waited two days, then I went downstairs and asked the landlady for some of her gin.

She said, "Chile, you ain't lettin one little ugly, poor man start you to drinkin are you?" She laughed.

I said, "No, I just thought I'd have a little drink. Maybe it would quiet my nerves." I was very nervous.

She laughed. "That's what everybody say! Quiet they nerves! Quiet somethin! Girl, you can't see when you sober! You sure nuff don't need nothin gonna make you lose whatever else helps you get around!"

This ole woman was makin me mad. I said, "You got some gin? Cause I can get my own!"

She say, "Yeah, that's better. Buy your own problems! Gimme the money, I'll get it for you cause I got to go out anyway." I did, and she brought me some back.

I went upstairs, poured my gin and played all the blues records we had. Over and over and over. One song: "The Blues Ain't Nothin But a Woman Cryin for Her Man." I wore that out. Then, "The Very Thought of You." I slept with that on real low. Maman was worryin bout me, but he couldn't help me even tho he patted and hugged me more than usual. He hadn't seen Skip as he usually did.

When I went back to the landlady for some more gin, she didn't laugh at me. She just sounded disgusted with me. Said, "Now, listen here, girl! You can't start gettin to be a drunk over that ole ugly dog that take you out sometime! What's wrong with you, losin your mind like this!"

I ask her, "What do you mean? You talkin bout Skip?"

She laughed. "That his name? Well, good looks sure did skip all over him! Went right on by, didn't leave a mark!"

I said, "Skip is a wonderful person!"

She said, "Well, everybody got somethin and, Chile, he sure need somethin! That is the ugliest man I have EVER seen! If I didn't drink this gin I'd a got sick when I first saw him! You oughta be glad you can't see! Don't have no babies by that man, chile. Do, they gonna be mad at you for the rest of your life!" She laughed again. I didn't like her at all.

I went to Jane's room fast as I could stumble up the stairs. I ask her what Skip look like. I told her what the landlady had said. I knew Jane wasn't all that smart, but I knew she knew bout looks. She had a smile in her voice when she told me, "I think he is beautiful. He handsome. He sure look like he sweet."

I thought, "Oh Lord, if he is beautiful no wonder he don't want me." Then I decided to go back to the landlady and ask her, "What do you mean he is ugly? What does he look like? He didn't feel ugly to me."

She answered. "He Black." But I liked Black. She went on, "He got a square, box head with a crooked eye in it and one straight eye."

But, I thought, he can see!

She went on. "He got the strangest lips I done ever seen! He Black, but his lips are pink!"

But I knew his lips were pink! I loved those lips!

She went on. "He got a nose that's goin everywhere all over his face! That is a ugly man, chile!"

But I had felt that wonderful nose. It didn't feel ugly. How does ugly feel?

She went on. "Cuts his hair in a funny way, too. Square, to match his head, I guess!" She laughed again.

But I was thinkin bout all those kind, wonderful thoughts inside the head she was laughin at.

She was going on bout ugly, but I left to go back to Jane. I ask her again bout how Skip looked. She said, again, "He is beautiful! He a man, ain't he? And he sure love you. You don't want him, you can send him over here to me. He is beautiful!"

I went back to my room and drank my gin and played my music. I wanted Skip to come back. I didn't care bout what nobody said. He had given me all kinds of pieces of life. And I wanted some more.

Bout two weeks passed before Skip came back. I didn't know much bout this kinda love before, but I do now. Love can be hard on you! I lost weight. I drank, didn't hardly eat. Didn't care bout nothin! Cept Maman. I was really sick. I didn't care if Skip was that Godzilla they talk about, I loved him.

When he came in at last, I grabbed him, hugged him, wouldn't let him go. Sent Maman off to the show. Poured my Skip a drink of gin, put on my music, took my clothes off, took his clothes off, got in bed and my own man made love to me. Softly, gently, completely. I didn't get scared, I didn't get nervous, I didn't get nothin but to feelin good. My body was happy and my mind was too. Cause Skip was back.

What do I care bout a crooked eye? I ain't got none. What I care bout a square head and face? Strange lips? What do I care bout a nose? Thank God he got one, that's all. What are all those things compared with a kind, lovin heart? And love. I was loved. My body was drenched with his and my soul so much I almost couldn't take all these wonderful, amazing, miracle feelins.

I thought of what my life had been and all I thought I would never have. I had my son, but I knew someday he would have his own and be gone to his life. I got terrified I would lose Skip even while he kissed me and loved me! When he called out my name, "Tine . . . Tine . . . Tine," it was the sweetest way my name had ever been said. I held him close, close, close to me. Chile, I loved him! I just loved him, that's all. Now, I do not curse, but . . . fuck the landlady!

Skip ask me to marry him. I said yes. We got married.

The landlady said, "That place is too small for all of you, and I will have to raise the rent."

I said, "I got a house. We'll move." I felt so good, I liked everybody!

I had Skip send the minister a letter. Then we called. Said, "Empty my house out. I'm comin home!" With a husband, chile!

We had some problems. Skip was worryin bout what work he could get in such a small place. Maman didn't want to leave his school. He was plannin to be a vet for poor people, or a doctor. He studied hard even with all those little extra jobs he had. Jane was goin crazy bout me leavin. And I didn't want the same thing happening with Jane that happened with Dancer, so I was upset.

My husband had a car. We decided to ride over to the house and look around the schools and places for work. We went, and I sat and twirled and felt my wedding ring all along the way.

Mrs. Minister was dead. I had wanted her to see my husband and my son. But I was sorry she had died. Mr. Minister was not doin bad. He was always off eatin at some of the flock's house.

There were some single women in his flock, all tryin to get him, he said, but he was better off single. Said, "The memory of my good wife keeps me from marryin again." I remembered when he hadn't remembered his wife when she was livin!

Mr. Minister seemed to be happy for me. He kept huggin Maman. He told Skip there would be plenty work. A lot of people were movin round there and if you can fix a car, you would always be workin cause cars always break down. Said he had told the people in my house to move and they were. Said my brother was round somewhere.

Then we went to the house. Skip and Maman said it was a mess. A lot of work to do. Saw the people who lived there and they said they was gonna move anyway cause the house was too broke down. Course they had been there, breakin it down, for bout thirteen years. Skip looked all round the place and even went under the house, takin Maman with him. He said he knew what he had to do.

The schools didn't look big enough for Maman, but Skip told him in three years, when he was sixteen, he would get a little ole car and be able to get around to where he wanted to go . . . for his future.

Sweet, sweet Jesus. I can not even begin to tell you bout my life and what all these new changes meant to me. I had a life. I even had a real future! My son was goin to have a better life. We could begin to think of college for him cause we had help. We had new love, more love, cause we had Skip. Skip was the most beautiful man in the world to me.

See, seeing people have to see things to believe them. Being blind, I have to believe things before I can see them. Skip was beautiful to me.

You can't understand what I mean less you have been in a

desolate place in your life at some time. My blindness was still like prison bars in front of me, to keep me inside for all the years of my life. Now, the darkness was still there, but Skip had the key to my prison. He opened doors. He was my new eyes. And he didn't HAVE to be. He WANTED to be. Just think of it. He loved me. He loved me.

How it feels to have someone take some work from your hands and say, "Don't worry bout that, I'll do it. Don't worry, don't worry."

Mmmmm, sweet Jesus.

Now, Jane was a problem for me. See, I knew her ways. And she thought Skip was beautiful. Now, she wouldn't mean me no harm, but she might do me some. Her mind just had somethin missin out of it.

Our little room was awful crowded. We had added a cot. Me and Skip never made love when Maman was home and since Maman liked to be round Skip, he was usually home when he was through school and his little jobs. Skip didn't stop him from workin, said that's good for a man. Only now Maman could keep and save his own money. But when we finally had the place to ourselves for a hour or two, here come Jane. Now, I loved my friend Jane, but—good grief!

I trusted Skip, he loved me. But I knew Jane, and it's a strong man can throw somethin off him. I told Skip, "Skip, I love you. I know you love me. I don't think you are a weak man, but . . . you are a man and Jane got a problem bout men." He started to laugh, I stopped him. "Wait a minute, hear me out. I trust you. I HAVE to trust you cause I can't see you nor Jane. BUT, I don't have to see to think. If I ever THINK somethin is wrong . . . Don't have to see it, just think it. . . . Blind as I am and as much as I love you and all you mean to me . . . I will leave you!"

Skip asked, "What is this shit?" And he wasn't a cussin man either.

I answered, "What it is is just what I said, that's all. Now, let's forget Jane and talk about our future." We understood.

I could now tell Jane she could move with us if she could work it out with her workers and everything. I could hear her callin her worker on the phone and talkin loud and arguin with her when she came by Jane's room. Whatever they worked out, Jane was goin with us. I didn't know what else to do! I knew Jane didn't have much life to look forward to and I didn't want her to hurt herself and I wanted to help her. I had enough happiness to share some. So there I was.

When the time came, we just went on and moved into our house. They got to workin on it right away. Jane and I cleaned up. I wouldn't let them kill any spiders, at least I told them not to, re-membering Dancer and her spider friend. After all the paintin was done, we put up curtains, dishes and everything. I put the braille books my husband had bought me on my own bookshelves.

Me and Skip had Mama's room. Maman had me and Phine's old closet room. Jane had Brother's old room. It worked out. Jane could go outside a lot now, cause wasn't nothin out there but trees and things. No man to run off with.

Maman decided he liked country livin. We had a garden started soon as we could. Skip bought me a bigger stove with the bells and buzzers and timer for my cookin. And a refrigerator. Said he knew he had been savin for somethin important. We hugged a lot. And now with a door to our bedroom, he could call my name when he wanted to. I liked that lovemakin stuff!

Then we got a dog. I named it Darlin cause I still loved Darlin.

One day, my brother showed up. I was glad to touch him again after so long. But I kept in my mind the fact that I could touch him cause *I* came back. He hadn't lifted one finger to find out where I was and if I was doin alright.

Brother wanted to move "back home." He said he had a room in another fellow's house, but that the fellow wasn't clean, stole his money, or his food. I blive they were lies. Any which way it was, I told him no. "No room, and everybody in my house brought in some money."

He called me "a cold-blooded bitch."

Then Skip said, "I know she your sister, but she my wife, too. Don't call her no bitch, please, cause I don't want no trouble with her brother." When he said *please*, it didn't sound like he was beggin either. Now.

I told Brother, only cause he is my mother's son, he could come eat with us on Sundays. He did. You know, when he was round Skip and Maman, he helped some, like in the yard, in the garden. He was tryin not to be so useless. He wanted a home. OR, he liked Jane.

You know, Jane could back up to a man and feel on him with her hand behind her. Maman told me that. I tried to keep her in the house with me when Brother was round workin in the yard with Skip. She always wanted to go outside. Sometimes I let her cause Skip or Maman was out there workin on some car. I knew Brother was sweet on her. I figured their minds were bout the same size, too. Anyway, Brother worked when he was round our house and he always went home at night.

Skip was doin alright too. People got to know he knew bout cars and buildin things. They kept him busy. He made money and liked bein his own boss. He welded me some pretty, thin iron rails that they said looked like room dividers, so I could move fast as I wanted to with only one hand on the rail stead of reaching out two hands with a cane to keep from runnin into things.

My life was so good I wished my mama had lived and could see the way me and the house was now. And see the garden, the lawn. She would have loved everything. But if she hadn't died, I'd never have left. I would have held her down too. I'd never have found Skip. Wouldn't have Maman. Oh! Life! How do people know what to do bout life!? Life goes on.

One day we had all had dinner and was sittin out on the porch. It was a Sunday. Each person had their own favorite chair. I like the swing with Skip on it with me.

Brother said, "Who is that comin down the road, walkin?"

I said, laughin, "Could be anybody!"

He said, "Look familiar, but I can't tell yet."

For some reason the hair stood up on my neck. I felt somethin. I asked, "Can you tell yet?"

Brother said, "Noooo."

I said, "It's Phine. I bet it's Phine." When she finally got here, it was Phine. My sister Josephine, come back home.

Now, I was glad to hear my sister again, cause she was my mama's child. But my life was full with happiness, my house was full with people I loved. Not one of em had let me down. Brother only visited.

My sister had left me. I don't care if it was on the church steps. She left me with $5.00 and fear. I'm not a cussin woman, but I said to myself, "Oh shit."

Of course I opened up my home to her. Brother started stirrin up some mess by sayin Mama had left what they thought was a rented house to me, tho he hadn't seen no papers, he said.

I ask him, "Do you want to keep comin over here to eat and visit?" He shut up.

I ask Phine while she still stood on the ground front of the steps, "Where you goin?"

She told me, "Here. Home."

I ask, "Where you been?"

She told me, still standin down there on the ground talkin in my direction, "Well . . . first . . . I left here and went to the city. I was goin to go learn me a skill, go to some school. Get . . . a good job someday. First . . . I got a job as a ticket seller at a movie show place. Then . . . the day school wouldn't take me . . . so I had to go at night. So I got a job workin as a domestic for a white family so I could go to school at night. But . . . my lady I worked for didn't like me goin to school. She was makin me miss all the time. I looked for another job but she always told em bad things so they didn't want me. So I stayed with her."

She stopped for a minute and I noticed the porch was dead quiet. I told Maman, "Get a chair for your aunty. She been walkin. Set it out there on the ground so she can tell me what happened to her after SHE LEFT ME."

He did.

I ask Phine, "You want some water?" She did. Jane got it for her.

Now, you may think that was mean of me the way I was doin my sister. But I, blind, have struggled on my own for fifteen years in this world. With no help but my son. She left me where I got my son, but she didn't know how it coulda turned out! How it had turned out! She had never checked back. Not once! See, I have learned to care bout a lot of people in my life, but naturally, I care bout who cares bout me! Only one good thing bout Phine was she did take me to that church and give me $5.00. She could have left me here, in the dark, with my then lyin brother. That was good . . . but it wasn't good enough.

She was ready to talk again. I said, "Go on, finish talkin."

She did. Said, "When I worked at the movie show, I use to get my pay, go to the bank and get all one-dollar bills, put em in my bed and sleep on em. My own money. I saved it in my room I rented from a old lady. After a while I got all quarters and spread them in my bed and slept on them. It was the first time I had money, my own money. Lots of pretty pieces of money. When I had to change my job and live on the place I worked, I had to hide it. I was too tired to play with it anymore. I bought my books tho. I got in night school. I don't know what I took nomore, cause I didn't know what I wanted to be yet. Didn't know what they would let me be. I . . . tried to study hard. They laughed at me . . . so much. They laughed at my bare feet. I saved my shoes for work. They laughed at my clothes. Didn't have many. They laughed at how I talked. When I answered somethin . . . they laughed at my answer. The teacher told me to keep comin . . . and I tried to. But . . . my lady kept wantin me at the house when my school time was. So I missed . . . a lot . . . too much. I couldn't keep up at nothin. I started hatin that white lady I worked for. She had everything. Why didn't she want me to have nothin? Didn't cost her nothin. Then . . . one day she had a party. She dress me like a mammy so I could serve em. I tried . . . I tried to do it, but they laughed. They all laughed at me!"

My sister's voice was so sad. So sad. My heart went to the bottom of somethin and hurt for her. I started to stop her from tellin us her story, then . . . her voice changed. Got hard. Had hate in it.

She said, "I started droppin things. My lady screamed at me. Called me lazy, good for nothin, stupid, all kinds of names. But I fixed her. I went and got her husband's gun and waited for her in the kitchen. When I didn't come out, she came in to scream at me some more. And I shot her."

Everybody on the porch moaned and groaned or whatever.

She didn't stop talkin. "I shot her feet. Cause she wasn't goin to walk all over me no more! I ran out of bullets in her feet."

I cried, "Oh Phine!"

She went on. "She didn't die, but they sent me to prison after I went to court. I never got my can of money back. Then . . . after two years, maybe three years, they sent me to the sane asylum. They let me out two days ago. I have found God now, so . . . I don't want to live in no city no more. They give me all the money I made in twelve years—$50.00. Then . . . I came . . . home. That's all. You all still here." I was crying for my sister. Then she said in a strange, little-girl voice, "How come nobody never did come see bout me?"

I rushed down the steps, holdin on that rail, and fell flat on my face again, but I crawled to my sister and held her. See, my sister could see, but she didn't understand life. I think I rather be blind and be able to understand a little bout this life we have to live.

I took my sister in, fed her, gave her Jane's room to share. We talked some more, cried a little. Then I went to bed. I was tired. I was also gettin to be a cussin woman. Then Skip put his arms around me and said, "Your mama would be proud that you are tryin to help your family."

I told him, "You and Maman are my family. They are my brother and sister. They got to get their own family!"

I went to sleep thinkin on just that! I wanted my life, my house and my husband to myself!

For the next two or three weeks, as I did my dishwashin or cookin and things, I was thinkin hard bout my brother and sister. All during that time, Brother was hanging round Jane and Jane was hanging round Brother when she wasn't knitting somethin for him. Phine was gaining a little weight and Skip said she was wearin the shoes he bought her and looked nice in the clothes I gave her. Me, giving her clothes! Phine began to take over most of the cookin and even did some cleanin of the house. She was glad to be home, to have any home at all. I didn't know what to do or if there was anything at all I could do to have my house and family to myself.

Then, sweet Jesus, the minister dropped by. I was rushin to tell Jane he was a preacher so she wouldn't back up to him (she told me she wasn't studyin nobody but Brother!) and the minister was talkin to Phine. I realized all of a sudden, Mr. Minister was a single man! Phine was single. I made up my mind to have a little talk with him, soon.

Since I was havin more trouble keepin up with Jane and Brother, I decided I would think on them first. One day I knew they were gonna catch that right moment and get somethin goin! So I had Maman take me over to old man Woods' house where Brother stayed. Maman said the house looked pretty bad. So I talked to the old man.

"Old man," I said, "You need a woman round this house."

He laughed a cacklin laugh. "Say I do?"

"I'l say you do!" I said. "This house is a mess! You need somebody in here to clean up and make it warm and cozy. Cook good food. Be company."

He cackled again. "Sho do!"

I turned to Maman, said, "What's in the sink?"

He answered, "Lotta dirty dishes."

"What's on the kitchen table?"

Maman answered, "Lotta dirty dishes and empty boxes and dirty ashtrays and empty jars and two beer cans."

I smiled. "What the rest of the house look like?"

Maman kinda laughed, said, "Pretty bad, Mama."

I turned to the old man again. "See? Mr. Woods, you need

somebody who likes to make a home. And ain't you lonesome? I know Brother is. He need company too."

He cackled again. "Sho do!"

I ventured out some. "I think I got one for you."

He stopped cacklin, said, "Who? Who you talkin bout? I don't want no woman worryin me to death! What you tryin to do in my house?"

I said, "Help you make a home in it for your old age to have comfort in. See, Brother live here and he may be marryin. He got to bring his wife to his home, don't he?"

The old man didn't say nothin for a while. Then, "Who this woman? She can't take over my house, you know. This MY house! I don't need nobody tryin to take over my house!"

I said, "Houses ain't meant just to be houses. House is meant to be a home. Your house is not a home. You too old to be up in here by yourself. You need hot food and a kind person round you. Ain't nobody gonna try to take your house. I promise you that. Why don't you just try it and see what you think? Come on, now."

He cackled again. "If I don't like it, she will leave? People hard to get out your house, you know!"

I smiled. "Try it for a while. You won't want to put nobody out cause you need the company and she is a nice woman. Knit sweaters and things for you."

I got up to go. He said, "You the blind girl what come back, ain't ya?"

I reached for my stick. "Yes sir, that's me. Now, they gonna get married soon, so you get ready for some company."

As I left, he was sayin, "Yes mam, yes mam. I sho will. But if I start to don't like it . . ."

I was down the steps, goin home to finish my job. "You will like it, you'll see! Bye now, I got to run."

I flew.

I went home and told Brother and Jane they ought to get engaged and get married. Told them between Brother's little work with Skip and Jane's check they could live better than they did now, apart. Brother thought he was movin in with us, but I explained everybody needs their own. Take Jane with him. Jane almost lost her mind. She nearly knocked Brother down huggin him. I think it was a good idea for both of em. She wanted sex, he sure had that. He wanted a home, she could sure make one for him and that ole man. All their brains bout the same size anyway, so they would all get along. We'd be here if they needed us. Brother's walleye just rolled round in his head happy.

They got engaged, got a license, and Mr. Minister married them, all in one week. I went to help her with her new home, but I didn't know nothin bout that house and she said I was more in the way. She was takin over. And doin a good job!

Now. It was time to go see Mr. Minister. I rested a few days from my last little job, then I had Skip drop me off at the church one day. After Mr. Minister finished telling me how well I was doin, and how God had blessed me, I told him how God was blessin him.

I said, "Mr. Minister, you know my son belongs to you. At least, you are the father of my son."

He tried to sound holy and shocked. "Sister Christine, I don't know what you mean. We took you in our house when you had no home and nobody. Me and my blessed wife."

I interrupted him. "That's when it happened, as you know. I know it was you, Mr. Minister."

He got a little less holy. "You are blind! It could have been anybody!"

"Well," I said, "It wasn't anybody, it was you and I know it."

He jumped up, said, "I think you better leave here with all your blasphemin me. . . ."

I didn't move. I said, "You know, I told your wife my son had five fingers. Well I lied, to keep from givin your house troubles. Maman was born with six fingers . . . just like you. And you brought me some money, thank you, cause you knew he was yours."

He sat down. Said, "That's not enough to go on to make a man a child's daddy!"

I said, "It is to me."

He ask, "Just why are you here tellin me this . . . now? Ain't you happy over there in your house with your family?"

I told him, "I preciate you lookin after my house for me so that now we have a home here. But I think you need a home too."

I felt him relax a bit. "Oh . . . I have a home, Sister Tine."

I didn't relax. "I mean a home with a woman in it. You need a wife, Mr. Minister."

He laughed. "You already got a husband, Sister."

I didn't laugh. "I don't mean me, Mr. Minister, I mean my sister, Josephine."

His laughter was gone. "Josephine? I ain't never been even round Josephine!"

I smiled to him. "Oh, she is very nice. Make you a good wife. And she has found God. She can probly help you find him where he really is, stead of round mongst your flock. She cooks, is clean, likes sex, quiet, and loves God. Be a fine wife! For you."

He said, like he had just put his foot down, "Girl, don't you and nobody else pick no cup for me to drink out of! Now, you go on home and take care your own business like you got some sense!"

I put my foot down. "Mr. Minister, I will take the medical papers I got to the police with my son's birth certificate. I will tell them you raped me. I will get out in front of your church on Sunday, lay on the ground and cry bout how you raped me years ago and never lifted one hand to help me nor your son. And . . . I am blind, Mr. Minister. That won't hurt me, that will hurt you!"

Mr. Minister almost cried. "Girl, the devil is in you!"

I just said, "The devil gets in all of us sometime, don't he? I don't like to do this to you, but I am fighting for my life, for my sister's life, and it ain't going to do you no harm either!"

He blew his nose. "I will let you know."

I just said, "I am not asking. I am telling. I'm goin to the police THIS mornin!" I wasn't tho. "You didn't give me any time to decide fourteen years ago."

His voice sound like it came out of a tunnel. "When is this 'weddin' sposed to be?"

I smiled to him. "Court her a week, get engaged, and be married the next week. See, I want this to be her idea, her doin. For her sake."

And that's what happened. My sister is Mrs. Minister now, and she is doin alright. She loves her own house. She loves God. She is just right for Mr. Minister. Maybe too good.

Last time I was over to the church, she told me, "God is good. All those years I didn't have nothin. Then, look at me. I come home and now . . . I got everything!"

Sweet Jesus.

I told her as I hugged her, "That's right! And now you got a chance to work hard for God and be a good Mrs. Minister."

We were on the steps of the church as I was leavin. I got in Skip's car, saying as I left, "Bye now, I got to run!"

After everybody was through gettin married, right and left, everybody and everything was quiet. Skip, me and Maman—my family—was home alone at last. My heart just burst with happiness and whatever ran out of it just warmed me all over and filled me with joy.

And thrills!? Plenty thrills in my life now. We got another dog. I call it Double Darlin. We got a cat, she got kittens. I got plants growin everywhere, Skip say I got a green thumb. I still make my rock art. Skip buys me pretty rocks and Maman makes my base for me. We eat, we laugh, we play, we fuss together. We are a family. I blive it's as good as a family can be in this ole world.

I think of my mama, and long ago, how I was scared of what I would do in this house, in the dark, with my brother and sister. I didn't know how I would take care myself, and here I have helped to take care them! I been blessed!

I can't see a thing . . . but I got feelings you wouldn't *believe*!

Well, I have told you all the things I do and all the things I have done. You know I am tired. Happy tired. I have to leave you now, but, as I am leavin you, I just want to say one thing I love to say.

Bye-bye, I got to run now!

ACKNOWLEDGMENTS

I shall always thank Alice Walker for her invaluable help, and Robert Allen's, in publishing my first book. Always.

Paris Williams, my daughter, who loves me and proves it.

Shy Scott, a sister, who continues much encouragement.

Mary Monroe, author, helps in so many ways.

Joyce Carol Thomas, author, always willing to give information, time, never changes. She is kind.

Mary Webb, author, realizes authors must make a living and tried to help me do that.

Patti Bloom, who kept her every word to me and searched for ways to help me.

Emma Rodgers, of The Black Image Bookstore in Dallas, who works so hard and does so much.

Lynn E. Higgins, attorney, always ready to help with information whether I was broke or poor.

Barbara Haley, lecture agent, who has done innumerable things to keep me before the public. She believes in my work. A special thanks to her.

My editor, Michael Denneny, who responds to my every need, understands, assists, encourages me in my low points, is honest and of invaluable help to me. I do thank God for him.

I would be remiss if I did not mention that Linda O'Brien of St. Martin's Press is one of the most efficient, considerate, kind persons. Helps without being asked. I will never forget her.

Sharon Larsen of California is another I wish to remember for her kindness and concern.

Every reader who has liked my work. I will never be able to thank you enough.

ABOUT THE AUTHOR

J. California Cooper is the author of four novels and seven collections of stories. She was honored as Black Playwright of the Year, and her work received the American Book Award, the James Baldwin Writing Award, and the Literary Lion Award from the American Library Association. She died in 2014.